M000306584

A GILDED CAGE

A GILDED CAGE

CHRONICLES OF AN URBAN DRUID™ BOOK 1

AUBURN TEMPEST

MICHAEL ANDERLE

DISRUPTIVE IMAGINATION

This book is a work of fiction. All of the characters, organizations, and events portrayed in this novel are either products of the author's imagination or are used fictitiously. Sometimes both.

Copyright © 2020 LMBPN Publishing
Cover by Fantasy Book Design
Cover copyright © LMBPN Publishing
A Michael Anderle Production

LMBPN Publishing supports the right to free expression and the value of copyright. The purpose of copyright is to encourage writers and artists to produce the creative works that enrich our culture.

The distribution of this book without permission is a theft of the author's intellectual property. If you would like permission to use material from the book (other than for review purposes), please contact support@lmbpn.com. Thank you for your support of the author's rights.

LMBPN Publishing
PMB 196, 2540 South Maryland Pkwy
Las Vegas, NV 89109

First US edition, September 2020
Version 1.03, April 2021
eBook ISBN: 978-1-64971-175-5
Print ISBN: 978-1-64971-176-2

THE A GILDED CAGE TEAM

Thanks to our Beta Readers:

John Ashmore, Kelly O'Donnell, Rachel Beckford, Jim Caplan

Thanks to our JIT Team:
Deb Mader
Debi Sateren
Dave Hicks
Dorothy Lloyd
Diane L. Smith
James Caplan
Jeff Goode
Billie Leigh Kellar
Paul Westman
Peter Manis

Editor
SkyHunter Editing Team

DEDICATIONS

To Family, Friends and
Those Who Love
To Read.
May We All Enjoy Grace
To Live The Life We Are
Called.

— Michael Anderle

CHAPTER ONE

E mmet stalls with his hand on the door. The trepidation in his eyes catches in the glow of the neon pub sign blinking 'Guinness' beside his face. "It's not too late, Fi. We can still make our escape."

I move in and block his retreat. He might have six inches and fifty pounds on me, but I can take him, and we both know it. "Four hours ago, you swore to be brave in the face of danger. You can handle this."

"I signed on for bank robbers and automatic weapons. What's awaiting me in there, not so much."

A stiff summer breeze whips a loose swath of auburn curls into my face. I trap it and tuck it back in my ponytail. "Sack up, mate." I lay the accent on thick. "Yer a feckin' Cumhaill. There's no need to fear the wind if yer haystacks are tied down."

He snorts. "You're getting scary good at the oul man impressions."

And that's why I am the chosen one to get Emmet here.

Resistance is futile when I dig in my heels, and my five brothers know it. "Onward, Cumhaill. There's a hape of people proud of you. For once, suffer through the attention and accept the compliments."

He doesn't budge, and he doesn't laugh.

I'm about to get physical when he holds up a finger to stop the assault. "At least swear you won't let them embarrass me. I haven't lived down going viral on my twenty-first birthday, and that was almost three years ago."

I catch my laughter as it pushes up my throat. He never figured out it was me who posted that drunken delight. "No promises. Da and the others headed over straight after your graduation. They'll be banjaxed by now."

The expression on Emmet's face is priceless. Still, he's stalling. I reach around him, yank open the stained-glass door, and shove him into Shenanigans.

The blissful aromas of pub fare and beer hit us at the same time the uproar of applause and hollering signals our arrival. With a hand on the hostess stand, I climb onto the bench of the first booth. After steadying my boots, I accept the tumbler of whiskey shoved toward me and straighten.

Finger and thumb together, I press them under my tongue and let out a whistle that could shatter glass. The music cuts off, and the room of loveable rowdies quiets.

I raise my whiskey. "To my brother, Emmet Cumhaill. The last man in the house to hit the city streets." I smile and call on Da's family motto to finish my toast. "May yer heart remain pure, yer limbs remain strong, and yer actions always be true to yer word."

"To Emmet!" Da says, perched slightly cockeyed at the end of the bar talking with Auntie Shannon. He raises his pint glass and offers the room a glassy-eyed smile. "*Slainte mhath!*"

"*Slainte mhath!*" I shout amongst the chorus.

Emmet gets a drink thrust into his hand and is swallowed by a crowd of friends and family and men on the force. As the fifth of Niall Cumhaill's sons to don a badge and gun to follow him into the city streets, great expectations abound.

And rightly so.

My brothers and da are solid men who live by a code and put their lives on the line every time they leave the house.

As much as I worry—and I do—I admire them.

The music blares back on, and I hop down from the booth to join the celebration. With the Celtic rhythm pulling me into its enthrallment, I sway my hips through the mass of familiar bodies and raise my glass.

"*Slainte mhath*," I shout.

The toast for good health comes back to me twentyfold.

I empty my tumbler in a greedy gulp, the velvety fruit flavor of Redbreast Whiskey sliding down my throat. It mixes with my cocktails from dinner and warms my belly.

The elastic slides from my ponytail with little more than a tug and I run my fingers through the lengths of my hair, setting it free for the evening.

Twirling on the dance floor, the upbeat rhythm of fiddle and flute feeds my soul as always.

Friends spin me and kiss my cheek as I cut through the dancers and head to the bar. It takes me an age to get there, but no sooner do I set my empty tumbler on the pitted wooden surface than Shannon reaches over and pours me another dram.

That's the beauty of Shenanigans.

There's no such thing as an empty glass in an Irish pub.

"What's the craic, Fiona?" Shannon reaches over to accept Da's empty pint.

"Not much beyond the obvious," I say.

"Did you and Emmet have a nice dinner?"

I take a swallow of whiskey. "We did."

"Sushi isn't dinner," Da says. "If ye'd gone somewhere with real food, we'd have joined ye."

I chuckle. "It's Emmet's night, Da. He wanted sushi."

"*Arragh*," he says, which is the Irish be-all and end-all sound when one of them is annoyed, disapproves, or is generally unhappy.

"You didn't miss much, Da, I promise. We came straight over. Are Kinu and the kids here?"

Shannon points to a booth on the back wall. My oldest brother Aiden is there with his wife and their two wee ones. As if he senses my attention, Aiden looks over and winks. I blow them a kiss and wave to Kinu and the kids.

He and I look the most alike. The oldest and youngest of six got Da's russet-red hair and bright blue, Irish eyes. Brendan, Calum, Dillan, and Emmet got Ma's raven black hair and eyes as green as shamrocks in the sun.

Still, there's no looking at any one of us and not knowing we come from Clan Cumhaill. Or as most pronounce it, Clan Cool.

"It's a shame Brendan can't join the fun." Shannon slides Da a refill.

My old man raps his knuckles on the wooden bar with a firm knock. "Safe home, Brendan."

Shannon and I follow suit and knock. "Safe home."

My second-oldest brother, Brenny, works undercover for Guns and Gangs. It's been four months since we've had him home. Da keeps tabs on him through his captain, so we know he's all right—and I saw him a couple of months ago while I was out on a run-around in town.

Honestly, his transformation when he's undercover is so impressive that I almost didn't recognize him.

But I did, so I crossed the street and headed into a store to let him pass without acknowledging him. Being raised in the culture, I'm as well-trained in police procedure as any of the six officers Cumhaill.

The only difference is, I don't make the Toronto streets safer. They do.

By midnight, the crowd is thin, the music slows, and Aiden and Kinu have long ago taken Meg and Jackson home to tuck them into their beds.

"So, Liam." I nurse my drink at the bar. "Are we keeping you from something important, cousin? You've checked your phone six times in the past hour and have one eye on the door."

Liam shuts the beer tap he's pulling and shoots me an ocular "fuck-you, Fi." It's a look I'm very familiar with, and I laugh. He checks around and finds his mom at the far end of the bar joking with Emmet, Calum, and Dillan.

He shakes off his panic and rolls his eyes. "One sec, and I'll top you up."

I sip from my tumbler while studying the faces of those still celebrating Emmet's progression from the academy to beat cop. Everyone's so happy and proud. I am too...truly.

Immersion in law and order is the lifeblood of our family. It's what we know. It makes perfect sense for Emmet to join the others. I considered it for a time—Da nearly shit a brick—so I discarded the idea.

Even if Da would allow it, which he never would, I don't think police work and I would be a good fit.

I'm not one for rules and regulations.

Liam sets five Guinness and a fruity abomination with an umbrella onto Kady's serving tray. When she heads back to her tables, he grabs the neck of the Redbreast bottle and comes over to my end of the bar.

Tall and fit, with brunette hair and ice-blue eyes, Liam's a handsome guy. It's not weird for me to think so. He's my cousin by circumstance, not blood. Our fathers were partners out of the academy, and they rode together for sixteen years. Our families grew up close, and after Mark was gunned down during a traffic stop, my parents stepped in to make sure Liam and Shannon weren't alone.

After Ma passed a few years ago, they returned the favor.

Liam stops on the other side of the bar, and the wonky energy he gives off raises the hair on the nape of my neck. When I look up and meet his ire, the pub spins in a pleasantly fuzzy tumble and swirl.

He lifts the bottle and leans in. "Shit on a stick, Fi. Quit setting my balls in a sling for shits and giggles. Seriously, you're a royal pain in my ass. If I didn't love you so damned much, I'd quit you."

I wave off the top-up and laugh. "Seriously, what's up with you?"

"Now that you're poking at it, my blood pressure." Liam has a great sense of humor and can take the piss better than most of us.

I lean back and smile. "How is it a great guy like you is still single? Are ye tryin' te break yer mam's heart?"

He snorts, grabs a bar towel, and wipes the taps down. "It's one of the great mysteries. I propose to every woman I meet on the first date, but none of them say yes."

"Yet."

"Exactly. What about you? Have any prospects made it through the Cumhaill screening process alive?"

"Not a one. The last one was messy."

"Not another musician."

I snort. "No, a part-time yoga instructor."

He laughs and wipes his hand over his mouth. "And your da found the man wanting, did he? I'm shocked. He's so accepting when it comes to you and the security of your future."

"I know, right? Too bad. He had a fabulous...body."

Liam laughs and nods at one of the regulars holding up two fingers. He pulls a couple of bottles of stout from the cooler, hands them over, and keys the charge into the register. "You're the great Fiona-freaking-Cumhaill. Raise the bar and find someone worthy."

"Oh, I did. I've decided the love of my life is Chris Hemsworth in character as Thor. If I can't have him looking pretty in leather and saving the world, I don't want anyone."

Liam checks on his mother again, then calls up the time on his phone.

"She must be one helluva booty call."

Liam waggles his brow. "Of the wildest variety, and if I don't leave soon, I'll be pooched to catch a bus uptown. Ma doesn't approve of me running the roads so late at night. She thinks I need to set my sights on a good Irish girl and make plans for a future."

I snort and hold up my fist for a knuckle bump. "Preach."

We're still chuckling when Da nearly slides off his stool down the bar. I launch to catch him before he embarrasses himself and us.

"Lightning reflexes, Cumhaill," Liam says.

"It's a gift." I'm not exaggerating. All of us have crazy-quick reflexes. It's a boon for them as cops. I guess, for me, it means I can catch my inebriated father when he slips from his stool. Yay me! "It's a skill honed from years of dodging my brothers' fists and tackles."

"The joys of being a one and only child."

Ha! Being Shannon's sole focus since her husband died is exactly his problem at the moment. "Hey, Liam, can you do me a huge favor?" I prop up my father and gesture for my cousin to join me in front of the bar.

"What do you need?"

"I'm a little gone for driving tonight. If I cover the bar with Auntie until close, could you take my car and drop Da at home? I'll be here anyway. Might as well make myself useful. I'll catch a ride with the boys, and you can drive it back tomorrow if that works."

That earns me a grin worth the next two hours on my feet. "For you, Fi, I'd walk on hot coals."

7

I snort, exchange my keys for his apron, and head behind the bar. "And that's why you'll never quit me."

By closing time, there are a dozen patrons left in the pub, and I start the final cleanup behind the bar. Shannon balances the waitresses' till and cashes Kady out for the night. Calum props a polluted but content Emmet in the booth by the door and starts lifting chairs. Dillan runs the hot water for the mop.

Each of the six of us has worked at Shenanigans at one time or another, so we all know our way around what needs to be done. Considering tonight's crowd was almost completely our guest list, helping out is a no-brainer.

"Why don't you head out, Kady," I say.

She watches me tie up the night's trash and nods. "Yeah. If you guys have things covered, I'm happy to cut and run a few minutes early. Thanks."

I follow her down the back hallway with the two large garbage bags clenched in my hands. She stops inside the door and grabs her hoodie off the plaque of wall hooks. After shrugging it on, she frees her long, blonde hair from the back. "Thanks for helping out tonight, Fi. It's always fun when your family hangs around."

Translation: I like it when your family comes in so I can stare at your brother. I smile. Kady's had a crush on Dillan for a donkey's age, but he is as oblivious as she is shy. They've each had enough time to figure things out.

I'll have to intervene.

The two of us step out the back door, and I follow her down the four metal steps and toward the dumpster. I heave my burden over the side of the massive green bin. My smile fades as my instincts kick in. The hair on my nape stands at full attention, and I turn.

A man steps out of the shadows in front of Kady.

"Hey," I snap while waving my hand to shoo him off. "This is a staff area. Go home and sleep it off."

The guy doesn't move, and Kady is frozen in her tracks.

I look around for something to use as a weapon, but Shannon is meticulous about keeping the dumpster area clean.

I hustle to get to Kady, but the stranger is closer. He grabs her and pulls her by the wrist toward the back lane. When they step under the light of the streetlamp, I recognize him. I felt his gaze on the bar more than once tonight while I was working and caught him staring.

Is he stalking Kady?

Far more Wall Street than mean street, he didn't set off my radar. Handsome, shabby-chic, and well-dressed, he doesn't fit the bill of the men in the mugshot books Da and Calum pore over some nights.

Stupid. So were Bundy, Dahmer, and Bernardo.

I glance toward the back door and curse. It's too far to get help and not lose track of Kady. Yelling won't do any good either. The music is still playing inside.

It's on me, then.

I hold up my palms and ease closer. Petite and willowy, I'm no one to be alarmed about, right? I study his hands and his hold. He doesn't have a knife or a gun out. That's a plus.

"How about you let go of my friend?" I make every effort to seem non-threatening. "It's been a long night, and you don't want trouble, do you? Kady and I will head back inside and forget you were ever here."

He chuffs. "Off ye go, then."

And leave Kady? Hells no. Had this been any other night, Kady would've thrown out the trash and been out here alone. Thank the luck of the Irish she's not.

"Look." I step closer and try to convey to Kady to remain calm. "You noticed a pretty blonde, and you made a bad decision.

If I scream, a dozen cops will flood out that door, and someone's liable to get hurt. Maybe you. Maybe her. You don't want her to get hurt, do you?"

His gaze narrows on me as his mouth quirks up at the corners. He's studying me studying him. He glances around the back lane and his smirk blooms into a smile. The car parked in the darkest spot between the light posts must be his.

His shoulders tighten as he secures his hold on Kady and moves to step back. He's going to make a run for it.

Some might think having five brothers pound on a far smaller and weaker little sister is terrible. At times, maybe it was, but I learned at a young age if I didn't fight back, I'd be toast. I can hold my own in an all-out fisticuff, and there's no way this shadow-skirting gobshite is making off with Kady while I still have an ounce of breath in my lungs.

When he checks over his shoulder, I seize his moment of distraction and launch. I run and use momentum to boost my impact. My pulse pounds through my veins as I connect. The moment of surprise is short-lived, but I manage to land a solid palm-strike to his head.

The hit shifts his focus from Kady to me.

Twisting her free of his grasp, I shove her toward the back door. "Go!"

The iron grip on my shoulder makes the world spin. Hot breath washes my cheek, and the scent of cinnamon and pine trees assault my senses. He shakes me like a ragdoll and my brain rattles in my skull.

I fight my way free, but the violence of it knocks me flying forward. Off-balance, I go down. The asphalt bites into my hands and knees, and I hiss. My palms take the worst of it, but I scramble into a crouch. He's between the pub and me, so my option is fight, not flight.

Game on, asshole.

With a banshee scream, I rush him, head down, shoulder-first.

He cushions the hit, and we fight and grope. I'm out-weighted and out-muscled. That's nothing new.

Hellcat works for me.

I'm clawing at his face while I slam my boot heel into the top of his foot. He curses and grips my elbow with bruising force and pulls me against his broad chest.

Twisting with all my weight, I make a solid grab for his crotch. My hands aren't big, but I grab all I can and squeeze like I'm juicing an orange to a pulp.

"*Bitch!*"

My knee meets his face as he buckles over. Then I start punching. I don't stop when he drops to the ground. I don't stop when he's got his arms over his head. Lost in a rabid rage, I lose track of the world around me.

The roar of fury brings him bursting back to his feet. He lifts me off the ground like I weigh nothing and slams me into the trunk of a tree. Pressed face-first against the rough bark, I try to push back.

I've got nothing left.

I twist in his hold but get nowhere. Where his palm presses between my shoulder blades, his touch burns my skin.

Prickly tingles zing into my cells, and my senses explode.

I groan, and he lets me go, sinking to a heap on the pebbled ground. My vision fritzes and my head goes wooly.

Blacking out is a bad idea.

I try to stay conscious, but…

"Ye've got fight in ye, kin of mac Cumhaill. I'll give ye that."

CHAPTER TWO

"What? And I'm hearing about it *now!*" My father's voice booms up the heating vent on my bedroom floor, and I track the sounds of his approach through the creaks of our old Victorian house. Depending on how mad he is, and how many stairs he skips, Da can make it from the kitchen to my room in anywhere from twenty-five to seventeen thundering footsteps.

It's a seventeen morning. Oh goody.

"Fiona Kacee Cumhaill!"

I stiffen in my bed and pull my covers over my head. It doesn't matter that I'm twenty-three and an independent woman. When he yells my full name, I'm back to being an eight-year-old girl caught red-handed, shearing Dillan's hair while he slept.

Well, he deserved it. He did the same thing to Walks With No Legs, my fancy-haired Guinea pig.

My door flies open and Da busts in, followed by Aiden, Calum, and Emmet. Aiden takes one look at the gauze wraps on my hands and curses. Da's expression darkens.

Calum and Emmet look whipped and contrite. I imagine they got a fair dose of our father's fury for not waking him up last night when we finally finished giving our statements and arrived home.

Before I get a word out, he erupts. "Are ye off yer gob? Ye stubborn, foolish wee girl. Ye coulda been killed."

When my father gets like this, it's best to let him have his say before trying any form of reason. It's a Borg "resistance is futile" thing. I sit up, nod when appropriate, and prop my pillows to await my turn to speak.

"—and then to learn that the boys found ye unconscious. What if that sonofabitch got ye into a car and made away with ye, or had a weapon? Have ye any idea..."

Now that I'm awake, I have to pee. I slide off my bed, shuffle into the ensuite that joins my room with Dillan's and Emmet's and close the door all but an inch.

Da doesn't miss a beat. Dressing-downs like this are a common enough occurrence that he knows I can still hear him. The onslaught continues while I empty my bladder, unwrap my palms, wash up, and rejoin them.

"—enough to worry about with yer brothers in danger every goddamn day, do ye think I need more on my mind? After yer mother..."

I sit on the edge of my bed and examine my scraped hands in my lap, biting my tongue.

He's winding down. My time is coming.

Auntie Shannon says I inherited the "can't be told" gene from my mother. I don't know if that's true, but if Ma was considered more stubborn than Da...well, that's saying something. I do remember she could give it as good as she got.

Yeah, maybe I am like her in that way.

"Da," I say when he's had the floor long enough.

"—brothers and I would do if he'd killed ye. Yer the feckin' glue that holds us together, Fi."

"And a person in my own right." I break his rhythm. "You forget that sometimes. Yes, I'm the keeper of the house, and it takes most of my time to sort you and the boys out, but I'm more than that. I'm tough and smart and as much a Cumhaill as any of you."

I point at Aiden, Emmet, and Calum, leaning against my dresser and door to ride out the storm. "You trust that they can take care of themselves in a scuffle, but I can too. I've got a stone fist and a fighting spirit the same as them. My instincts are sharp and my reflexes quick. And I'm smart."

"That's just it," Da snaps and scrubs a hand over his morning stubble. His hair is sticking up all cockeyed and at odd angles like a crazy russet rooster. "Yer too smart fer yer own good. Ye can take care of yerself, but yer too sure of it. Ye have no fear, and that's not good. Ye've never respected danger, Fi. It's like yer temptin' the Fates to test ye."

"I am not." I'm pissed at how blind he is. "I assessed the danger to Kady. There was no time to get help, and the man was unarmed."

"Ye *assume* the man was unarmed," he snaps. "He held Kady as a shield between ye. He coulda had a gun at his back or a knife in his pocket, but ye were so damn sure ye could handle things yerself, ye rushed him like a novice fool."

I jut my chin as his disapproval hits. "And if it had been Calum or Emmet in that alley instead of me, you'd be whistling a different tune. You'd be patting them on the back saying, 'Good on ye, boyo. Ye got the girl safe home. We'll catch the man responsible in the days to come.' But because it was me, I'm an eejit to think I could do the same."

Da's finger comes up in the air between us, and his cheeks flush red. "Don't throw yer feminist shite at me, Fiona Kacee. I work with women in uniform every day and trust them in any situation. They're trained and competent and know what they're up against."

"But I *don't*? Da, I grew up in this house. I've seen the horrors you face and heard the stories the boys tell of their shifts each day. Hell, I learned enough working behind the bar at Shenanigans to write fifty true crime novels."

"Hearin' and knowin' are different, *mo chroi*." He loses steam by calling me his heart. "Ye take care of yerself better than most, I'll not argue that. Because of it, Kady is safe home. I'm proud as blazes of ye for lendin' her aid, but no matter how sexist or unjust it is, yer a wee thing in a world of monsters—a Chihuahua ready to take on Rottweilers. If ye don't learn to respect the danger, it'll get ye. Like it or not, that's the truth of it. There is *always* someone bigger and better prepared for the fight."

"So what?" I launch to my feet and throw up my hands. "I should don my apron and resign myself to cooking and ironing for you lot the rest of my life? If Ma hadn't died, I would've gone to college and struck my own path. Filling this house with a family to take care of was *her* dream, not mine. I'm capable of doing great things too."

"Do ye think me daft?" Da drops his pointing finger and scowls. "It's not fair that ye had to step in and take care of yer brothers and me, but it's the way of it. Yer mam's death left shoes to fill and broken hearts to mend. Ye've done better at both than any of us had a right to expect. If yer ready to take on the world, I'm all for it. Still, we need ye alive to do it."

Not often does Da let feelings crack through his crusty shell. I'm not prepared for it. Angry I can handle. Sharp retorts, I've mastered. Admissions of his vulnerability after losing our mom has me looking at the door for a quick escape.

Only, there's no escape.

Aiden is blocking the door with his muscled arms crossed over his chest. Emmet and Dillan are standing beside him looking as lost by the turn of conversation as I feel.

I can't look at them or I'll start crying, and I'm not crying because I'm mad. I step back and frown at my father. "I do see the dangers, Da—honest, I do—and I respect them. I can't let that stop me. If you think honor and doing what's right is only for the

Cumhaill men, you're cracked. The same blood runs in my veins as yours. The same teachings were drummed into me. I care about people as much as any of you."

"More." Emmet pushes off the dresser to straighten. "That's what scares us, Fi. You care about people more than any of us, and don't hesitate to stand as the shield between an innocent girl and her attacker."

"We don't want to see you hurt, baby girl." Aiden comes over to squeeze my hand. "If you feel like life's leaving you behind, carve out something for yourself. We'll all pitch in to make it work for you. Just be safe about it."

Calum pegs me with a look so haunted my chest tightens. "When Kady screamed for help, and we saw you lying on the ground by that tree so still…" He shakes his head. "Jaysus, Fi. You can't put us through that shit again."

Da nods. "After every shift, I come home knowing as soon as I see your beautiful face, the darkness of my day will dissolve. You're our touch-stone, Fi."

Emmet joins the love-in and kisses the side of my head. "Even though you're a total pain in the ass."

Calum nods. "Absolutely the worst."

It's close to one that afternoon when I hear the throaty rumble of my muffler grumbling along the back lane and pulling into my spot. It's tough to find parking in the city, so by the time Aiden, Brendan, and Calum needed to get around, Da moved the back fence forward and paved a section of the lawn so they had space behind the house.

We're luckier than most. Being the last house on the street before the ravine, we also have a little dirt lane that runs up the side of the house. It's not for parking, but we often use it for short-term stops when friends drop by.

I finish with Emmet's uniforms and hang them on the hooks at the bottom of the stairs. Our house, a quaint Victorian built in Cabbagetown in the 1840s, isn't fancy but has character. It's an old, brick semi-detached with four bedrooms upstairs and a basement finished with a pool table and enough workout equipment to open Cumhaill's Gym if policing doesn't work out in the end.

Who needs more than that?

"Fiona?" Liam lets himself in and is jogging up the back hall looking panicked when I step out to meet him.

"I'm fine—" I'm caught up in his arms as he gives me a quick hug, then eases back to take inventory. He touches the bruise on the side of my face and scowls at the road-rash on my palms. I regain possession of my hands and step back. "Seriously, I'm fine. Your mom told you I take it?"

He nods and pulls me into the kitchen. "I'm sorry, Fi. If I hadn't skipped out—"

I wave that away. "It's nobody's fault except the weirdo in the alley. Even if you were there, I would've still taken out the trash. S'all good."

He sits me down at the table and busies himself at the counter. He's as comfortable in our home as we all are in his. "I'm making hot toddies. Talk to me and keep talking until I believe you're all right. Tell me what happened."

I give him the full recap. Explaining everything for the eleventeenth time increases my sense that I'm missing something —something big.

"And you saw him inside earlier?"

"Yeah, a Tyson Beckford-type drinking Redbreast in booth nine."

"Who's Tyson Beckford?"

"Beautiful, black supermodel for Polo, piercing eyes, easy smile…ring any bells?"

He makes a face at me. "Sorry. I'm not up on male models, but

I do remember a slick-looking black guy set up in nine. Pissed me off that we were busy and he sat alone and taking up a booth for six."

"Yeah, that's him. Hey, did anyone check on Kady?"

He grabs two glass mugs and the honey out of the cupboard. "Mom called this morning and told her to take the night off. She refused, of course. Dillan said he'd stay with her for the day and escort her in for the dinner shift."

I picture how protective of Kady my brother got after hell broke loose. "While the two of us gave our statements inside after I came to, it was like a switch flipped for him. Kady was shaking and about to crumble into a heap of tears, and he finally saw her —like, *saw* her."

Liam measures the shots of whiskey and mixes our drinks with a stick of cinnamon. "Mom said he volunteered to take her home and stay with her."

I accept the drink and inhale the honey-lemon glory of it. "Yeah. D's good like that. The patience of a saint, that one. He'll play the part of her loyal watchdog for as long as she needs to lean on him. Then, it'll be more, guaranteed."

Liam settles across the table and smiles. "Thank fuck. That love match was a long time in coming. Every time Dillan came in the bar, Kady became half as productive. It had to happen sooner or later."

"You're not kidding. Hey, speaking of love matches, how was your night?"

Liam fills me in on the PG broad strokes of his evening, but the tension of his worry never eases. After our second round of restorative whiskey drinks, I can't take it.

"Stop worrying. I *am* fine."

He arches a brow. "That might work on your family, Fi, but I know better. Tell me what you're *not* saying. You know I'll keep your secret."

I do. Liam's good that way. I stare into those ice-blue eyes and my guts twist. "It's going to sound crazy."

He shrugs and leans back in his chair. "With our families, what's not crazy?"

True. "Okay, so, last night, I thought it was simple. A crazy guy assaulted a pretty girl, and I got in the way."

"But you don't think so anymore?"

"I've been running it over in my head. I'm going into the station this afternoon to go over my statement and sign it. I was trying to remember every detail because more comes to you once you settle down and your mind unlocks."

"And you remember something new?"

"A couple of things."

"Like?"

"He never hit me or raised a hand to me. I punched him and sacked him and kneed him in the face and he never once returned the favor."

"Maybe he was busy trying to subdue you."

"Why not hit me? He had a foot on me and was strong. He pinned me against the tree out back for like, five seconds, then walked away. Why?"

Liam's getting angry again. I watch the mottled flesh of his cheeks darken. "What else did you remember?"

"Not remember. Found."

"Found? What do you mean?"

I get up from my chair, give him my back, and pull my shirt off. Clutching the fabric to my front, I swing my hair away from my shoulder blades.

"What the fuck is that?"

"My question exactly."

The legs of his chair scrape on the floor as he gets to his feet. He's taller than me—most people are—so when he takes a good look at the Celtic knotwork tattoo that spontaneously appeared on my back, he has to bend to do it.

"Does it hurt?"

19

"No, but I feel it. It tingles like it's squirming up from beneath my skin. Like it's alive somehow."

"That's not gross at all."

"Right? This morning when I had my shower, I saw the faint outline of the tree of life. The triquetra came around lunch. What does it look like now?"

Liam brushes a gentle sweep across my skin, and my cells light up inside. It's the same sensation I got when the handsome weirdo in the alley pressed his palm there.

"The tree is a brilliant, shamrock green, the triquetra a shimmering royal blue, and circling the whole thing are the words, *Glaine ar gcroi. Near tar ngeag. Beart de reir ar mbriathar.*"

"Well, shit." I flap my shirt in front of me and shuck it back on.

"You know what that means?"

"If you'd spent more time paying attention during Irish classes instead of flirting with the girls, you'd know what it says too." I free my hair and face him. "It's three sayings, and it means purity of our hearts, strength of our limbs, and action to match our speech."

His gaze narrows on me. "That was your toast last night for Emmet. Do you think that has something to do with it?"

"Indirectly. It's the three-part family motto of Da's people back home in Ireland. How weird is it that a guy gets the better of me in a dark alley, presses his hand on my back, and leaves when I pass out?"

Liam crosses his arms and frowns. "I, for one of many, am damned thankful that's when the asshole took his leave."

"Me too, but how do you explain a family crest magically appearing on my skin hours later?"

"I don't... I can't."

"Yeah, me either." I'm still standing there thinking about last night when the man's voice drifts into my head. It was right before I passed out. He leaned close and whispered in my ear, *"Ye've got fight in ye, kin of mac Cumhaill. I'll give ye that."*

I blink, and my entire body tingles. "I need to speak to my father right now."

The Fifty-first Division Headquarters, where Da has served since he graduated from the academy almost thirty years ago, is a bustling, gritty old law enforcement center on Parliament a block south of King. It's a heritage building, with decorative masonry, arched windows, and an interesting roofline that looks more like a turn of the century bank than a police station.

There's limited parking in a public lot, which is nice, but what I love most about the place is that across the road there's an original city fire hall complete with shiny brass poles and a Dalmatian named Pongo.

It's hot—in fact, I'm cooking with a cotton shrug on and annoyed I have to wear one. With the foresight of not wanting to strip my shirt off at da's station, I wore a strapless tank with an airy knit sweater. Even that's too much.

"It never gets old, does it?" I lock my car and Liam and I cross in front of the fire station.

For once, I'm more interested in getting inside to the air-conditioning than watching the fireman with no shirts polish their trucks.

Liam follows my gaze and chuckles. "I'll take your word for it. I've never gotten weak in the knees for a pec wink."

I laugh. "Sucks to be you."

I wave to Greg working the door and head straight up the staircase on the left. Da knows I'm scheduled to go over my statement, so of course, he's working in-house for the afternoon.

"Hey, kiddo." Da's partner Marcus lifts his gaze over the monitor of his computer and gives me a once-over. "I heard about last night. How are you?"

I glance at the concerned faces of two dozen cops I've known my whole life and smile. "Right as rain, guys. Seriously. You know us Cumhaills. You might be able to knock us down, but you'll never be able to keep us there."

"Good girl." Marcus points across the space. "You're set up in meeting room two."

I weave my way through the warren of cubicles with Liam on my heels. "Meeting room two is good. The walls are mirrored so I can read his reaction. There's no way he can front when he sees the tattoo."

"Do you hear yourself, Fi?" Liam casts me a sideways stink eye. "In what world would Niall Cumhaill be associated with a man who attacks his daughter in an alley?"

I pause with my fingers curved around the handle. "Only one way to find out."

CHAPTER THREE

I'm fuming mad by the time I drop Liam at Shenanigans and park in my spot behind the house. The back door is propped open to catch a breeze, and I fly inside, nearly bowling Emmet down as he comes out of the kitchen. His hands are full, two sweating beers in one, and a bowl of nuts in the other.

"Whoa, Fi. Where's the fire?" He shifts to avoid a full-on collision, and a wave of nuts washes the rim of the bowl. They rain down on the hardwood, scattering at our feet.

I am about to let loose on what a royal shitshow my afternoon was when a squirrel runs over my foot and starts chattering madly at my brother.

"What the fuck!" Emmet yells, backing up fast.

Calum jumps through the doorway to the den, spots the squirrel, and squeals like a five-year-old. "Is it rabid? Give it nuts, Emmet. Give it all the nuts."

Only my lightning reflexes save the bowl and its contents before my twit brother dumps the nuts on the floor. "I washed that damned floor yesterday. If Slappy Squirrel wants nuts, she can eat the ones you already dropped."

As if agreeing with me, the little brown rodent chirps and

23

switches her tail at them. In a flurry of grabby hands, she gathers the discarded peanuts, pockets them in her cheeks, and trots back outside. At the door, she sits back on her haunches and chatters something at me as if it were the most natural thing in the world.

Calum waits until the wee beastie bounds off the back steps before he hustles past me to slam the door. "Okay, that was bizarre."

My mind stalls out. "Believe it or not, that doesn't top my list of bizarre today."

Calum takes the beers from Emmet and points for him to go back to the kitchen for more. "Did something happen at the station? I figure you'd be used to that particular brand of strange and unusual by now."

"It did, and I am."

I accept the beer he offers and plunk into what is known as my chair. It's a pretty blue reading chair that our mom bought for herself a year or two before she died. Because of its delicate lines and it being the only dainty thing in a house with six men, they leave it for me.

"Okay, what did I miss?" Emmet comes in with another beer and a bag of chips. "What has your freak-o-meter redlining?"

I take a swig of my beer and set the bottle on the side-table coaster. "This morning after I showered, I found a gift left behind from the man who attacked me last night."

Both of them tense and I wave away their panic.

"Nothing too horrible but look at this." I peel off my sweater, gather my hair to the front of my shoulder, and turn so they can see.

"He inked you?" Emmet says.

"Sort of… I guess. Only it isn't a tattoo, and it's been getting darker and more detailed all day. It doesn't hurt or need to heal. And look at what it says."

They both lean in and read the Irish.

"I don't get it," Calum says. "You've been branded with the Cumhaill family motto? Why? By whom?"

"That's what I wanted to know. I showed it to Da at the station this afternoon, and he went into complete lockdown denial. Then, he checked his watch and suddenly had things to attend to. He left, denying he knew anything about it."

"Maybe he didn't," Emmet says.

"Emmet, he left me to go over my final statement without him being there."

Calum frowns. "Okay, that's weird. There's no way he'd leave the details that might catch that guy to anyone else. He'd want to be there for sure."

"Still," Emmet says. "Do you think he knows more than he's admitting to?"

"Who's not admitting to what?" Dillan says, coming in from the hall. Calum and Emmet catch him up, and I show him the tattoo. "Oh, if the oul man told you he didn't know what that is, his pants are on fire."

"I knew it." I drop my hair, still incensed that he lied to me, then ditched me to avoid answering my questions. Doesn't a girl have a right to know about her mysterious mugging tattoo? "What I don't know is why he lied, what the tattoo means, or what the hell a guy in the alley did to make it appear?"

"I can't help you there, but I know he's lying about not knowing about that image."

"How can you be so sure?"

"Because I've seen it before. When we were kids, Aiden and I got into his things from Ireland. We found a cool dagger at the bottom of his trunk. That Celtic tree is the image stamped into the leather sheath."

"So why not tell me? What's the big secret?"

Dillan shrugs and accepts the beer Emmet hands him. "I dunno. What I do know is, Da would never let his shit put you or any of us in danger. If he didn't know the connection before you showed him your back, he does now. Give him a chance to sort it out and see if he comes back to you with an explanation."

"Like I have any choice in the matter."

The doorbell rings and I head to the front of the house to see who it is. Emmet and Calum both cut me off and practically body-check me into the wall to take the lead. "What? Now I'm not allowed to answer my front door? Boys, get over yourselves."

"You can never be too careful," Calum says. "Maybe the squirrel told his friends about how good our nuts are, and they've circled back for more.

I laugh. "First off, *you* are nuts. Second, do you think if the neighborhood squirrels have organized they would use the doorbell to ask for more nuts?"

"That was one freaky intelligent squirrel."

"What the hell are you guys talking about?" Dillan asks, looking utterly lost.

Emmet has already answered the door and is talking to whoever it is. He leans back, his grip still firmly on the door. "Fi, there's a registered letter here, and this guy wants you to sign for it."

Dillan and Calum both eye the delivery person up and down like he's a person of interest in a potential crime about to be committed. Only when they've thoroughly reduced the poor guy to a nervous wreck, do they let me go to the door.

Calum frowns. "Registered mail? Could this day get any more bizarre?"

I sign for the letter and roll my eyes. Save me from well-meaning men. "Registered mail isn't common in our life, but it isn't bizarre."

I open the manila envelope and pull out a folded piece of paper. No, it's not paper, it's thick and textured like a sheet of old, handmade parchment. "Okay, maybe it's a little bizarre."

Emmet looks over my shoulder and points at the green wax

seal holding the ends of the parchment closed. It's the same tree of life and Celtic logo that I now wear on my back.

"Okay, Calum, you're right. It's full-on bizarre."

"What does it say?" Dillan asks when we return to the living room, and the four of us sit and reclaim our beers. Condensation made wet rings on the coasters, and I'm thankful that the boys are house-trained enough that they use them. Coaster training took a lot of yelling and more than one bloody nose to get it through their thick heads. I exchange my beer for the letter, wipe my fingers dry on my jeans, and break the seal.

"The writing is fancy," I say, studying the smooth lines and long tails and curls of the penmanship. "It's inked in some kind of calligraphy." I read the first couple of lines in my head, stop and start back at the top reading aloud. "Okay, boys, you're not going to believe this…"

My dearest Fiona,

Forgive the bluntness of this letter arriving unsolicited and likely unwelcome to yer home. If I were not yer granda and fast approaching the end of my time on this earth, I would never introduce myself in such a manner.

A lifetime ago, your da and I parted ways. True to the passions of our family, it was a heated and vocal event. We pictured his future differently and he left Ireland, never to return. The rift broke his mam's heart, and I've long regretted it.

When Aiden was born, I tried to make it right and haven't stopped trying for almost three decades. To no avail. I wish with everything in me that yer gran and I could've watched yer family grow.

Ye must know by now yer da is a stubborn man. He'll not hear my apology, so I beseech the youngest and most soft-hearted of my heirs….

Come home, mo chroi. Visit an oul man before the final set of his sun. There is much I need to teach ye about yer heritage. There are heirlooms that belong to yer family. It would ease my passing to know they were in yer hands.

To Aiden, Brendan, Calum, Dillan, and Emmet: I'm proud of the men ye've become. Yer calling to do right warms my heart. I've followed ye all from a distance, watching, and hoping that one day we'll meet.

All my love and devotion,

Granda,

Lugh Cumhaill

P.S. If ye mention this to yer da—and I'm sure ye will—know that he'll forbid ye to come. I'm sorry to put ye in the middle of such a situation. It's that important.

Dillan reaches toward me, and I pass him the letter. "We have a gran and a granda in Ireland? Why didn't we know that? Why don't we know them?"

"Because the bastard disowned me," Da snaps while storming in from the den's open doorway. He snatches the letter from Dillan's hand, looks it over, and huffs. "If he's not my da, then it stands to reason he's not yer granda."

"But, Da," Calum says. "It sounds like he's sorry and tried to make it right. Don't we get a say in this?"

Da grips the letter tight in his fingers and rips it in half. Then, he puts the pieces together and rips it again. My heart lurches with each renting tear, and I want to snatch the bits from his hands. There's no point.

Rip after rip after rip; the pieces grow smaller.

My eyes sting, and I blink back tears. "You had no right to do that. That letter was addressed to *me*. Maybe I want to hear what Granda has to say. Maybe I want to hug my gran and see where you grew up. What's so wrong with that? Were they horrible to you?"

Da scowls. "Och, of course not."

"So, if they simply wanted a different future for you and you stood your ground and built the life you wanted, why can't you make amends and let us get to know them now?"

My father takes the confetti bits left from my letter and stuffs them into his pocket. "Because I know the man, Fiona. The moment he gets his claws into one of my kids, he'll size ye up for a future ye never wanted. The same future I walked away from thirty-five years ago."

I chuff. "Da, the man doesn't know us. He doesn't hold designs on our plans."

"And ye'd be wrong on all accounts if ye believe that," Da snaps, the vein on the side of his head throbbing. "Forget hoppin' the pond fer a grand family reunion. It won't be like that. What he offers, yer best without. The only truth in that damnable letter is that I *do* forbid it. Ye won't go to him. Ye won't speak to him. And if he was here and says he has no watch, yer not even to give him the time of day."

"Come on, Da," Emmet protests. "He can't be that bad."

"He's worse. Trust me. Ten minutes in the door and he'll have yer sister's future planned and her head filled with tales of Cumhaill family traditions. I'll not have it." He gives us all a final glare. "That's the end of it. I'll not hear another word on the matter."

We hold our breath as he storms off.

The front door slams and I wince, anticipating the shattering of glass. By some miracle, it doesn't come. I sink into my chair and cast a glance at my brothers. "So, we know where Da stands on the matter."

"I guess we do," Dillan says.

I pick up the manila envelope from where it fell down the crack of my chair cushion and feel something else inside. "Do any of you know where Da was raised? Maybe we can research the area and contact Gran and Granda ourselves. How many Lugh Cumhaill's could there be in Ireland?"

Calum laughs. "That's our Fi. Deadset on doing the opposite of whatever she's told *not* to."

I ignore the jibe, my mind still spinning. If my tattoo links back to our family heritage and Da refuses to tell me what that's about, maybe Granda knows. Spontaneous branding isn't normal. If my GQ mugger did something to me, I want to know what.

"Look." I scan the room. "Don't tell me you all aren't curious. We have grandparents—people who want to get to know us. People who tried to play nice and make amends with Da, but were refused. If Granda is dying and reaching out, it has to be now. We should try to find him."

Dillan curses. "Did you miss the part where the top of Da's head blew off and splattered the stucco? He stood here two minutes ago and forbade us from looking into this."

I pull the rectangular slip of paper from the envelope and study it. "Okay, I won't research him. Are you happy?"

Dillan's gaze narrows. "No. I know that look—we all know that look. You have a bad idea festering, and it's going to bite us in the ass, I know it."

I hold up a paid travel voucher in my name for a flight to Kerry, Ireland. "Well, if we know the bite is coming, why play it safe? Who's driving me to the airport?"

CHAPTER FOUR

I quickly realize it's one thing to get fired up and hop on a plane to find my long-lost grandparents, and quite another to face an airport carousel, jetlagged, three thousand miles from home, and realize that no matter how long I stand here, that chute won't barf out my suitcase.

"Sorry," the attendant says when I explain things to him. "The baggage claim office is there. Queue up, and they'll take down yer tale of woe."

I follow his pointed finger to the small line forming at the counter on a sidewall. The half-dozen people there look as tired and frustrated as I feel.

I sigh and join the line of misery.

One thing I love about living in a city and working at a pub is having a broad sense of the people in the world around me. Humans are an eclectic lot from the myriad of their natural features, skin colors, accents, friends, lifestyles, clothes, and choice of drinks.

It all goes to tell their story.

Deep down, we are all the same. The subtle differences are the spices that make the stew of life rich with flavor. I cherish Da's

31

accent and quirky sayings, Aiden's wife Kinu bringing Japanese culture into our family, Calum and Kevin being free to live their love without judgment.

On any given night at Shenanigans, there are a few gregarious beauties, a few awkward but wonderfuls, and a few who would rather be left to themselves to sink into the background and get steaming drunk.

You learn a lot about people from behind the bar. The same can be said when standing in a line. As one passenger after another records their lost luggage and peels away empty-handed, I distract myself by studying them.

There's a well-tailored businessman next in line. He has a faint tan line where his wedding ring usually sits on his finger, and there's an indent if you look. Newly divorced maybe. Hoping for a little Irish adventure during a business trip more likely. He's a looker. I don't suppose he'll have much trouble finding a good time.

The woman next seems quiet and not all that put off about losing her luggage. She gives the name of a local bed and breakfast and asks directions to the taxi stand.

Then comes a red-faced man irate about his golf clubs not arriving on his golf vacation. Yeah, that sucks.

I occupy myself watching the other luggage losers and try to guess their stories. When I'm next up, I glance at the woman behind the counter.

My world goes wonky.

Maybe it's the jetlag that throws things off or perhaps the past two days are catching up to me, but I widen my stance to keep from keeling to one side.

I notice her hair first, long, and ruler-straight. It's so black under the fluorescent lighting it shines blue. When she turns to her printer, I trace the fall of the cut to a sharp line at her backside, which, from one female to another, looks amazing—more amazing than it should, given the unflattering fabric of her airport uniform.

When she turns back, I get my first direct glimpse of her face. I'm stunned, mind-numb. Something primal inside me bursts to life. *Danger, Will Robinson.*

I'm not into girls but to say she's Hollywood starlet material is to insult her ethereal beauty and grace—she's a freaking angel. *It's not real. She's not human.*

I shake off that lunacy and try to slow my crazy train. My exhaustion is obviously making me loopy.

She finishes with the irate golfer and has somehow tamed the raging beast. He turns away from the counter, looking love-drunk with a dreamy expression on his face.

"Grand. Now, what's yer story, dearie?"

Oh gawd, she's even more mesmerizing when her attention is focused. Her eyes are such a light blue they're almost silver. When her gaze locks on mine, every hair on my body stands on end.

"Are ye all right?" she asks, her voice a warm caress. She waits, her eyebrows arched expectantly. I feel strange. Not a normal odd, but a panicky, run for the hills weird. She frowns. "I take it ye queued up fer a reason, did ye not? What have ye lost?"

My mind. I tear my gaze away from her radiance and focus on the laminated images of baggage on the counter. I point to the one that most resembles my suitcase and offer her my boarding pass. "It's like this one, number six, but red."

She takes my dog-eared flight stub and starts to fill in a claim form. Her mouth tightens when she's writing my name, and she pegs me with a look. Her silvery eyes glitter with—I'm not sure what—hostility, concern, curiosity?

"And where will ye be stayin' while yer here, Fiona Cumhaill?" The intensity of her gaze makes my skin tingle. I break the connection to watch the silver tip of her pen glide over the page as she records my information.

"I'm not sure. It's all a little undecided right now." I desperately want to get away and have no idea why.

For the next few minutes, her pen flows in a graceful cursive, as efficient as it is hurried. When it jolts to a stop, she tears off the top copy and pushes it at me. "Next."

I take my paper and put some distance between the creepy, ebony-haired angel and me. In an effort not to look back, I check that she's gotten everything right and notice the digits of my cell phone.

Shit with sugar on top. I left in such a rush that I have no travel package. *Awesome.*

I make a mental note to go online and amend that before I have to sell my firstborn to pay the bill. No doubt, my phone will ring the moment I take it off airplane mode.

I likely have fifty hostile and frantic messages too.

Wait. Maybe *not* having a package is a good thing. It gives me an excuse to never take it off airplane mode.

Thinking about Da's ire doesn't improve my mood. He'll be raging mad that I went against his wishes and came to Ireland. More than angry, he'll be disappointed.

I swallow and head into the loo to freshen up.

It's not like the six of us are obedient children—far from it—but when push comes to shove, we respect when our father lays down the law for Clan Cumhaill.

He has the final word. No argument.

I've never blatantly crossed him before, and the betrayal of trust twists my guts tight.

Still, those same guts tell me I need to be here.

I need to unravel what my dark and dangerous, back-branding, mugger has to do with a family I know nothing about. What does the symbol mean? Why do I feel so strange since it appeared?

"He called me kin of mac Cumhaill," I whisper to myself in the mirror as I wash my hands. I mulled everything over in my mind a million times on the plane. In the city, work-life, and with everyone who knows my family and me, I am simply Cumhaill.

Da has buried most of our family history from the first day he arrived. I doubt anyone in Toronto knows our traditional Irish name—mac Cumhaill—except for a shadow-creeping hottie in fine clothes.

Exiting the loo, I shrug my computer bag higher onto my shoulder and stare at the security exit into the arrivals area. The flow of arrival traffic has thinned to a trickle of the last few stragglers.

The businessman has struck up a conversation with the quiet woman, and the two of them are lost in conversation as they slip into the same taxi. I wonder if he's accompanying her to her bed and breakfast. My instincts say yes.

The red-faced golfer still looks dazed and oddly blissful. Before the ebony angel, I would've said if looks could kill, the Kerry Airport arrivals area would be heaped with bodies. Now, it seems all is right in the world.

I let him pass, creeped out by the energy he gives off.

Alone in the corridor, I draw a deep breath and decide I've stalled long enough. When the automatic doors *whoosh* open, I draw another steadying breath and step over the threshold.

As stupid as it sounds, although no one knows I'm coming, my heart sinks when no one stands waiting for me. No lovely old couple is wringing their hands with the excitement of meeting their granddaughter, no limousine driver in a black hat holds a sign with my name on it—Cumhaill or mac Cumhaill—okay, I've watched too many RomComs with that one.

Still, I regret my lack of impulse control.

I'm in a foreign land with no idea of my destination, no luggage, no cell package, and no idea where to start.

I am as alone as alone can be.

"Och, stop the lights. Yer not the weepy sort, are ye? Ye look like yer ready to fall to bits, and I'm not the man for tears and carryin' on."

I blink at the crusty Irishman stepping inside the glass entrance. He wears the same impenetrable scowl I've seen every day of my life, and it doesn't matter that I've never met the man, I rush forward and hug him tight.

The stiffness in his frame tells me he is as uncomfortable with PDA as his son. The tingling in my skin tells me whatever weirdness is taking hold of me is getting stronger.

Ouch. Like, really strong.

Is he triggering it, or is it this place, or is it me?

The lights flicker and hum above us. I glance up, and the fixture bursts into an explosion of sparks. I pull away from my grandfather while ducking the raining fireworks. "What the hell?"

"Come. That's our cue to leave."

Another light hums and flickers. It bursts and explodes the same as the first. My cells fire with energy and I feel it building inside me. "Am I doing that?"

Granda places a firm hand on my back and shoves me outside. He seems more anxious about the pyrotechnics than me. When we stop, twenty feet from the building, he scans me with an assessing gaze and his brow pinches.

I finger my hair and straighten my shirt. "Sorry. I'm a bit crumpled and frazzled by exploding lights. Not the best first impression."

"Arragh," he mutters. "Forget the lights. I'll take ye, crumpled or not. By the fates, ye have the look of yer gran, that's fer sure."

"I look like her?"

"A great deal. My Lara is a wee russet beauty with a fire burnin' inside her, too."

I study the nuances of my grandfather's features and try to see myself in him. He's classically handsome in a worn leather jacket sorta way and has my bright blue eyes. "Except for the dark hair, you're the spitting image of Da."

He chuffs. "One might say he's the spit of me." There's an awkward pause, then he huffs. "So, how is yer father, then?"

"Grand. A pain in my ass every day."

"So, moving across the world changed him none."

"I don't suppose anything could."

"Ye have a point. That boy was always stubborn as rocks." Granda looks me over again and offers a sad smile. "I wish things had been different, Fiona. Yer gran and I ached to know you kids."

And now you're dying. I pat my bag, thankful I kept my most important possessions as a carry-on. "There's still time. I brought pictures, and the boys sent quick notes of hello."

He looks at the concrete walkway around my feet, then scowls toward the building. "And is that all ye brought? Ye seem to have forgotten yer bits and bobs."

"There's a problem with my luggage."

He nods. "I'm sure we can make do. Come, we should strike off. We live a fair whack away, and yer gran will be bustin' her buttons until I get ye home."

I take one last look at the airport and can't say I'm sad to leave it in the rearview. Between lost luggage and the ebony angel and exploding light fixtures, I'm ready to put some distance between us.

It's not an auspicious start to my quest for answers.

I have more questions than ever.

CHAPTER FIVE

G randa and I leave the terminal and venture into the deep, darkening dusk of the Emerald Isle. Sixteen hours ago, I entered an airport surrounded by the cacophony of a metropolis, the hum of cars on the highway, and city lights as far as the eye could see.

Emerging from Kerry Airport is like stepping into an alternate reality. The rolling green and beige hills stretch off into the distance, the only cars are parked neatly in one large lot out front, and there aren't enough people here to fill Shenanigans on a Friday night.

"This is us." Granda points at the dust-covered blue Land Rover parked in the lot.

"Ah, ye found her," an elderly man shouts from a few rows over.

"That I did," Granda shouts back with a wave.

For the third time in an hour, my skin tingles with awareness like I'm becoming some kind of freakish energy antenna. My reaction stems from the little man. Why? What is it about him that has my Spidey-senses tingling?

He's incredibly short, with snowy hair tucked under a crooked hat. His chinstrap beard outlines a round face, mischievous blue eyes sparkling behind rimless glasses, and ends on each side of his face at his noticeably small ears. If it weren't totally cray-cray, I'd say he's one of Ireland's fabled old leprechauns.

Granda opens my door and shoves me inside the truck.

"Hey," I say, "enough with the shoving."

He leans into the open window, so close, his two eyes merge into one. Scowling cyclops is not a good look for him. "It's not polite to stare, young lady. Or did yer da fail to teach ye basic manners?"

Before I respond, he pulls out of my window, rounds the hood of the truck, and offers another wave. "Take care!"

"*Slan,*" the man says, his gaze locked on me.

I force a smile and wave, making certain not to stare.

Granda slides in, turns the key in the ignition, and pulls away with unveiled haste.

I grab my belt and buckle up. The smile pasted on my face fades away as the engine's throaty growl pulls us away from the sleepy airport. "What's your problem? What did I do?"

"Don't play daft, Fiona. No matter how angry yer father is with what we are, I don't believe that if ye have the sight, he hasn't taught ye better than to slight a Man o' Green."

I blink at him. "That *was* a leprechaun?"

He chuffs. "Let one catch ye callin' him that and ye'll learn yer lesson quick enough. The proper term is a Tuatha De or Man o' Green. The 'L' word will get ye cursed to dig earthworms with yer fingers for the rest of yer life or polishing beetles ye pick from dung."

I run my fingers through my hair and try to focus. Whatever this energy is inside me, it's much stronger here. I scratch the flesh of my arms and try to pull air into my lungs.

I can't breathe.

Leprechauns are real?

What the hell was the woman at the baggage claim? Because sure as shit, she wasn't human. "Wait. You said 'what we are.' What does that mean? What are we? What's the sight? How did I make those lights explode?"

Granda pulls the truck onto the shoulder of the two-lane road and turns his full attention on me. It strikes me then that he's awfully fit and muscled for a man who claimed to be dying.

Oh, gawd. I'm a fool. Da warned me not to come.

Liam's words ring in my spinning head. He's right, Da would never be tied to a man who'd attacked me in an alley...but maybe Lugh Cumhaill would.

I try to fill my lungs, but the oxygen doesn't come. The inside of the truck swirls and my breath starts to hitch. I fumble with the handle on my door, but my hands are trembling too much to coordinate my escape. "What's going on? Are you really dying? Da warned me this was a mistake. What do you want with me?"

The scenery spins and a firm hand presses on the back of my neck. Granda pushes my head down between my knees and curses. "Breathe, *mo chroi.* I'm sorry. I thought ye knew. I'll explain everything once we get home. Just breathe. Yer gran will have my hide if yer in a state when we get there. I swear, yer as safe as safe can be. Just breathe."

I'm not sure how long it takes before my breathing returns to normal and my world stops tilting. I'm in Ireland with my grandfather and leprechauns are real and "we are" something, and there's more to tell me...

When I sit up, the countryside is full-dark, and the pitch surrounding the truck makes things that much creepier. I don't want to talk about what's happening while vulnerable in the darkness. Too late, I worry about venturing into Nowhereland with a man my father left behind without a backward glance.

Then again, da said his parents never mistreated him.

A GILDED CAGE

They saw his future differently. That's not so bad.

I pull my shit together, straighten in my seat, and clutch my bag against my chest. "If you don't mind, I'd like to meet my gran and have a cup of tea now."

Granda nods and gets us back on the road.

We drive along in awkward silence while I sort through things I need to address. Whether or not whatever's happening inside me has to do with them, forging a relationship with my grandparents is important.

I'm in Ireland, meeting my father's family—*my* family. That's huge. "Thank you for coming to get me."

Granda nods again, his eyes on the horizon. "We're thankful ye came. And to answer yer question, I *am*, but I'd rather not be."

"I'm sure that's true."

"It's a complicated situation, and we'll get to the meat of it when we know each other better, but I didn't bring ye here on a lie. If I don't get the help needed, I'll be dead within a month, maybe sooner."

"Then get the help you need."

He slows the truck and hits his indicator, taking us off the main road. "I'm trying. It's complicated. We'll talk about it more another time. Fer now, let's celebrate yer arrival."

We ride along for a while, and I watch the road illuminated in the pool of our headlights. "How'd you know what flight I was on? Da destroyed your letter, and I didn't know how to contact you."

He casts me a glance I recognize well. It's my father's "think about it" look. I do, and there's only one explanation. "Da called you in a frantic fit."

He dips his chin, his attention on the road ahead. "The neighbors, actually. We're having some power troubles at our place at the moment, but he did manage to get a message to me, and I rang him back."

"And? On a scale of one to ten, how furious is he?"

"Time and distance haven't changed much with Niall. I'm still evil incarnate, but apparently, he is willing to deal with the devil to ensure his daughter is not lost and alone in a strange land."

My guilt over sneaking off behind my father's back increases tenfold. "Yeah, that sounds like him."

The tires of the Land Rover crunch over the dirt and gravel of my grandparent's long laneway. Although I can't see the landscape, I know they live in the remote countryside. Unlike in the city, where day or night lights lead the way, here it's only the truck headlights and the light of the bulbous silver moon. It's eerie, dark, and nothing I could ever get used to.

"This is us," Granda says.

We drive through an arched opening in a tall, shrub wall and I lean forward in my seat. It's amazing. White faery lights hang in playful swoops along the inside edge of the shrub wall. They ring the bottom edge of the house's roofline too, and the pathway that welcomes us in.

The one-story home is built into the side of a grassy hill. The rounded stone walls create an organic architecture while the thatched roof undulates over the different sections like a gnome's floppy hats.

OMG. My grandparents live in The Shire.

Granda catches me staring and grunts. "It's nothing like a city house, I know, but ye'll do well not to judge. Our home is a treasured part of yer gran, and it'll cut her deeply—"

"It's incredible." I unbuckle my belt and slide out my door, mesmerized by the sprawling stone cottage. "It's like something out of a dream."

"Och, well, it's home, is all." He swings his door shut with a clang and drops the keys into his pants pocket. "Come, yer gran is likely dizzy with impatience by now."

I follow Granda down a cobblestone path lined with blooming flowers. The scents of greenery and blossoms fill my senses and go a long way in settling my nerves. Ivy hangs in front of the handcrafted wooden door, and Granda waves his hand. "Out of the way, ye wee nuisance."

The vine flaps its leaves and twines up and over the rounded top of the door. If I didn't know better, I'd swear it listened to him. I'm lost in the wonderment of that thought when we step inside.

I squeak as I'm caught up in a breath-constricting hug.

"Lara, don't crush the girl. She's had a day."

Gran pulls back, and I blink. Wow, Granda is right. Other than her hair being white and pulled back beneath a daisy laurel, the similarities between us are astonishing.

She casts her husband a look, and her brow crinkles like my father's. "Ye took yer sweet time gettin' home, oul man." Then her attention shifts to me and her expression smooths out. "Are ye hungry, luv? Will ye take a cup of tea and some supper? Ye must be famished."

My stomach is so empty it's cannibalizing itself, but it's customary to refuse the first offering of Irish hospitality. I hold up my hands. "Don't let me be a bother. I'm fine."

"I insist. It's hot and ready fer ye."

"All right, thank you. I'd be happy to eat."

Gran takes me by the wrist and practically drags me through the house at a jog. The front and side walls of their home are stone, and they're covered in living plants toward the back.

We pass the wide trunk of a tree growing in the middle of the living room, and I'm staring backward at that when the succulent, buttery scents of colcannon and fresh bread hit me.

My stomach lets off a thunderous roar as we arrive in the kitchen. I blush and place a hand over my rumbling belly. "That smells amazing."

"It was one of yer father's favorites."

"It still is, although ours doesn't smell half that good."

Gran winks and starts dishing out heaping bowls. "I'll teach ye a few family secrets while yer here and ye can surprise him when ye cook it next. How does that sound?"

"Wonderful." With my emotions bubbling up, I swallow and try not to think about Da. I already broke down in front of Granda in the truck. One fall-apart is quite enough. Gran seems to sense my battle with composure and sets the bowls down to hug me.

This time, her embrace doesn't threaten to crush my ribs. The burning tingle of my skin subsides, and my restlessness eases in a rushing wave of warmth and nurturing energy.

"There, now. That's better, is it?" She squeezes my hands before turning back to the stove.

"Much. Thank you."

I accept two steaming bowls of the potato and cabbage dish and head to the table. The kitchen and living room beyond are spacious and furnished in wood, stone, and living things. The glowing light from a dozen lanterns placed around the interior gives off a mystical, old-world feel.

It's quaint and welcoming—much like the two of them.

The table is set with flowers and candles, and Granda points to my place. "Set those down, and we'll wash up and settle in fer the night."

Granda leads the way to the loo and points inside the door when we arrive. "We have runnin' water heated by pipes between the stone of the south wall, compostin' toilets, and pretty much every convenience yer accustomed to other than electricity."

No electricity? It strikes me then, his comment about power troubles and not having a working phone, the candles and lanterns twinkling in the corners, and Gran standing before a cookstove. There are no candles in the bathroom, and still, a warm glow lights it.

I lift my gaze and stare at the ceiling. This part of the house must be under the hill. The roof is blanketed in spongy green moss bursting with buds and blossoms. It glows iridescent white, blue, pink, and green, giving off as much light as anyone would need. "What is that?"

Granda follows my gaze and smiles. "Bioluminescent fungus. Nature provides a great many wonders if ye take the time to learn about them."

"How is it possible?"

"Ye asked me in the truck what we are. Well, Clan Cumhaill, from as long ago back as the Middle Ages, are druids. Our family and a few others in the area live in the ways of the ancient Keepers of the Earth. It's something yer gran and I are proud of and part of the reason I contacted ye. I'm eager to teach ye more about yer heritage."

Okaaaay. Not sure what to do with that, but after the past couple of days, I'm willing to suspend disbelief.

Druids.

All right, it could've been worse.

I blink up at the ceiling and my skin tingles. I reach up, and the glowing light intensifies. The fungi, flowers, and foliage are woven together in a symphony of living architecture above our heads.

I trace the twining branches and blooms, sensing playful confidence in every nuance of them. "This might sound crazy, but I feel like the plants are aware of me somehow."

"Of course, they are. Every living thing has a predisposition to seek and sustain life. To do that, all things have intelligence, instinct, or awareness on some level. Think of plants reaching for the sun or roots reaching into rich dirt."

"Why haven't I sensed it before now?"

Granda nods and points inside. "I'm sure yer bubblin' with questions, and we'll get to them all. Wash up. If yer dinner gets cold, yer gran will take it out on me, and she's a fierce one when she's vexed."

I chuckle and close myself into the washroom, my mind spinning. Druids. My father's parents are—and all our family before them were—druids.

Crazier still—I lift my arm to the ceiling, and a little vine comes to hug my finger—I think it's catchy.

CHAPTER SIX

I wake to the scent and sound of bacon frying and a swath of golden sunlight blinding me. The blazing rays stream through all three of the round, portal windows in my room—the same one my father grew up in. I stretch and force myself to sit. Last night is a bit of a sloggy-brain blur. I met my grandparents, and we ate until I almost burst, then they took me next door to their neighbors and let me call home—I had to leave a message. Because of the time change, everyone was at work—then the night fell away in jetlagged exhaustion. I remember the most important part, though.

We're druids.

That's something Da might've mentioned in the last twenty-three years. I rub my hands over my face and shake myself awake. I still feel like something the neighbor's cat hacked up on my back porch, but like Calum always says, there's nothing bacon can't fix.

"Howeyah," Gran says as I shuffle into the kitchen.

"Howeyah," I say back.

Gran's in good spirits, radiant in a cornflower blue dress and humming a jaunty tune. Today, a grapevine wreath decorated with sprigs of wildflowers replaces her daisy laurel. I pride myself on being a live and let live kinda girl, but if this is what "druid" means, it's not for me.

Hard pass on converting into a flower child.

I'm far more endless night than sweet delight.

The kitchen skylight is open, and birds fly in, pluck seeds and cut fruit from a serving bowl set out for them, then zoom out as if it's the most natural thing in the world.

"Ohmygawd...Gran, you're Snow White." I slap my hand over my mouth to catch my laughter and can't believe I said that out loud.

Gran giggles and her laugh sounds like a cheerful birdsong. "Och, not me, but Neve was a powerful and respected druid. Jacob and Wilhelm Grimm came upon her in the forest one day and the rest, as they say, is history."

Seriously? Huh, who knew?

Gran studies me, standing in front of her in Granda's t-shirt and clucks her tongue. "I'll have Lugh call the airport this aft and see about yer missing bag." She hands me a plate of bacon and tilts her head to the table. "Fill yer gob, missy. The day is fast slipping away."

"Sorry, I'm usually an early riser."

"Och, well, I'm not a traveler myself, but it's said a good laugh and a long sleep are the two best cures for anything."

I set the plate of bacon on the table and sit in my spot. Both the other places have been cleared. "Just me then?"

"It is. Go on, now, help yerself."

I lift the lid of an old-fashioned tureen, heap my bacon plate with baked beans and eggs, and top it off with grilled mushrooms and tomatoes. "It must be the fresh country air because I can't remember ever being this hungry."

Gran smiles. "I'm happy as a lark to keep ye fed. Make sure ye tell me if ye have a preference."

I finish chewing what is in my mouth and swallow. "The only

one of the six of us who fusses about food is Emmet and only because he has a tricky stomach. I'm good. It feels weird though, filling my face while someone else cooks. I'm happy to earn my keep when you're ready to put me to work."

Gran chuckles. "No fears there, luv. Lugh will keep ye plenty busy in the days to come. There's so much to do and little time to do it."

Right. Granda said he only has a month left to live. I wonder more about what's killing him, but he said it's complicated and he'll tell me in time. I respect that. I scan the inside of the expansive cottage and look out the windows. "Where is he now?"

She drains the bacon grease into a container and takes the dishes to the sink. I can't tell if her sudden frown is related to my question or an egg-crusted plate giving her a hard time. "There's been a bit of a stir about yer arrival. A couple of the local druid families want to come by and give ye a scrutinizing once over."

I look at my reflection in the mirror, then down at the t-shirt I'm wearing. I'm a freaking disaster. "When's that?"

Gran shakes her head. "Don't worry. I pointed out that everyone will gather at the Rose of Tralee Festival in a few weeks and they can meet ye then. That gives ye time to gain yer footing before yer put up fer display."

I exhale. "Thanks, Gran."

She turns from the dishes and winks. "My pleasure."

I finish my meal and join her at the sink. After slipping my empty plate into the sudsy water, I start clearing the table. "So, what's the plan for today?"

Gran points at a box sitting on the living room sofa. "I had Lugh dig out a bin of Niall's things from long ago. Take it into yer room, have yer shower, and see if ye find anything ye can wear today. By the time yer dressed and ready, I'm sure yer granda will be back."

Fresh from the shower and dressed in a pair of my da's old khakis belted around my waist and a black t-shirt tied at my hip, I feel almost human. There is a ton of good stuff in the box Gran gave me—a bag of marbles, toy figurines, yearbooks, mementos from places he worked—but I've wasted enough of the day already and opt to snoop through my father's childhood when I have more time to soak it in.

With my hair tied back and new spring in my step, I head out to find my grandparents. I smile simply thinking that word—grandparents. I am in Ireland with my grandparents.

How freaking cool is that?

"Great timing," Gran says, her arms full as she heads through the living room toward the front door. "Help an oul girl out and grab the last of the lanterns, will ye?"

I hurry to open the door for her, slip on my shoes, grab my sunglasses from the pocket of my purse at the door, and hook my fingers through the handles of the last five lanterns.

"Line them up, here, luv." Gran points to the stone half-wall that borders a little patio area in front of the house from the grassy lawn beyond.

I set my lanterns by the others and let them start soaking up the sun's rays to use inside tonight.

"Right, then." Gran picks up a cutting basket with a set of pruners. "That's done. Let me show you around."

I fall in step, taking in the natural solitude. It's a huge property bordered at the front and sides by the tall, thick hedge we drove through last night and a dense grove of trees beyond the back lawn. The shrub wall runs along the front and reaches off on both sides. It has a completely different feel to it than the city. "How close are your next neighbors?"

Gran points off to the right. "The O'Rourkes are a cock-crow that way, and the Fowlers are three times that over there." She tilts her head in the opposite direction.

I see nothing beyond the top of the hedge other than the soft green hue of Irish hills stretching lazily into the distance. With no idea how far a cock-crow is, I figure I'll learn as I go. "And are they druids too, your neighbors?"

Gran smiles. "Most in these parts are simply culchie folk. As far as others like us, there are eight other families scattered across the isle. With heirs and descendants, that's likely a few hundred all total."

"And do all descendants get the druid gift?"

"Och, not at all. And as the years pass, that number dwindles. As the span of natural spaces disappears across the lands, so too does the fae magic, it seems."

"Across the lands? They're not all here in Ireland?"

"Och, that they were, luv. Many believe emigration is as much to blame fer the loss of magic as the lost wildness. Over the centuries, druids have married and moved to become Bretons, Cornish, Manx, Scots, and Welsh."

Gran sets her basket on the stone half-wall and presses her palms together. In a deliberate pattern of finger movements and sweeps of her hands over the plants, blooms bud and open. The power of her nurturing energy tickles my skin and raises the hair on my arms.

She takes my hands and presses my palms together as she did. "Like this, luv. Palms together for the first position, then one full circle of yer fingertips…not that way, withershins."

"Withershins?"

She holds up her finger in the air. "Clockwise is this way. Withershins is this way."

"Counter-clockwise."

Gran smiles. "Druids, pagans, and those of the fae prefer withershins. Right then, hands in the first position. Try again."

I press my palms together and follow Gran's motions. Together we tend to her flowerbeds, relocate the weeds from the garden to their designated weed bed, and fill her basket with fresh tomatoes, cucumbers, and berries.

Gran's in the zone. It's as if the earth and plants feed her soul. It's cool, but...

"Don't take this the wrong way, but what's the point? What do druids do? What's the relevance of connecting with weeds and making friends with moss?"

The breeze picks up and treats us to the floral aromas of what I can only describe as content plants.

"Don't look at it as what we do, but who we are."

"Okay, so who are we?"

She leans back against the stone wall, and the sun warms the crinkles at the sides of her eyes. "Fae energy is the *prana* of the earth, the life source of growth, the intelligence of animals, and the breath of plants. It is the essence and spirit in all nature. Fourteen centuries ago, during medieval times, druids were named as the protectors of that energy. Because of our dedication to preserving such a fragile resource, our ancestors were rewarded with heightened abilities. Those gifts help us fulfill our calling."

"And that is what's been tingling inside me for the past couple of days—my calling?"

She nods. "Yer natural power woke, but Lugh holds yer true magic. The innate gift ye possess is much stronger than what's normally felt from a spontaneous bloomer. Lugh mentioned he got cross with ye yesterday at the airport. He didn't understand this is all so new for ye."

"Whatever it is, it burst to life three days ago, and I don't understand any of it."

Gran takes my wrists and presses my palms to the mossy ground. "Empty yer mind of the noise that buzzes inside yer head, no questions, no expectations, no turmoil. Nature will explain more to ye than I ever could."

I close my eyes and do as she says. Maybe it's here or gran's gift calming me or simply focusing on nature as she said, but a connection builds beneath my palms. It amps up, zings from my hands and up my arms.

All at once, I am aware of the living force that is nature.

From the rich earth beneath my fingertips, to the detritus and worms burrowing below the dark soil, and the moisture seeping drop by drop to offer the grass sustenance.

"Can ye feel the strength of the sun's rays feeding the plants and trees and wildlife?"

"I can."

"That's the power of the Earth Mother, our Divine Goddess."

I embrace the connection with the source energy, and it invades me. Heat surges from my arms into the core of my body, and I gasp when it fills my lungs.

"Relax, luv. Druids are the conduits of earthly power. It will never harm ye as long as ye hold it in yer heart with reverence. Accept our Lady's gifts and let her ignite your cells and wake ye to yer calling."

I focus on gran's instruction, and after a long moment, nature's lifeblood pulses freely in my veins.

"That's right. Now open yer eyes."

I'm half-afraid to see the mundane world and lose the radiant beauty I see with my mind's eye. Seeing the world doesn't ruin anything. The grass, the trees, even my hands are pulsing with a breathtaking aura.

"Is this real?"

"It is. Now, relax into the magic of it all and reach further. Don't push. Simply let yer essence seep out like the tide ebbing away from the rocky shore toward the sea. Once ye free yerself, ye should be able to feel the wee creatures of the forest."

I focus on a little pigmy shrew rooting beneath a pithy log. Beyond that, a fox plays in the afternoon sun, and farther still, a deer forages for leaves.

It freezes, wary of a snapping twig in the distance.

I feel the interconnectedness of it all—the web of life and the interdependence each component has with another. "It's incredible."

"It is at that. Now, I'll leave ye to it. Spend as much time as ye like. Allow the Divine Lady to know ye, and she'll do the same. Yer one of her custodians now. Ye'll need to build a relationship." The pressure of Gran's hold on my hands releases and the drop in magic is jolting.

Gran is powerful—far more powerful than she looks.

I settle into the magic of the moment, memorizing how my body tingles, how the fragrant breeze crawls across the hairs on my arms, how nature's magic warms a part of my insides I never realized was cold.

Eventually, I sense it's time to release my connection, and I end my first true commune with nature. Jazzed, I find Gran tending to the plants that line the side patio.

"How was it, then?" Gran asks.

"It was… I can't even describe it."

"To be awed is a description in itself."

A little brown furball crawls up onto the stone half-wall near us, his tiny nose rooting around before him. Right before he gets into trouble with a vine of deadly-looking thorns, Gran lays her hand flat, and he crawls into her palm.

"Druid power stems from seven different disciplines. It's not all or nothin' mind, there is a great deal of crossover, but most have an affinity for one over the others. My primary discipline is natural magic—zoology, herbology, and botany. My gift enhances my connection with flora and fauna."

She kisses the little shrew and places him back in the flowers. "Lugh's primary is knowledge, past, present, and future—meta-composition, epistemology, ancient civilizations, prognostication. He's the historian of the Ancient Order."

"And my da?"

"Och, that's the rub of it. Niall's gifts fell squarely in physical magic—combat, weaponry, survival. From the time he took his first steps, he had a gift for archery and was wicked deadly with a staff. He would've gone far."

I fail to see a modern use for wicked stick-whacking skills other than Olympic piñata bashing, but I bite my tongue. "He did go far, Gran. He's a great cop. Being a fighter in the middle of a rolling countryside wouldn't have been enough for him. It makes sense that he ended up where he did."

"From yer viewpoint of not knowin' what it means to be a Cumhaill, maybe. From yer granda's point, Niall thumbed his nose at us and tossed our heritage like it meant nothing."

I disagree, but this is a forty-year feud I'm not about to weigh in on. "What do you think my primary discipline is?"

"Good question," Granda says as he joins us. "I asked a friend talented in such things to join us at the rings to help sort that out. Are ye set to go meet him?"

CHAPTER SEVEN

Granda laces his fingers to walk hand-in-hand with Gran as we cross the back lawn. It's sweet. They're sweet. It's not long until our path ends at the top ridge of a sunken circle. As the land slopes away from us, I find what my grandfather must have meant when he said the "rings."

Like an ancient Greek amphitheater plucked from history, three cylindrical rings cut deep into the hillside. With each three-foot drop into the descending landscape, the rings tighten, and the valley narrows. At the bottom, a flat circle of manicured grass lays dotted with equipment and supplies.

"Let the games begin." I jump down the first three-foot drop.

I leave my grandparents as they head for the stairs, jog across the three feet of grass, then jump down to the next level. I jog the plane of that tier and drop again. After hopping off the third ring, I arrive on what must be the training floor of this pagan arena. The tools Granda intends to use to test me lay in wait: weapons, seeds, a few tools I don't recognize, some polished rocks—

"Skunk!" I scramble up the stone wall to the next tier.

The stocky rodent raises his white head, two distinct black

strips running from his muzzle to his ears. "Skunk? Are ye daft? I'm not a feckin' skunk."

I yelp and stumble back onto my ass. "Talking skunk!"

Gran giggles and waves off my warning. "Don't panic, luv. Animals talk, and many druids possess the ability to hear them. Except, Dax isn't a skunk, he's a badger. Come here to me, now, my girl, and rest easy. Dax is a dear friend. He's my animal companion."

Seriously? How is it that my father was raised by Dr. Doolittle and we weren't allowed anything larger than a Guinea pig growing up? And why are they looking at me like I'm the crazy one?

Sticking close to Gran, I hop down to the training circle. "No worries. Hakuna Matata, right?"

My grandfather smiles. "Well, ye seem to have inherited some of yer gran's nature magic. That's a start."

The badger snuffs. "Did she, though, Lugh? She doesn't know the difference between a badger and a skunk."

"Och, give her a chance," Granda says. "She was raised in the new world—in a city no less."

The badger shakes his long snout. "The poor thing."

I roll my eyes and step over to take a closer look at the weapons. I recognize some of them from Calum and Emmet playing Dungeons and Dragons when we were young—a club, dagger, quarterstaff, sling, spear.

"Sorry I'm late. I—"

The familiar male voice directly behind me triggers every defensive instinct I possess. I drop, sweep the guy's feet, and sucker-punch him in the groin.

"*Arragh!*" Gran shouts.

"*Fuuuuck,*" the man wheezes. My back-alley mugger curls up like a shrimp and gasps for air. "*Again,* with my knackers. What is wrong with ye, *woman?*"

Granda blinks at me, his bright blue eyes as wide as saucers. "Well, ye've got quick reaction time. There's that, too."

It's a good fifteen minutes before Sloan Mackenzie, a.k.a. my back-alley groper is sitting up on the tiered wall and ready for proper introductions. Although he's upright, the twitch in his lip and tightness in his dark brow speaks to him not being one of my biggest fans.

That's fine. The feeling is mutual.

"Sloan, ye've had the pleasure of meetin' my granddaughter, Fiona," Granda says, amusement thick in his voice. He gestures from the tall, dark, and stupidly handsome Sloan to me. "Fi, Sloan has a unique ability to assess latent druid abilities. I asked him to approach yer family in the city and see which of ye possess the most raw potential."

"Approach? Ha! Manhandle and molest me, you mean."

Sloan grunts and rakes rough fingers through his impossibly black hair. "Don't flatter yerself, Cumhaill. I assessed ye inside the pub along with yer brothers. A pat on the arm here, a hand-shake there, a brush of yer back as ye sashayed yer ass across the dance floor. Ye came up the winner of the Cumhaill lottery, so I tested yer abilities out back."

"Except I didn't *have* abilities until you branded me."

"Brand ye?" Granda says, his forehead creasing with violent speed.

I untuck the knot of my t-shirt and give them my back. Reaching behind my head, I swipe my hair out of the way and pull the cotton up my ribs until the summer breeze cools my shoulders.

Gran gasps. Granda curses.

Sloan sputters. "I did *not* do that."

"*Bullshit.*" I turn to Granda and appreciate the level of alarm on his face. "That beauty started burning the moment your boyo here did whatever he did. Now I'm tramp-stamped."

Sloan growls. "First off, I *didn't* do that. Second, as tramp stamps go, yer about a foot too high."

I drop my shirt. "Whatever it is, it started wriggling to the surface the moment you touched me. Ergo, *you* did it. Why do you think I raced here? My da made like he had no idea what it is. I know damn well it's the Cumhaill crest, so I came to learn what's been done to me."

"Yer not quite right, *mo chroi.*" Granda looks pale. "It is the crest our family displays with pride, but it's not a Cumhaill crest, it's a Fianna crest."

"Okay, so what is that?"

"The Fianna were the highest order in druid history—and somehow ye wear their mark."

I throw up my hands. "Awesome, so what the hell does that mean?"

"Well now, that's the rub of it, isn't it?"

Although I want to despise everything about Sloan Mackenzie, he's somewhat helpful to Granda during my assessment session. Kinda. Sorta. I guess. He's even more useful standing in as my opponent while testing my offensive abilities. Sadly, no matter how much energy I put into the staff, dagger, or sickle I'm swinging, I can't land a solid blow.

Granda does, however, appreciate my dedication.

"All fight and no finesse," Dax grumbles.

"Says the mouthy skunk from the peanut gallery," I drop to the manicured grass, sweating and gasping for breath. "When you can pick up a staff and fend him off better than I can, then you get a say, rodent."

"And no manners," Dax adds.

I snort and roll to my knees to swig back some water before I face Granda's next feat of fancy. "Ha! Me? I have fuzzy slippers back home with more manners than you."

"Enough, you two." Gran chuckles. "Fi, come here to me, luv. I want to test yer sensitivity to stones."

I take another swig of water and go to Gran.

After tugging the silk tie free from the velvet bag I saw in Da's box of keepsakes, she pours out six polished globes of different colors and sizes. "Do ye know what these are?"

"Da's marbles?"

"In a fashion. These are druid spell stones. Every druid selects theirs when they begin to learn spells and casting. Since yer energies seem very similar to yer father's, for now, I'm sure ye can use his."

"What?" Sloan says, his face screwed up. "You're letting her use spell stones? Her gifts woke less than a week ago."

"And whose fault is that?" I say.

He flips me a middle-fingered salute. "I understand there's a time constraint here, but Lara—"

"But nothing." Gran looks cross. "Fiona shows unprecedented potential, and these stones hold the energy and alignment of her da. She'll be fine."

"And what about the rest of us?"

"Yer concern is noted, son," Granda says, his voice firm. "Go ahead, Fi. Listen to yer gran."

"All right." Gran settles onto the grass and runs a hand over the marbles. "Humans are composed of more energy than matter, more spirit than physical substance. Casting stones allow us to focus our energies and essences to mold them into a change of form or intention."

"Us humans or us druids?"

"Both. People from all walks of life and many religions use stones fer strength. A chakra bracelet to ward off negativity or gemstones in yer pocket for the desired effect. Many carry a citrine in their pocket to draw wealth or amethyst to help with healing."

I nod. "A waitress friend from Shenanigans wears a chunk of unpolished emerald in a pendant. She's convinced it will bring her true love."

"Exactly. Depending on the stone, its origin, the energy deposits, the veining of other minerals, and a hundred other factors, a stone's power fluctuates. Cross that with a human's physical and mental energies and the relationship between a person and their stones becomes specific. Add to that a druid's connection with the natural world, and we can amplify that power to conform to our will."

"We can do magic spells—like *witches?*"

Sloan and Granda both make a face.

"From an uneducated point of view, it would seem similar." She throws them a look. "Our magic is far more nature-specific. The point is that druid magic is enhanced by our casting ability, and because of that, amazing things are possible when we learn to harness our powers."

I study Da's marbles and fight not to burst into a fit of giggles. I'm learning magic. Hermione Granger's got nothing on me. Liam is right.

I am Fiona-*freaking*-Cumhaill.

When I look at the stones, the power emitted by those energy-giving globes calls to me. Excitement and adrenaline feed my cells, and I scoop them up.

"NO!"

A chorus of shouts rent the air.

A surge of power shoots up my arms and into my chest. It bursts out of me in a sonic wave. It ripples the air with violent force and knocks everyone tumbling backward.

I blink, stunned. Thankfully, no one looks injured. Man, my cells are thrumming with power.

"Oops. Sorry."

Sitting cross-legged on the patio an hour later, I close my eyes and focus on the one casting stone I'm allowed to hold from Da's bag of marbles. Apparently, I jumped the gun by grabbing them all at once. Novices can only focus the energy of one at a time. *My bad.*

In my defense, they kinda buried the lead on that.

So, here I sit. A malachite casting stone warms my palm. A little flowerpot sits patiently in front of me. And a pissed-off badger glares at me with his beady black eyes.

"You don't need to stay, you know?" I toss him a sideways stink eye.

"And give ye the chance to cheat? I don't think so."

"I'm not going to cheat, zebra face. And the fact that your mind went there says more about you than me."

Dax rolls back against the stone wall. His hind leg arches up, and he scratches the underside of his chin with his claws while flashing me his furry male bits. "No place to be at the moment. Might as well keep an eye on the city girl."

I roll my eyes and check the binder for the words of the spell. Not that I need to, there are only a few.

An inch and a half below you go
Snug and fed, and time to grow

I stare at one fat white bean lying on top of the black soil, the shot glass of water beside me, and the beam of sunlight about to move beyond the surface of the café table. In another fifteen minutes, it'll be too late. My bean won't get its time to sunbathe, and it won't grow.

C'mon, Fiona. You can do this.

"Okay, it's Jack and the Beanstalk time."

I close my eyes and let the malachite's energy warm my palm while Gran's teachings rerun in my head. Casting stones focus our intentions and amplify our power to influence. Set my intention. Ask the fae energy to comply. Project my casting energy to the object.

In my mind's eye, I envision the bean wriggling down beneath the soil. It's rich and dark and full of nutrients needed to promote growth. Focused on my intention, I rub my thumb over the globe in my hand. *Please sink into the soil little bean.*

I crack my eye open, then sigh. "Nothing?"

"Yer as daft as it gets, girly. Yer a novice. Ye have to speak the words, ye feckin' eejit."

Damn it. Okay, I envision the bean wriggling into the rich soil, and I rub the malachite in my palm and say...

"An inch and a half below you go,
snug and fed, and time to grow."

This time, when I open my eyes, my bean has nestled itself under the dirt. I fight the urge to jump up and happy-dance and read over the next two lines. "Okay, part two."

Staring at the glass of water, I swallow and focus on the malachite stone, and read the spell aloud.

"Water, cleanser, quencher of thirst,
Let what is dry be nourished to burst."

My heart races as the water level in my glass empties.

"Okay, take it home." I check that the sunlight is still over the pot, read the last two lines of the spell, and roll the marble between my palms.

"Sunlight, warmth, bringer of drought,
Bolster the seed, and make it sprout."

After a few moments, I squeal.

Clutching the pot in both palms, I hurry toward the house, my green beansprout waving proudly in the air.

"Suck it, skunk."

CHAPTER EIGHT

I wake in the dead of night to the deafening crack of lightning striking close to the house. The impact shakes my bed, and the scent of burning ozone singes my nostrils. Gran shouts in the distance, and I jump out of bed. Maneuvering halls I'm not familiar with, in the void of light, means I move slower than the rush of adrenaline fueling me demands.

Still, I find the handle of my bedroom door with only a brief groping in the shadowed darkness. Out the door, I see things more clearly, led by the glow of the phosphorescent fungus of the ceiling in the loo.

Gran's and Granda's room is at the end of the hall. By the time I get halfway there, my grandfather is hushing his wife. "Don't cry, *mo chroi*. I'm sorry the lightning gave ye a fright."

I stop. He doesn't sound hurt or afraid so there's no reason to intrude.

"Ye need to tell her, Lugh," Gran whispers, her voice thick with tears. "All of it."

"We mustn't overwhelm her."

"Ye mustn't wait. Ye'll die, ye stubborn eejit."

His throaty chuckle drifts to me in the darkness. "There's still time, *mo chroi*. She's here. That's what's important."

I straighten and shuffle silently back to my room. What aren't they saying? What is more overwhelming than what I've already learned?

My door snicks shut, and I burrow beneath the old quilt on my bed. With everything in me, I wish I could talk to Da. I haven't needed to hide under his covers to weather a storm in over a decade. If it were an option, I'd be there now.

Over the next three days, my grandfather and I work out in the training arena for hours every morning, then I help Gran in the gardens after lunch, and take a mid-day snooze while Granda visits the homes of others of the Nine Families and tries to figure out why I spontaneously wear the mark of the Fianna warriors.

Thankfully, I'm excused from those meetings for now, although he did take a picture of the tattoo and Sloan has to go with him to verify his part in triggering it.

Ha! Sucks to be you, Mackenzie.

And although I've initiated a dozen conversations about learning more, there's no mention of "all of it" or the underlying reason of why they brought me to Ireland. I've interrupted a few whispered conversations that end the moment I walk into the room, but that's it.

I refuse to believe it's anything nefarious.

They genuinely love me and want me to learn about my heritage—and I am game to learn more—so, it grinds my gears that they're holding back.

"But if we don't figure out the tattoo thing," I say on the afternoon of the third day, "does it matter?"

Granda's face screws up like he swallowed a swig of sour

milk. "How can ye ask that, Fi? Ye've been honored with the mark of our ancient order."

"And no one knows what that means," I say as I head to the gazebo. I'm sick of hearing about the mark but can't say that out loud, or it'll crush him. "For the most part, the questions I came with are answered. I miss home. If we don't figure it out before I go back, it'll have to remain one of life's mysteries."

"Back to the city, ye mean?" he says as if I've slapped him across the face. "Ye see and feel how magical Ireland is fer ye and ye'd consider going back?"

"Consider it?" I stop beneath the shade of the gazebo's thatched roof and face him. "Granda, I came to visit you and Gran and learn about my heritage. I always intended to return to Toronto to resume my life."

His expression contorted. Yep. That was the look I was trying to avoid. Now he's crushed. "Ye'll be the death of me then, will ye?"

I stiffen. "That's not fair, and it's not true."

"It's completely true. I hoped ye'd rise to be more than yer da, Fiona. Now, I see yer the same. Both of ye selfish and stubborn."

A rush of energy ignites inside me, and I raise my finger. "Okay, stop right there. Be mad at me all you like, if you're disappointed. But if you talk shit about my father, I'm on the first flight home."

He pales. "And run off to the city to ignore yer family duties and gifts like he did?"

"In a heartbeat."

His gaze hardens as he clamps his fist at his sides. "I expected more of ye, Fiona. I thought ye understood."

"Maybe I would understand if you told me what's going on. Stop manipulating me. I don't like it, and I certainly don't deserve it. Stop treating me like a child."

"Maybe I would if ye stopped actin' like one." He stomps off, muttering under his breath, and I collapse into my hammock.

Strung pole-to-pole under a thatched canopy like the roof of the house, this hammock has quickly become my favorite location for a lazy retreat.

I groan as I swing. Thought I understood? Ha! I understand nothing. I'm stranded in the land of fae magic and druid gifts and miss everyone so much more now that I need them to talk to.

It's been five days since I left home.

Five long, torturous days since I connected with my life.

Without electricity, I can't charge my phone, or email my family, or check in on what's been happening since I left. Brenny is deep undercover, and Emmet's new on the job. So much can happen so quickly, and I worry.

I could use their phone, but it's a party line with their neighbors, so I can't talk about anything private and the time change makes things so difficult.

As much as I'm trying to honor what Granda and Gran want to teach me about our heritage, what does it matter in the big picture? Being branded a druid warrior is cool—I guess—but I totally see why Da left to build his own life.

"What's the point of being an ancient keeper of the druid ways when the rest of the world is happening everywhere but here? In a world that needs change, why don't druids stand up and make a difference?"

And what difference would ye make?

The voice in my head sounds similar to when Dax speaks to me. At the same time, it's different.

I look around but don't see any lemmings or pine martens or irate badgers. Still, Sloan said communication is growing inside me which means I should attract an animal companion at some point soon.

I search the trees close to the edge of the gazebo. A lynx would be cool. Maybe too conspicuous when I go home.

Can I take a wild animal into Canada?

I'd look that up, except, um...yeah, no electricity.

Hellooo? Yer boring me, Red. I'll give ye ninety seconds to impress me. Go!

Well, all righty then. "If I had powers like my grandparents talk about, I'd help people."

Och, like I haven't heard the world peace angle before. Try something original.

Tough crowd. "All right. I'm good under pressure. I helped a friend get away from a mugger last week, and I liked the taste of it."

So, ye'd be a guard? Like yer da?

I think about that. "Like that, but no. There are so many more things police could do if they didn't have to follow regulations and protocols. I'd stay outside the constraints of that."

Ye aim to be a vigilante then?

I blink. "I wouldn't go that far. There's an alarmingly big gap between justice and law."

An important distinction. The two are not the same. And yer da, he's strong in physical magic, is he?

I push my toe against the wooden floor to swing the hammock. "Yeah. That's what Gran said."

And do ye have his gifts? If yer aimin' to take a stand, ye'd better be able to take care of yerself in a donnybrook.

I glance around, wondering about the animal I hear. "I've shown affinity in three of the seven disciplines so far. I'm attuned to plants and animals, I'm a decent fighter—although I attribute that to twenty-three years of older brothers—and Sloan feels illusion growing."

Are you hoping for an animal companion?

I shrug. "It might be better if an animal selects me once I get home to Toronto, so it blends with the city surroundings."

The bizarre scene of the squirrel running in the back door of the house last week suddenly makes sense. I was raving mad and likely throwing off animal communication vibes. Did I draw her to me? Could I?

I imagine how badly I can freak out Emmet and Calum if I organize the community squirrels to come for their nuts.

"Excuse me, fair Fiona."

I jump, and my heart pushes at the base of my throat. A huge red deer with a massive rack of antlers is standing with its head inside the gazebo. He's muscled and majestic and pee-your-pants terrifying—especially standing three feet away. "I am Eli, of the Kerry herd. I must speak to your grandfather about a matter most urgent. Is he here?"

My first instinct is to roll out of the hammock and run. Except, a quick escape from it seems unlikely. I picture myself face-planting and making an easy target for a good hoof-stomping.

Besides, you're never supposed to turn your back to a predatory animal. Are gigantic talking reindeer predatory?

I have no clue.

"Eli, you frighten the poor thing," a doe says, sticking her head under the canopy of the roof. "Breathe, child."

The male takes a step back. "The red deer of Kerry would never harm a Cumhaill."

I draw a breath and pull up my big-girl panties. "Sorry, I'm new to the whole druid, talking animal thing. I'm Fiona."

"Eli," he repeats. "Patriarch of the Kerry herd and this is my mate, Fawn." As he introduces them, both deer fold their front hoof under their knee and dip their heads in a bow.

"It is an honor to meet you, Fiona Cumhaill," Fawn says.

I try to wrap my head around this being my new reality. Snow—freaking—White. No matter what Gran says, it feels like a fairy tale. "It's a pleasure to meet you, too."

They both straighten, and I try not to stare—Granda made that point clear enough—but holy hell it's hard not to when an eight-foot-tall and equally as long deer stands directly in front of me with horned spikes raised above his head.

I tilt to the side and ease out of the hammock. "Granda was

getting ready for a trip to town. We're headed to the airport to pick up my lost luggage and then to Tralee for supplies for Gran." I'm rambling. The deer king and queen don't care what our errands are. Right. "I'll get him for you."

The giant deer swings his muscled neck out from under the gazebo and follows, plodding up the cobbled path. The *click, click, click* of their steps at my back punctuate our trip to the house. I try to keep a steady pace and not to let my nerves get the better of me.

Did ye know that click noise isn't their hooves but a tendon stretching over a bone in their hoof? The animal voice says in my head. *Gross, when ye think about it. And hello. Good thing they're not predators. No sneaking up on prey with that racket.*

I smile over my shoulder at the two deer. They don't seem to hear the other voice. Good. Let's not call the eight-foot beastie with a rack of daggers pointed in every direction gross, shall we?

"Eli," Granda says while standing at the dropped tailgate of the truck with Sloan. The two of them seem deep in a heated chat, but both rebound well to our arrival. "To what do we owe the pleasure of yer visit, my friend?"

Eli dips his chin. "Good afternoon, Master Cumhaill. May I have a moment of your time?"

Granda sobers. "Is something wrong?"

The deer dips his chin. "I'm afraid there might be."

As my grandfather withdraws to the shady side-lawn with two of Santa's helpers, I realize this is the first time Sloan and I have been alone.

Ask him how his ball sack is. He'd appreciate that.

I cover my burst of laughter with a cough and slap my chest. "Sorry," I choke, "spit went down the wrong pipe."

Sloan seems more interested in what Granda and Eli are discussing than me choking to death at his feet.

"So, what were you two arguing about?"

He arches a brow looking less than amused. "It seems he'd

rather not spend the afternoon in a truck with ye at the moment. He's ordered me to take ye on yer errands."

"Hard pass." I wave him off. "You're free to go."

"Only I'm not," he huffs and cuts me with a glare. "Yer grand-father is a Master Shrine-Keeper of the Druid Order, and I'm a Seventh-Level Apprentice."

I snort. "And I'm a half-orc cleric with a leather fetish on a quest to find the enchanted chest of jibber-jabber."

He doesn't seem to share my amusement.

"C'mon, you realize you sound like a sixteen-year-old LARPer when you say shit like that, right?"

He grabs my wrist and yanks me around the back of the truck. I pull my arm free, but there's no getting past him unless we throw down. The idea has merit.

He leans in, and I feel his energy activating my gift. "I get that ye don't respect the Order, but Lugh Cumhaill is a huge feckin' deal in our world. How do ye think it makes him look when his heir cracks wise about what we are?"

I roll my eyes. "You missed the point, dickwad. I was making fun of *you*, not him."

"Oh, I heard that. I also heard ye threaten to leave it all behind and run off home. If it wouldn't kill him, I'd say good riddance, but I respect the man too much to watch him die. Now, like it or not, it's the two of us for the afternoon. Grab yer bag and hit the loo because I'm not making stops. I won't drag this excursion out any longer than we have to."

CHAPTER NINE

The trip to the airport is an ode to silence. Neither of us utters a word, and from what I can tell, that suits us both. It's not until Sloan turns off the Land Rover's ignition that I realize it's me who must break the deadlock of wills. "Look, I don't like you and you can't help the attraction you're fighting for me, so we just have to work through it."

The look he spears me with is so utterly furious I bust out laughing. "Okay, neither of us likes the other much—that's a given—but I'd like you to come inside with me."

"And why on this blessed earth would I do that? I'm not yer bellhop, and I'll not be carryin' yer bag."

The last thing I want to say is that the baggage lady scares me, but—"The baggage lady scares me."

Now it's his turn to laugh. "Scares ye? The mighty chosen one of the Fianna warriors?"

"You know I had nothing to do with that. As far as I know, some trickster god crossed the wires on the cosmic tattoo printer and is laughing his ass off while everyone else is trying to figure out how to take it back."

"Finally." He slaps the steering wheel. "That's the first sensible thing you've ever said. Agreed. It's one massive cosmic prank."

I let him have that one. "Still, when I arrived last week, the woman working the claims counter set off every warning bell I have. It was before I knew about any of this. She's not human, and I'd rather not face her alone not knowing what she is or what not to do around her. It would ruin my weekend plans to be eaten by a fae monster."

He grins. "That would improve my weekend."

Fine. Whatever. I won't beg.

Da says I need to ask for help. I tried.

I'm halfway to the entrance doors when my escort for the day catches up. His legs are longer than mine, and his stride easily leaves me hustling to keep up. When we arrive at the door, he reaches around me and opens my way to the building. "To be clear. I'm here for Lugh and to find out how big a dosser ye are. So, go on now. Tell me about the female who gave ye a fright."

I describe the ebony-haired angel as we walk and after a moment he stops and pulls me out of the flow of traffic. "Did ye mention any of this to Lugh?"

"No. With all the other weirdness filling my days, it didn't come up until this afternoon. I would've told him, but he pawned me off on you."

Sloan frowns. "And yer sure she was influencing them?"

"Yeah."

"And yer sure she reacted to yer name and asked where ye'd be stayin' while yer here?"

"Yeah."

He presses his hand to the small of my back and turns us back the way we came. "I don't like it. Let's go."

"*What?* Why?"

Sloan's usual cocky veil is gone. His dark eyes are darker as he hustles us back through the doors. "Because whether she's a siren, a silkie, a succubus, or the fucking faery queen, she took notice of ye. I'm not prepared to defend ye in a public place if she has designs on ye. It's a good thing ye didn't know where ye'd be stayin'. It left her waitin' fer ye to return to collect yer bag. It's too dangerous."

"So, I forfeit my capris and yoga pants for my da's forty-year-old khakis and Van Morrison t-shirts?"

We're back to the truck, and the alarm beeps off to welcome us back. "It's temporary. Trust me. There could be a trackin' spell on yer suitcase, a mocker on yer clothes, a compulsion fer ye to harm yer granda—"

"Wait, first off, what is a mocker?"

"A hex."

"Seriously? People can do that?"

"Of course. Stop thinkin' like a civilian."

"Easier said than done. I've been a druid for like two minutes, but whatevs. More importantly, why would someone want to hurt Granda?"

Sloan opens my door and waits for me to get in and buckle up. "I told ye before. Lugh Cumhaill is a big deal in our world."

"Yeah, but that's nothing new. Have hostile fae come at him before now?"

"Not overtly. Not yet."

"You say that like you're expecting it."

"In a way, we are."

"Well, there are more direct ways to get to a man than using my underwear." I shake my head and wave that off. "Ew…bad choice of words but you get what I mean."

"I do." Sloan slides into the driver's seat and starts things back up. "But Lugh's never been this vulnerable before."

"Because of me?"

He tilts his head and frowns. "Not directly, no. The fact is, Lugh is dying, and beings from the Unseen Realm sense the volatility in the balance. Those seeking power and change might think yer the way to get to him or stop the balance from being righted."

I drop my head back and sigh. "Fine. Let the succubus bitch have my gitch. I'm getting used to the hippie grunge look anyway. But there is one thing I want for the sacrifice."

"Och, and what, pray tell, is that?"

———

It doesn't take long to get from the Kerry Airport to the suburbs of Tralee, and by the time Sloan pulls up in front of an old, stone cathedral, I've come to terms with forfeiting my clothes to keep my grandparents safe. Surprisingly, despite his declaration of no stops, he agreed to my condition.

After we finish our business in town, he'll take me to an internet café or coffee shop to plug in my electronics to recharge. I desperately need to reconnect with the modern world. And who are we kidding—I miss my Cumhaill men.

"Welcome to Ardfert Cathedral." Sloan gestures to the gray-stone ruin of a massive old church. He feeds the metered parking, and we're on the move. "From 1117 to the 1800s, this church stood as the seat of the Kerry Diocese. Built-up, marauded, burned, and rebuilt more times than you could imagine, when it was abandoned as the keystone of faith in this part of the country, the druids moved behind the scenes to have it claimed as property of the Irish nation."

His long strides and brisk pace leave me falling behind.

I need a minute to take it in. It's massive and beautiful and holds so much energy my blood fizzles in my veins. The main part of the church has no roof or windows, but the stone skeleton fires my imagination to life.

We walk around the ancient sandstone bones of what looks like a Romanesque or Gothic section to the south transept. It's the only part of the historic site that seems to be in current use. It houses a small parish church.

"We'll only be a minute." He lifts his chin in greeting to a woman as we walk right past her. Once clear of the reception, we walk to the end of a private hall and stop in front of a solid stone wall. Sloan places his palms flat on the surface. He must be accessing his powers because mine ignite in response. A doorway appears, and we descend a set of circular stairs.

The basement of the church is dimly lit and smells of musty stone. "It feels more like a wine cellar down here than any church basement I've ever been in."

Sloan chuffs and swings a tapestry rod to sweep the woven fabric in an arc away from a stone wall. "I'm not surprised ye'd think so."

"What's that supposed to mean?"

"It means yer from Canada, eh? It's a country founded in the late eighteen hundreds. Yer land has no depth of history. Yer culture practices no long-standing traditions. And yer people have no understanding of the power of what came before."

"Hello, judgy much? I'll have you know that Canada prides itself on being a great melting pot. We haven't got one practice of tradition. We have dozens—Greek, Italian, Irish, Chinese, Japanese, Portuguese—everyone is welcome to live freely and recognize their beliefs. Immigrants can speak their language, believe in their gods, and do it without judgy assholes looking down on them for not having been there for a thousand years."

He shrugs. "Is yer basement dry, bright, and comfy?"

"It is. What's wrong with that?"

"Where's the character in that? Where's the meaning behind things?"

"Where's your head? Wait, there it is—stuck up your Irish ass. Do you honestly think you're better than me because you have mold in your basement?"

"I do."

"You're an idiot."

He shrugs and starts drawing sigils on the stone wall with his finger. As his touch passes over the stone, a golden trail of light illuminates. The power he emits makes the hair on my arms stand on end.

"You don't need to say words?"

"I don't. Reciting spells is first and second level stuff—before the magic has sunk deep into yer bones." When the first symbols are connected tail to tip, they burst into a brilliant glow. Sloan moves his focus to the right and starts again.

"Call me a judgy asshole if ye like but time and history enrich druid connections and bring true power. Yer already at a disadvantage because yer da neglected to educate ye. If ye expect to be able to do anything beyond parlor tricks, ye need to stay here and learn from Lugh."

The "while he's still alive" goes unspoken.

It guts me to think of leaving when Granda only has a couple of weeks left. And after he's gone, Gran will need support. I went through it with Da when Ma died. I know how desperately she'll need support after losing her husband.

"I suppose I can give him a couple of weeks."

The second sigils connect and burst into a glow. "Give yer head a shake. Lugh's a Master Shrine-Keeper. The wisdom he has to impart will take decades to learn. I've seen his teaching goals. He sees amazing things in yer future."

My da's words come back to haunt me. *"Because I know the man, Fiona. The moment he gets his claws into ye, he'll size you up for a future ye never wanted."*

A rush of dizzying heat swells up from my chest to my head. I press a hand against the wall to steady myself, but the wall dissolves as it did upstairs. Stumbling from the loss of support, I'm about to take a header into Ali Baba's treasure trove when Sloan grabs my wrist.

"Careful. Don't touch anything."

The panic about Da's warning is shoved to a back-burner of my mind as I take in the shelves overflowing with gem-studded golden treasures, relics, parchments, glittery stones, and what I can only assume are...potion bottles?

"Toto, we're not in Kansas anymore."

Sloan scowls at me. "Yer so strange."

I blink and raise my hand to our surroundings. "Sorry, I've never been inside Gringotts vault before. Sue me for being mind-blown that druids have access to a crypt of golden treasure."

"Lugh is a Master Shrine-Keeper. How did ye not realize that involves a shrine to be kept?"

I never thought about it. I guess that makes sense. "So where did it all come from? Were druids big into pillaging back in the day?"

Sloan ignores me entirely which is better than us interacting. He searches a shelf against the far wall, takes out a piece of paper, and frowns. "Okay, where are you?"

"Where is who?"

"Not who—what?"

"Okay," I say, rolling my eyes. "Where is what?"

He turns the paper around to show me a picture of a rectangular wooden box with a brass, snarling wolf crest on the front. "Yer granda sent us to fetch this."

I take a closer look at the box, and start to help with the search. I'm deeply focused on the hunt when suddenly, I don't want to be here.

I rub at the tingle spreading over my arms. "This place gives me the creeps. Let's get gone before I hurl."

"Yer nauseous?" Sloan turns to me with the box in his hand. I don't know what he sees, but by his response, it can't be good. "Did it come on quick?"

"Very."

"Have ye any other complaints?"

I swallow and brush a hand over my moist brow, sinking to the stone floor. "Dizzy… Oh, gawd. I'm gonna puke."

"No, yer not." A blur of Sloan pushes the box into my arms. The whirl of him wildly swirling his arms in the air doesn't help the slosh in my belly. It does, however, reform the stone wall and seals us off from our exit.

He kneels, looking freaked and takes my wrist.

"Seriously, Sloan," I choke. "Back off. You're in the splash zone."

With the steady rhythm of a metronome, he *tap-tap-taps* at the base of my wrist below my palm. On principle, I want to object to him touching me, helping me, and in essence being anywhere near me, but I can't.

I stay slumped over while he repeats the process twice more. "Any better?"

"Okay, yeah, thanks. You can treat the flu?"

He glares at the stone of the treasure room wall and frowns. "No, but I can ease yer reaction to a hex."

"*What?* I've been mockered? How? Who? What does that mean?"

He straightens and rushes to the curio cabinet with all the little potion bottles. Grabbing a blue bottle with no label on it and a sprig of dried leaves, he presses them in my hand. "Ye need to ingest two sips of this and four leaves of that."

He gets up and starts his symbology designs on the inside of the stone wall.

"What's happening?"

This time when he ignores me, I don't take it personally. Instead, I uncork the little potion bottle and take a whiff. "Oh, *dayam*, that smells like a cat's asshole."

"I don't care how ye know that. Just drink. Two sips if ye want to come out of this whole."

I take a page out of his book and flash him the bird. Okay, two sips to rid me of a hex. "I can do this."

"Quickly, Cumhaill."

Okayokayokay. I pinch my nose, tip back the bottle, and swallow. Once. Twice. Hacking and sputtering, I fight the convulsions of my throat to heave it back up. I press my fingers firmly over my mouth and will the elixir to stay put.

All right, now the leaves. "Four leaves, you said, right?"

"Four."

Not knowing if it's four large leaves or four small ones I need, I split the difference and select four medium leaves. Channeling my internal koala, I wad them together and start chewing. "Okay, that's nasty."

A chalky bite of bitterness makes my tongue numb, but I keep chewing. "See what a good patient I can be?" I gag and have to spit the pulpy mash into my palm.

The surly one is right, Fiona, the voice says in my head. *Ye need to get those leaves down yer gullet.*

I look around the treasure room, and there's no way an animal companion could be sealed in here with us. So, what's the voice? Deciding I must be on the express train to Crazytown, I trust my imaginary friend's advice and get back with the cud-chewing. Yum.

By the time Sloan finishes playing magical finger-painting with the wall, my head is clear, and I'm sitting up feeling a lot more myself. "Thanks for the save."

Sloan nods but still looks pissy. "I wish I knew what happened."

"I thought you said I was hexed. If I swallowed that wad of manure for no reason—"

"Settle yerself. I know what it was. What I don't know is who cast it on ye, why, and if they're still out there."

They are. Don't let him lower the wards on the tomb or ye'll have more than a mocker to deal with.

"Is there another exit?" I force my gaze to focus on him. "Maybe a back way out of here?"

Sloan frowns. "I'm a wayfarer, so yeah."

It strikes me then, whenever Sloan's around, the focus is on me and my abilities. What are his? "What does that mean? What discipline is that?"

"Healing and Spiritual," he says. "I have a bit of healing but far more spiritual. I sense the powers of others, am strong in memory magic, dream manipulation, and can teleport."

"Teleport? Okay, let's go with that." I wriggle against the shelf propping me up but can't ease the itch on my back. "Although I feel better, I'd rather not face another attack and do back-to-back challenges on Fear Factor."

"I doubt whoever it was is out there," Sloan says. "They did what they came here to do. The curse found ye and solidly took hold."

"And why did someone puke-hex me?"

He shrugs. "Stuck in here without knowing who did it, it's impossible to guess. Lugh might know more."

"Then let's take the escape hatch exit and go ask him."

Sloan frowns. "The escape exit will cost us the chance to search the site. We're best to wait a few minutes and go back the way we came. That way, I can see if there are any clues to what happened."

Bad idea. Have him scry the basement. He'll find three hostiles lying in wait.

"Before we drop the wards protecting us and the contents of this vault, do you have a way to check that the coast is clear? You know, to be sure there isn't an ambush."

He tilts his head to the side as if considering. "I could scry the area and have a look-see."

"Perfect. That's my vote. Let's err on the side of caution. My Spidey-senses are tingling."

CHAPTER TEN

"I'm sorry your truck got left behind, Granda," I say while sitting at the kitchen table, twenty minutes later. "And I'm sorry for us fighting before I left. I'm frustrated, and I miss my family, but that's no reason to talk back to you in your house."

Granda lets off one of those Irish harrumph noises that can mean anything based on the situation. I think this one says, "It's okay, Fi. I was a mouthy, stubborn, old coot and shouldn't have taken a cheap shot at yer da."

At least, I hope that's what it means.

"What matters is that yer both safe home." Gran setting a mountain-high plate of stew and biscuits in front of both Sloan and me. "Sloan was right to portal ye straight back, luv. Yer far more important to us than a hape of steel and rubber."

By the scowl on Granda's face, I'm not sure he agrees.

"My computer bag was in the back seat." I pull apart my biscuit and reach my knife toward the butter. "Do you think anyone will steal it?"

Sloan scoffs. "This is Kerry, not Toronto. People here are raised to have a sense of honor."

I set down my fork so I'm less tempted to skewer him with it.

"And what, people from Toronto are morally corrupt? We're Canadian's, for shit's sake. We're loved around the world for being kind and polite, you judgy dickwad."

"Polite and kind, ye say. Right. How could I miss that?"

"Well, I was never hexed in Toronto, so there's that."

"Back to the problem at hand." Granda waves a hand between us. "Tell me again what ye saw when ye scried outside the shrine."

I go back to focusing on my dinner, not keen on revisiting the sensation of being hexed. It's ridiculous. Who hexes people anyway? Apparently, dark faeries who have a thing against Clan Cumhaill.

Sloan finishes describing the two men he saw.

"But ye sensed a third?"

He nods. "I did, but he had a shadow silhouette up so I couldn't see him."

Her, the voice says in my head. *The third was a female.*

"Her," I repeat. "The third was a woman."

"How do ye know that, luv?" Gran asks.

I chew my biscuit. "Something inside me says so."

Granda doesn't look at all pleased. "Shadow blocking isn't a dark fae gift. A female using it is even rarer."

"Sexist much?"

Sloan meets Granda's gaze, and the two of them share a silent conversation that I'm left out of. Whatever that's about, neither of them is happy about it.

Gran either. "It's time, Lugh. Ye've unwittingly made her a target. She has the right to know all of it."

I sit straighter. Finally. "Tell me, what don't I know?"

Sloan picks up his plate and his Guinness and stands. "I'll leave ye to have this conversation in private. I'll be on the patio if ye need me."

My grandparents watch him go, and my stew sinks heavily into the pit of my gut. I wriggle against the back of my chair to scratch my shoulder blades but still feel uncomfortable. "Whatever it is, say it. How bad can it be?"

Granda laces his fingers on the table before him and straightens at the head. He draws a deep breath and exhales. "All right. Here's the rub of it. Ye asked me why I'm dying, and what the help is I need to keep that from happening. The whole truth is that I'm dying because of yer father."

"What? Bullshit. Da would never—"

He holds up his hands, and I bite my tongue.

"Before yer father left, we had quite a row. He said a great many things, and so did I. The result was that I stripped him of his powers and cast him out."

"Yeah, he said you disowned him. He also said if you weren't his father, then we weren't your grandchildren."

Gran stands and busies herself with the dishes.

Granda purses his lips and frowns. "I was a rigidly stubborn man back then, and my behavior is nothing I'm proud of. What I never anticipated was how that moment of bad behavior would affect my life physically as time passed."

"Shunning Da ties to the dying part of things?"

He nods. "Druids are meant to pass their gifts on to the heirs born with druid ability. It's a wee spark of energy when a child is born, but it grows. When I took Niall's powers from him, he was well on his way to becoming a great druid. His powers merged with mine, and as a man thirty years ago, I was able to absorb them."

"But not now?"

"As well as my powers growing with age and experiences, once Niall started having children, his powers divided and expanded, ready to share with you six. Every one of ye has the gift, Fi. In this time of dwindling lineage, it's a rare and precious gift."

I blink, imagining our six sparks of power growing inside him as well as Da's and his. "It must be getting pretty crowded in there."

His smile is sad, and for the first time, I see how tired and near his end he is. "It's grown to be too much for the frailty of my aging body."

"So, you need Da to take his powers back so he can give us ours and you don't overload?"

"That was my intention over the past thirty years, but Niall made it clear he has no interest in unburning the bridge."

"Did you tell him you're dying because of it? I know Da better than most. There's no way he would ever let you suffer for the sake of his pride. He'd sacrifice anything to make things right for a member of his family."

Granda nods. "Maybe, but would he give up you kids to come back here and live this life in my stead? I am the Master Shrine-Keeper for the Ancient Order, Fiona. It's our duty to carry that mantle in perpetuity."

My mind stalls out on that.

I can't even imagine having to stay here to...

"You need him to leave us? But he's our everything. He watches over the boys on the job, and keeps the neighborhood on track, and is the one people come to when they're in a jam. He's more than our Da. He's the pillar holding up a large part of our community."

"And it does our hearts good to hear it," he says, genuinely pleased. "That's why I thought maybe I should approach one of his children instead."

Da's warning comes back full force. He does have designs on my future. "You want me to stay here *forever?*"

"It would be a sacrifice at first." Gran reaches across the table to hold my hand. "But if ye took the burden of yer da's power and that meant for yer brothers, Lugh could live years more. He could teach ye what ye need to know and I would help ye after he's gone."

My gaze skitters toward the door, then toward my bedroom. The girl in me wants to run and hide, but the fighter in me knows they didn't ask me this lightly.

Granda will die within weeks if I don't agree.

The druid energy intended for my family is killing him. Whether Granda meant to or not, he sacrificed his health so Da could live his life and become our everything.

Granda is Gran's everything, too.

But asking Da to come back here is about more than losing him. He keeps my brothers safe. He leads them by example. He's needed there.

What do I contribute to my life and community? I love my family fiercely, but am I indispensable? I think about my Da and my brothers, and Shannon and Liam.

Can I give them up?

The burgeoning hope and expectation in my grandparents' gazes make me want to scream. How dare they ask this of me? My guts twist. And Granda called *me* selfish.

They love their life as much as I love mine.

"I can't talk about this right now. If you'll excuse me, I need time to think."

Fiona, wake up.

I stir from a restless fit of sleep, tangled and tied down by a twisted quilt and sheets.

Fiona, open yer eyes.

I scrub a rough hand over my face and blink at the darkness. Gawd, I feel like I've been run over by a garbage truck and tossed in with the rest of the trash.

Fiona, ye need to wake Lugh. The mocker is building back and yer in trouble.

I'm still trying to make sense of the warning from my mysterious animal companion when my stomach lurches in a violent churn, and I rush for my door. Thank the stars for phosphorescent fungus because the glow of light is the only way I make it to the toilet before I hurl.

Pressing my palms on the seat, I brace myself as Gran's stew and biscuits make an unwelcome return. My ab muscles tighten, and I retch again. The quakes take me then.

Red! Call fer help.

"I'm busy," I whisper, setting my head onto my arm. My head is a tidal wave, my skin achy, and my back is on fire.

Busy dying. Now, get over yerself and call Lugh.

Man. Why are animal companions so snarky? Okay, fine. I might be in trouble here. "Gran... Granda..."

My voice is weak. I haven't got the strength to push out more than a squeak. I swallow and try again, but my voice won't carry. I push forward, and my stomach continues to empty.

Red, I need ye to repeat what I say. Chun liom a bheith faoi cheangal. Ta dha cheann acu, fuaim mo chinnidh.

I do my best, my mouth stumbling over syllables as my strength wanes. The moment I speak the last word, I gasp at the invasion of another entity bursting into my body.

What did I do?

Before I can think anything more about it, I collapse to the floor.

"Don't move, luv," Gran says close to my ear. Her voice is muffled like she's speaking to me from a distance. I fight to follow the warmth of her gentle hand on my shoulder, and she comes into focus. Oh, she's been crying.

I blink at her, my cheek cool against the polished wood of the kitchen table. "What happened? Why am I laid out like Sunday dinner?"

Someone touches my back with an icy gel, and I stiffen.

"Relax, Cumhaill," Sloan says from somewhere out of my line of sight. "My da is a healer. He's taking the bite out of the rash on yer back."

"It's a fair bit more than a rash," the man says above me. "The girl's been cursed to within a breath of her life."

I close my eyes and sigh. "I thought I was hexed. Are you saying Sloan made me drink liquid manure and chew those nasty leaves for nothing?"

"Ye *were* hexed, ye ungrateful witch—"

"Enough," his father says, silencing his son. "Sloan was correct. Ye were hexed, and now yer cursed."

"A double-whammy. Yay me."

Sloan chuffs. "It seems I'm not the only one ye rub raw."

I groan. "Who else did I piss off?"

"My question is what was the purpose of two spells," Granda says, "and why didn't they work?"

"Don't sound so disappointed, old man. I'm rather pleased they didn't."

Gran chuckles. "He's not disappointed, sweet girl. Quite the opposite. The fact that yer body held back a dual magical attack for this long speaks of great natural resistance. Sloan cleared the mocker's effects, but didn't realize there was a curse running along with it, too."

Rude. Seems like overkill...well, thankfully not.

No-kill tonight, folks. Score one for the good guys. "Okay, yeah. I'm with Granda. Why go for a twofer and why didn't it work?"

Sloan's father secures a compress on the affected skin between my shoulder blades, then tightens the towel that I'm lying on around my back. He and Gran help me sit up, and I tuck the corner of the cloth under my arm to keep it from slipping.

Growing up with five brothers, I'm not overly shy, but I'd

rather not parade the girls in front of Granda, Sloan, and his father.

"Hello, Fiona," Sloan's father says while thumbing the bottom lids of my eyes to check them. He's tall, jogger-fit, and possesses the same chiseled features as Sloan, although his skin is a great deal darker than Sloan's warm mocha shade. And by the way he's eyeing me, suffers from a serious lack of humor, like his son. "I'm Wallace Mackenzie."

"Wallace is the Master Healer in the Order, luv." Gran hands me a cup of honey tea. Then, she gestures to a fierce-looking Asian woman by the fridge. "And this is Janet. Sloan portaled his parents here the moment we called."

"Thanks for coming," I say, my head still a little groggy. "So, what do you think this is about?"

Wallace frowns and turns to address my grandfather. "My best guess is the tattoo acted as a shield to the initial attack. From the energy siphoned off the festered skin, and her symptoms, I'd say the mocker meant to sterilize her from being a vessel for druid power and the curse was a backup which activated to kill her when the hex failed to do its job."

"Kill her?" Gran says. "It was intended to do this? What on earth is going on, Lugh? No one has dared come after a member of the Ancient Order for centuries, and now there's been two attempts in as many days?"

"Two?" I ask. "What was the other one?"

Gran frowned. "That's why Eli and Fawn came by yesterday afternoon, luv. They wanted to tell yer granda that a member of the Kerry herd saw someone in a cloak tampering with the wards at the back of the property."

"When I stayed behind and sent Sloan with ye to town," Granda says, "I spent the afternoon rebuilding and reinforcing the wards."

"Who's doing it?" I ask. "What do they want?"

Granda pauses, and I notice he has the same vein by his left temple that pulses when he's pissed that Aiden and Da have. "I can't say who, yet, but why is clear enough. Some of the dark fae races want out from under the watchful eye of the Order. I assume news of my ill health is out. It seems they intend to keep my position vacant when I'm dead."

"And they need me to either be a magical dud or die?"

Granda nods. "That's my take on it."

"And it almost worked," Gran says. "If we hadn't been woken up and found ye when we did, ye would've been too far gone for Wallace to revive ye."

I frown, remembering a foggy version of my night. Me slumping beside the porcelain god, trying to get their attention. "I didn't think I called you loudly enough to wake you."

Granda pops a brow. "Och, that wasn't what woke us. It was Dax and a gigantic brown bear facing off in a fur-flying fight at the foot of our bed. When did ye bond with a battle beast and why the fecking hell didn't ye tell us?"

I look from him to Gran to Sloan to his father. "What's that now? I did what?"

"Don't play dumb, missy," Granda says. "Ye can't bind yerself to an animal totem without convincing the beast and speaking the binding spell."

"I don't get how she did it at all," Sloan snaps. "It takes a fourth level druid to summon elemental spirits, and she hasn't even accepted her heritage powers. How could she possibly have the strength to lure, trap, and bind an animal as powerful as a bear spirit?"

I snort. "I honestly have no clue what you're raving about, but it's hilarious that it makes you so mad."

He's talking about me.

I blink. *Hubba-wha?* "My imaginary friend is a spirit bear? News to me."

Sloan rolls his eyes and looks at his father. "Do you see what

I'm saying? She's practically brain-dead and supposed to be some great druid messiah? It's ludicrous."

"You're ludicrous," I snap, making a face at him. Okay, not my most mature comeback but hey, half an hour ago, I was dangling over the rim of a composting toilet looking into the dark precipice of death.

Granda clears his throat, a look of stern disbelief etched on his face. WTF, how is this my fault?

"Okay, so, yeah," I say, setting my teacup down on the table. "I chatted with an animal companion a couple of times. I thought it was weird that he never came out of the bushes or showed himself, but hey, he could've been shy. Sloan said I might attract attention, so be open to it. That's what I thought it was. I may be naïve, but I'm not duplicitous. I certainly didn't lure him, trap him, or bind him."

Sloan snorts and throws up his hands. "Then how do you explain a giant brown bear—an animal which is extinct in Ireland and has been for donkey's years—racing into Lugh's and Lara's bedroom on yer behalf?"

"I'm not saying it didn't happen, only that it didn't happen the way you're describing it. I *didn't* bind him. If anything, he bound me."

Cue more screwed up faces of disbelief.

"It's true. He woke me up tonight when I was sick and said I needed to get help. When I was puking and getting weaker, he told me to repeat what he said if I wanted to live. I did, and so I did."

"How stupid do ye think we are?" Sloan shouts.

"Them, not so much. You—very." I grab the tuck of my towel and drop to my bare feet. My legs wobble under my weight, and I'm glad to have the table to lean against. "Believe what you want —you obviously will anyway—but I'm telling you the truth."

I blink against the sting of tears and feel my new companion growing growly and restless with my upset. Why aren't my grandparents sticking up for me? Don't they believe me? I search their faces, and the answer is plain.

No, they don't.

I press a hand against the ache in my chest and try to breathe. "I didn't ask for any of this, and if a magic spirit bear wants to be my friend and save me from being murdered by your enemies over a world I know nothing about, then fine, I'm happy to have at least one person on my side."

"Fiona, luv," Gran says.

I hold up my hand, my heart too battered for one night. "Whether you meant to or not, you two dragged me into a mess of danger and obligation. You accuse me of luring, trapping, and binding, but I didn't. You did."

"Watch yer tone, young lady," Granda snaps.

I wave off his warning, my hands shaking. "I came here, excited to meet my grandparents and instead, you used family honor and magical wonder and guilt to coerce me into being the heir you need. Now, you point fingers at me and accuse me of being a liar when things don't make sense to you? Well, screw that! Guess what?" I swipe the heat of traitorous tears from my cheeks. "None of this makes sense to me."

CHAPTER ELEVEN

By noon the next day, I've cried myself to sleep, woken angry, indulged in a massive pity party, and run out of steam. I'm starving. I'm bored. And I'm not looking forward to facing my grandparents. It's not that I said anything I don't think is true, it's simply that I shouldn't have said it—at least not in anger and not in front of mixed company.

Sprawled sideways on my bed with my photo albums open and glossy images of my family smiling up at me from every page, there's nothing I want more than to go home.

"As much as I love the druid stuff, I don't belong here."

That's plain. And as much as I feel yer angst about disappointing yer gran and granda, yer happiness matters too.

"Is that selfish?"

Not from where I sit.

"That's okay with you? Leaving everything you know?"

I didn't bond with ye to cavort across the rolling hills of Ireland fer the rest of our lives. I've done that fer far too long. I'm ready for adventure and conquest and all the city offers.

I lay there for a long time, staring into the eyes of my father. He chose his path and walked away. From what I've seen, he lived the life he was meant for. "I'm meant to be a daughter and a sister and an auntie. As honorable as all this Master-Shrine Keeper stuff might be, it's not who I am."

Then speak the words and let them be so.

I kiss my fingers and press them to our family picture. "What happens to you if I don't become the mighty druid they want me to be?"

I accept who ye are this minute. Ye needn't put on airs and be what ye aren't. Even without Lugh offloading powers into yer system, yer a druid by blood and by nature. We are bound. All is well.

I'm glad about that. "Hey, would you come out of me, so we can properly meet?"

Are ye easily scared?

"Not as a rule. You?"

What's there to be scared of when yer the disembodied essence of a beast that's been extinct fer centuries?

"Good point. Well, we have bears where I come from. You won't shock me. Just don't eat me. Deal?"

Wouldn't dream of it. You're my ticket to freedom.

It's weird to feel another entity maneuvering inside a body I've spent twenty-three years living in solo. A flutter builds in my chest, a gentle pressure in my lungs, then the pressure pops.

I stare into the whiskey-colored eyes of a nine-hundred-pound bear that even standing on all fours comes up to my chin. "Wow, you're bigger than I expected."

And that is what every male wants to hear in the bedroom of a lovely lady.

"Funny guy." I chuckle as I check him out. He fills the room, and although there is enough space for both of us, it's claustrophobic with him out.

Despite my assurance to the contrary, I thought I might be intimidated. I'm not. He is part of me. Somehow, I know that on an instinctual level. I lift my hand but hesitate before reaching forward. "Do you mind if I touch you?"

I thought ye'd never ask.

"Flirt."

It's been centuries since I held physical form. I want to feel the breeze blow through my fur and tear at the rich soil with my claws as I run, and mount the round haunches of females and rut until I drop.

I hear the longing in his voice. It's sad. "Well, I'm not sure how to get you laid in a country where bears are extinct, but when we get home, we'll work on it, I promise. I'll be your wingman."

And I yers.

I let my hand sink into the depth of his thick pelt. He is soft, shaggy, and smells of spruce needles and clean outdoors. My fingers knead over the coarse brown guard hairs, and through the sultry underfur beneath. "You're incredible."

I am, at that.

"And humble too." I revel in the juxtaposition of touching the two textures of fur, tough and coarse on the outside, decadently velvet underneath. "What's your name?"

Among bears, I was known as Himself. Among the countryside folks and in legend and song, they called me Bruinior the Beast or Killer Clawbearer.

"Wow, okay. Those are aggressive. They don't roll off the tongue though. Maybe for a new life, you should have a new name."

Ye said ye need yer animal companion to blend in the city. What's a good name for that?

I laugh. "I think blending is out."

Leaving my bear companion in my room to stretch his paws, I grab a clean outfit and make it into the bathroom without running into anyone. Winning! If I can pull myself together before the awkward morning after face-to-face, all the better.

Under the hot spray of the shower, I lament how often I

laughed at Liam's "morning after the night before" stories. The grass is not greener on his side of the fence.

"What about food?" I ask after finishing with the daily battle of pulling a brush through my hair fifteen minutes later. "Do you eat?"

Bear twitches his moist black nose in the air and nods his massive head. *I think so. Dunno. This is new to me.*

"Cool. Finally, I'm not the only one figuring things out while everyone around me knows what's going on. Come on. I'll heat you some stew and biscuits."

The house is quiet as we make our way to the kitchen and I take that as a good sign. Maybe my grandparents feel as bad about last night as I do. I hope so.

Well, I'm not hoping that I made them feel bad, but I am hoping they finally see things from my side. I set out two plates and head over to the fridge. Taking out the leftover stew, I grease a pot and dump it in to heat up.

As the air fills with the rich scent of meaty gravy, my stomach growls. I can do this. I'll eat, apologize for my outburst last night, and explain that as much as I wish I could stay and be the dutiful druid they hoped—I can't.

That smells amazing.

I nod and dish us each a full plate. "And tastes twice as good. *Slainte mhath.*" I set his plate on the floor and sit at the table for mine. "Why is it that stew tastes better the second day?"

Another of life's mysteries, I guess.

It doesn't take long before our plates are empty and I'm staring out the kitchen window while washing our dishes. Movement by the tree line brings my attention to Gran and Granda coming out from the grove. Like always, they're holding hands as they stroll across their property, enjoying each other's company.

Barmaid, fetch me some ale. That stew left me parched.

I arch a brow at my bear and fill a large bowl with water to set on the floor. Ha! How crazy is that—*my* bear.

"I can't keep thinking of you as Bear," I say as he lifts his big, boxy head with water dripping off his maw. "Let's try out a few names until we find one you like."

Where should we start?

"I don't know. Bears are Ursidae. Do you like Sid or Ursi?"

Not really.

"Winnie, Ted, Fozzie, Yogi, Baloo?"

He lifts his lips and shows me his monstrous teeth. *I'm rethinking eating you.*

"Tetchy. Okay, for now, let's go with Bear."

I straighten, a strange sensation crawling over my skin.

It reminds me of how it felt those first days after my druid side woke and my Spidey-senses were tingling off the charts. "Do you feel that?"

Feel what?

I turn to the window and scream as a blue bolt of lightning rockets out of the sky at my grandparents. My heart pounds behind my ribs as the interior of the house passes in a blur. I'm outside, running around the house and toward the back lawn as another blue bolt shoots at me.

The tackle comes hard and fast.

Taken to the ground by a grizzly bear leaves me dizzy and stunned.

Stay here. Yer not ready to take on a magical attack.

His words ring in my ears, and it takes me a minute to clear my head. I want to argue, but he's right. There are men in black cloaks throwing lightning and fireballs at my grandfather, and the only thing I can do is make a bean sprout.

By the time the world stops spinning, Granda has one hand above his head, holding a protective dome around him and Gran, and is spellcasting with the other.

He's incredible.

My hippie flower child image of him is forever shattered.

He's a freaking wizard.

My legs are still firmly in wet noodle territory, but I force them to hold my weight and stumble forward to take cover behind the stone half-wall of the garden. A flash of light beside me has my fight and flight response kicking in.

Thankfully, I realize it's Sloan before I give him a cheap shot to the crotch. His dark eyes widen as he takes in my state. I point to the melee unleashed on the lawn. "Go. Help them."

I give the guy credit. From the moment he teleports and sees me, to the next, he catches up on the situation and rushes to my grandparents' aid.

Da has said a million times that fights in real life aren't like the ones you see on TV. In most of the altercations he's involved in or is called to break up, the physical conflict is over in minutes.

Minutes feel like years when your grandparents are under attack.

Granda keeps Gran safe and calls on defensive spells.

Bear slashes at a magical shield between him and three attackers. He seems to be making headway and keeps them busy instead of advancing on my grandparents.

Sloan raises a wall of stone from the ground, shielding them long enough for Granda to push Gran free of the dome and shift to an offensive stance.

I burst out from behind my shelter and run to meet Gran. For a woman in her seventies, she's impressively fit.

"Gran, are you okay?" I gather her in my arms and tug her out of harm's way.

"I'm ragin' mad, luv." She tucks behind the stone wall with me. She holds her hand out and closes her eyes. When a pine marten scurries to her feet a moment later, my mouth drops open.

The little guy is calm as can be.

Doesn't he realize the world is filled with killer blue lightning and battle bears and fireballs exploding in the air? Gran picks up the rodent and turns it to speak directly to him. "Lugh and I are under attack. Send help."

I'm not sure what the brown ferret can do to help, but when she puts him down, the cobblestone walk shimmers, and he disappears. "What the..."

"Animal messenger," Gran says as if that explains everything. Without waiting for my response, she shuffles to the end of the patio wall and places her palms flat on the ground.

Her power tingles over my skin as a rumble builds beneath us. Gran's lips move, but she's speaking so quickly and softly in Irish, I can't translate what she's saying.

"Away with ye, now." She sends off a rippling pulse of earth. The grassy tidal wave rolls across the back lawn toward the attackers. Their focus splits as the ground beneath their feet heaves and knocks them off balance.

A moment later, a half-dozen flashes fire on the back lawn. Members of the Order flood the yard.

In a matter of a minute, it's obvious the tide has turned. "And the good guys win." I stand.

Gran turns to answer, and her eyes grow wide and wild.

I sense the surge of magic behind me a second too late.

The searing pain of steel piercing my flesh sucks the breath from my lungs. At the same time, the roar of a murderous bear fills my ears.

I grip the bloody blade where it rips through my shirt. My hands are slick as I drop to my knees. All I can think of is that I've ruined one of Da's shirts.

CHAPTER TWELVE

I regain consciousness lying on a brocade and velvet coverlet in a room Sloan would describe as having more historical charm than anything in my trifling new world life. Which is to say the place is old, smells slightly musty, and the stone walls are crumbling bits of detritus onto the floors.

"Bear?" I whisper. "Are you here?"

I am. I feel yer heart picking up speed, but there's no need. Yer as safe as ye've ever been.

I lift the blanket off my chest and brush my fingers down the cotton nightie I'm wearing to probe my side. "Somebody patched me up again?"

That Wallace fellow from the other night.

"So, what happened after I got shish kabobbed?"

I'm sorry, Red. I felt yer fear a split-second before yer pain. I took care of the woman who skewered ye, but it shouldn't have happened. I failed ye.

"No. You saved my grandparents. That's exactly what I wanted you to do. We'll figure out how to work together so no one gets hurt. All's well that ends well. And you took care of Lady Stabby McStabber."

Messy, that bit. Then yer surly man from the shrine portaled yer family here.

"Gran and Granda are here too? Are they okay?"

Yer gran seemed well enough. Last I saw, yer granda wasn't long fer this existence.

I bolt upright in the bed and hiss. Wallace may have patched up the hole in my side, but I feel like I've been dragged through a knothole. "Where are my clothes?"

Burned, I believe. Surly boy did leave ye a present on the wee table though.

I slide off the bed and catch sight of a red suitcase sitting on an antique table beside the closet. No. It's not *a* red suitcase—it's *my* red suitcase—and it's sitting next to my computer bag. "Thank you, baby Yoda."

Rushing barefooted across the patchwork of fancy area rugs, I close the distance between me and my long-lost belongings. I pause with my hands in the air. "I take it Sloan and his people removed all hexes, curses, and bad juju my things might carry?"

That's a sound bet.

"Good enough." The first thing I do is pull the adapter power cord out of my bag and plug in my laptop and phone. "There you go, babies. You must be so thirsty."

With the flashing green lights signifying my electronics are juicing up, I move to my suitcase. The luggage lock is gone, but that doesn't surprise me. If Sloan was right about the creepy woman at the airport, she probably snooped inside the moment my bag caught up to me.

I give the contents a quick inventory, but everything seems to be here. *Awesomesauce.* After grabbing a fresh bra and panties, I whip off the borrowed nightie and slip into my clothes for the first time in…six days? Seven?

I free my hair from the neck of a navy and teal tank, pull my Lululemon yoga pants up my thighs, and shrug into a zippered hoodie. A glance into the mirror makes me smile.

"There I am. I was beginning to worry I'd never feel like myself again."

A knock on the door makes me jump. "I spelled the room to let me know when yer awake. May I come in?"

I roll my eyes at the back of the door. "You may. And you should be safe from scorn for at least ten minutes. Thank you for retrieving my stuff."

Sloan strides through the door, his gait stiff, his shaggy black hair damp as if he's fresh from the shower. Unbidden, my thoughts take a quick turn toward what that would look like. Dammit. There's no getting around him being a hottie.

"Are ye in pain?" He frowns at me and snaps me from my naughty daydream. "Ye've got a strange look on yer face."

I wave that away and give him my back while the heat of my blush colors my cheeks. Studiously, I fold the cotton nightie someone loaned me and shake my head. "How's Granda?"

"That's why I've come." Sloan's voice doesn't hold its usual condescending edge, and that scares me. I turn, and the sympathy in his eyes makes my fear ten times worse. "He'll not last long, I'm afraid."

"Was he injured in the attack?"

Sloan leans back against the front edge of the chest of drawers and stretches out his long legs. His feet are bare, and I curse my hormones.

Sexy guy in jeans and bare feet, that's not fair.

"The attack forced him to abandon his hold on the energy overwhelming him to protect yer gran. He hasn't got the magical strength left to harness it. It'll kill him within hours."

Hours? My heart aches for the loss of a grandfather I'm only beginning to know. Poor Gran. Poor Da. The two of them might be equally stubborn, but Da will regret not making things right before Granda dies.

"I fetched yer belongings as a sort of peace offering," Sloan says. "The other night, ye said some things that rang true. Ye were brought here with an end in mind and judged fer not warmin' up to it. It wasn't fair. And, fer my part in makin' ye feel deceived, I am sorry."

"It's not that I don't want to help. It's—"

"I get it. It took me a bit to get there, but if our roles were reversed, I couldn't give up Ireland and who I am fer someone I met a week ago and a life I never wanted."

I draw a heavy breath. "Thank you."

He dips his chin. "Don't thank me yet. I also think yer stubborn and short-sighted, and ye fail to see how shunnin' yer heritage damages something larger than ye realize. I took it fer selfishness until now, but after yer outburst the other night, I think yer merely ignorant."

"If this is you giving me a pep-talk, you suck at it."

He rolls his eyes. "Ye locked onto what ye'll lose and aren't willin' to see another solution—one that saves Lugh."

I cross my arms over my chest and lift my chin. "Well then, by all means, tell me what I'm missing, oh wise one."

Fifteen minutes later, I'm waiting outside the door to the guest room where Granda is dying. I shake my hands, searching the long, stone hallway of the MacKenzie castle while waiting for Sloan to join me.

Are ye sure about this, Fi?

"Yeah. Sloan's right. It's win-win."

Fer now. But not—

"Let's focus on now. Otherwise, I might chicken out."

Sloan rounds the corner with the wooden case we retrieved from the shrine tucked under his arm. "Are ye all right, Cumhaill?"

I nod. "Not even close."

He smirks. "Yer so strange."

I knock and walk, letting myself into Granda's room. Gran looks up from where she lays next to my grandfather lying unconscious on the bed. He looks awful, like, end of days awful. "Och, Fi, I'm glad to see ye up and about, luv."

My guilt over hoping that Gran and Granda felt bad for putting me in this position dissolves the instant I see her puffy, red eyes. What wouldn't I do to save Da or one of my brothers? Nothing.

"Gran, I'm so sorry."

She shakes her head and sits while opening her arm for me to come to hug her on the bed. "There's no need fer ye to apologize. We've had a great run, Lugh and me. And our love made Niall and by extension, you six. No regrets."

Hugging Gran brings back the painful loss of my mother. It's agony when you're the one left helpless on the sidelines.

Except I'm not entirely helpless.

Not this time.

I swallow and straighten. My resolve is solidifying. "Okay, Sloan, let's do this. Gran, you're going to get those extra years you and Granda were hoping for."

Sloan sets the wooden case on the bed and passes his hand over the howling wolf insignia. When the magical lock on the box clicks open, he eases the lid off to reveal two black metal crowns adorned with Celtic symbols and gemstones.

He passes one to me and one to Gran.

Gran looks at me, surprise, worry, and hope warring for dominance in her expression. "Are ye sure?"

"Sloan suggested a compromise I think I can live with. In any case, it'll give us time to think of a better solution."

She swallows, and I see how torn she is.

"It's okay, Gran. I'm making this choice knowing what it could mean. It's not coercion or guilt—okay, it's a little bit guilt, but mostly it's because I think it's the right choice for you, Granda, and Da."

"Ye failed to mention the most important person this affects, luv. Ye can't do this if it's solely fer everyone else."

I shrug. "I can't say I'm thrilled, but I'll deal. Ye might be able to knock down a Cumhaill, but ye'll never be able to hold one down."

Gran nods. "Thank you, *mo chroi*. I swear to ye, I'll move mountains to ensure ye never regret it."

After seeing her ripple the ground to topple our attackers, I believe maybe she could move mountains. Taking the steel ring, I place the ancient laurel on my head. "Okay, let's get this power transfer party started. Sloan, you have the floor."

"Yer off yer nut," Granda says when I finish laying out the terms of my offer four hours later. It took longer than we expected for him to wake up, but he suffered the strain of the overload for decades. No one is sure how much damage it did to his insides. "Either yer a druid or yer not. Ye can't take on the kind of power we're talking about, then flit off to North America and expect it to thrive."

I shrug and move the tea tray off the bed and onto the dresser. "It's a moot point now because it's a done deal."

"Druids draw power from the ancient fae grounds and the groves which sustain us. Ye can't be what we are in a place strangled by buildings and asphalt."

"No. *You* can't be a druid there," I say. "Ireland is in your blood, and it feeds your soul. To me, the city is the beating rhythm of my heart. It's my energy and life. It's everything I need to thrive—my family, Shenanigans, my creaky old Victorian house, my old, rusty car."

"It's not the same at all."

I grab a cookie off the sweets plate. "Says you. How many druids do you know who have ventured off to live in the urban streets?"

"None. That's my point."

"No, that's *my* point. If no one's ever tried, how can you be so sure it can't work?"

Granda huffs and looks at his wife for support.

Not happening. Gran is with me on this. I saved her husband's life, and she's firmly on Team Fi for however I want to play this. "Granda, I have Da's power and the sparks that belong to my brothers and me. I'll stay long enough to get a handle on things. I'll train. I'll grow strong. And then, in two or five or ten years down the road when you're gone, I'll preserve our duty as Shrine-Keeper."

"Lugh." Gran sits on the opposite side of the bed. "Try it Fiona's way first. It gives ye both time to see who's right. Fiona needs to adjust to her power and grow into the warrior she's marked to be. She misses her family."

Granda's scowl is one for the ages. "And how do I explain this at the meeting of the Nine Families next week at the Tralee Festival?"

"Ye'll think of something. The point is, at least yer alive to speak to them. That's what matters most."

"How's the oul man?" Sloan asks as I leave my grandparents to themselves for a while. I don't know how long he's been waiting out here, but given the dedication he's shown to my Granda over the past week, probably the entire time.

"Stubborn and annoyed with both of us for doing the transfer behind his back but strong enough to tell me I'm a daft eejit for thinking I can go home."

Sloan pushes off the wall. "With the siphoning of power, at least he won't shatter all our light fixtures. Mam strengthened the wards against power surges just in case. Lugh's now known as the destroyer of light."

I laugh. "Is that why there's no electricity at their house? Granda blew it up?"

He nods. "He became a gigantic lightning rod about eight months ago. Yer gran took it in stride, but I think she misses watching HGTV and her News One on the telly."

I'm still giggling over my nature-powered gran watching HGTV when we arrive at my bedroom door. "Thanks again." I head inside. "Seriously, you saved his life as much or more than I did. I owe you one."

He hesitates, looking expectant.

What? He doesn't think... Yeah no, owing him one doesn't get him an invitation into my bedroom.

Hells to the no.

"We should start yer training straight away." He derails my delusion.

"Thank goodness."

"What?" he says, frowning.

"Nothing. Sorry. What were you saying?"

"Yer training. I realize we're oil and water, but yer cells are surging with more power than any novice has ever had thrust into their system. Add to that yer bound to a greater bear spirit, and yer body must be humming. Ye'll need basic training right away, and Lugh will be in bed until tomorrow at least. We should start right away."

Oil and water are generous. Sloan and I are more like kerosene and flame. "All right. Grant me internet access, and I'll try to behave long enough to learn something."

"Grant it yerself, and we'll call it yer first lesson." He steps past me and heads for my computer. "Come on, Cumhaill. Yer a conduit of magical energy now. Internet passwords are beneath ye. Think like a druid."

Think like a druid, eh? This could be dangerous.

"Okay, let's fire up some magic."

CHAPTER THIRTEEN

"Cumhaill, meet Manx, my faithful animal companion." I watch in wonder as a lanky lynx lumbers out of the woods behind the Mackenzie manse—a.k.a. Stonecrest Castle—and trots over to where the two of us are set up in the outdoor training ring. Covered in a long, gray-gold coat, the cat pads closer with the ease and grace only a feline can pull off.

When he sits directly in front of us, Sloan scrubs over the fur on his head, scratches his black-tipped ears, and pats his cheek. "Manx and I partnered up eight years ago on my eighteenth birthday. I'd be lost without him."

The genuine warmth in Sloan's ode to his companion shocks me more than a little. The guy does have a gooey center underneath the crust of all that autocratic bullshit.

Who knew?

I hold out my hand for Manx to sniff. "Hello, Manx. My goodness, you're handsome. With your beautiful coat and sexy green eyes, I bet you get all the neighborhood puss—"

"Don't ye dare finish that." Sloan scowls at me. "Manx isn't a neighborhood tom. He's a majestic and highly-trained magical familiar."

I flutter my lashes, feigning awe. "Well, sorry. I didn't mean to offend. It was going to be a compliment."

"And taken as such," the cat says while dipping his chin. "Excuse Sloan. He's too serious for his good."

"Don't I know it. Someone should pull the broomstick out of his ass."

"I'm afraid it's too integrated into his personality. He'd collapse without the support."

I laugh, but sober when I catch Sloan's reaction.

He purses his lips and his eyes narrow on me. "Don't ye dare turn my companion against me, ye wee bitch. One minute in yer company and my only true friend is talking yer smack? I'll not have ye ruinin' him."

"I'm sorry." I mean it. I offer him a genuine look of apology. "He's gorgeous. You should be proud."

"I'm sorry too, sham," Manx says. "After everythin' ye said about her, I thought a little humor might be great craic. My mistake."

Cue an awkward pause.

The flutter of my bear inside me precedes the pop of pressure in my chest. A split-second later, he's standing in the battle ring with us, and the awkward pause breaks.

"All right, more introductions. Sloan and Manx, this is my animal companion, Bear."

He growls. *Bear is what I am, not who I am. If ye don't like Bruinior the Beast, can I not be known as Bruinior the Brave since I saved your grandparents?*

I shake my head. "No."

What? You don't think I was brave?

"Of course, I do. All right." I give my attention back to Sloan and Manx. "Please call my animal companion Bruinior the Brave."

Sloan rolls his eyes. "Next lesson. Yer bear is not what druids consider an animal companion. He's a battle beast or a bound spirit."

"He's an animal, and he's my companion."

"True enough, but he's intended to be used as a weapon. A tool fer ye to use. Not a companion."

Bruinior bares his teeth and lets out a growl that rumbles deep in my chest. It's scary to see him being aggressive.

Sloan looks equally affected.

"He doesn't appreciate your opinion on that. So, to keep you from getting chomped or stomped by an irate bear, let's go with him being an animal companion."

Sloan rolls his eyes. "Why am I not surprised that the bear spirit that chose ye is as unruly and independent as his master?"

I walk over, wrap my arms around my bear's neck, and giggle while rubbing my face into his fur's lush depths. "Consider us well-matched."

"Yeah." Bruinior waves his maw in the air. "What she said."

I hear his voice outside my head and straighten. "You can talk out loud?"

"If I wish."

Sloan nods. "Another difference between animal companions and yer battle beast—"

My bear's growl cuts off his words.

He swallows and lets out a long-suffering sigh. "Sorry. Yer non-traditional animal companion is that because yer spirits are bound, ye can communicate with or without words."

"Cool. And others can only hear him if he speaks aloud?"

"Right."

"Can I speak to him in my head? You know, so no one hears what I'm saying?"

"Of course. If it's possible to quiet yer mouth and yer mind at the same time."

"I've never tried it, but I think it's possible."

"Good, then do that now. Ye should sense a path in yer

thoughts that leads to the bear. Access it and say something by thinking it to him."

I step in front of my furry partner, and he sits on his round rump. Even sitting, his face is almost on the same level as mine. I look deep into his warm, whiskey-gold eyes and feel the connection of our strengths.

I think you're freaking awesome.

Yer not so bad yerself, Red.

My smile spreads so wide it hurts my cheeks, and I blink back the sting of tears. "That's so cool."

Determined to be the best I can be for not only me but my bear, I let my future settle into place. I'm a druid now—no regifting—so, I'm gonna rock this shit.

"Okay, Sloan. What else have you got?"

It's dark by the time Sloan and I finish druid animal companion 101 and head inside. I pass on joining him and his parents for a late dinner and opt instead for a turkey and swiss sandwich and a beer. Sloan says he envies my choice but says no more than that. On the way back to my room, I check on Gran and Granda, then close myself in for some much-needed alone time.

Well, not alone. I have a bear companion.

But enough privacy to face a call home to Da.

I kick off my shoes inside the door of my room, set my plate and beer on the bedside table, and gather my computer and phone for a long-overdue catch up with life.

After a long pull of ale, I activate a cell travel package and take it off airplane mode. "Here goes everything."

Go n-erie an t-adh leat.

I chuckle at his wish of good luck and hit send.

"Granda is doing much better," I tell Da once I've filled him in on the past week's chaos. "He says we'll portal back to their house in the morning. Wallace is confident that by then, he'll be back on his feet and fighting fit."

"Feckin' hell, Fi," he says for the twentieth time.

"I know." I hear all the things he's also saying in those three words. "I get this isn't what you wanted for him or me or even you, but it is what it is. I'm committed now, and I'm good. You'll see."

"This should never have fallen at yer feet."

"I've got it, Da. Don't blame yerself."

"I will because it's my fault."

"I don't see it that way."

As stubborn as my father is, we both know I'm a good match for him. He's smart too because he gives up. "Two weeks. Ye promise?"

"I promise that's my intention." I'm sadly aware my best intentions seem to blow up in unexpected and spectacular ways here. "We have the Tralee Festival in a few days and Granda says I'll need to meet the heads of the Order. Then some time for fallout and preparing for my return."

"If ye don't come, I'll be on the doorstep to drag ye back where ye belong. *Shite*, Fi, we miss ye somethin' terrible."

I swallow past the lump of emotion blocking my throat. "Me too. Two more weeks. It'll be better now that I have my computer back and my phone package. I'll make sure to keep them both charged. Now that Granda's not exploding the lights, he's turning the electricity back on. We're rising out of the Dark Ages."

"Fine," he says, although he doesn't sound happy. "Tell that connivin' bastard I want ye brought home by a wayfarer. I understand the power it'll cost, but I'll not have ye trapped in a tin can in the sky with dark fae and their ilk wantin' ye harmed."

I take another swig of my beer and chuckle. "I'm sure I'd be all right. I have a bear inside me ready to burst out and protect me."

"And how does that keep ye from fallin' from the sky?"

"I suppose it doesn't."

"A wayfarer, then."

I consider that. "Well, I *would* like to avoid running into that luggage lady."

"Did they send someone from the Order to investigate who she was?"

"I'm not sure. Sloan got my suitcase, so I guess so."

"Well, I grew up with Janet and Wallace. If their son is a thing like them, he'll be sharp and serious and graspin' the druid world with both hands."

"Yep. That sounds like Sloan."

"Well, all right, then," Da says. "I'm countin' the days until yer home. And if ye can get here faster, all the better."

"I love you too, Da."

"Safe home, *mo chroi*."

I end the call and swipe at the few tears that escape. Two weeks. I can do that. Setting things right with my father makes staying easier and harder at the same time. Auntie Shannon used to say that the universe compensated a little for losing our mother by giving us the world's greatest father.

I won't ever argue.

Hunkered down on my fancy-schmancy bed, I chew the last bite of turkey sandwich and open my email browser. I stare at the blank screen as I consider everything I need to tell my brothers and Liam. I won't tell them everything—I'm saving Bruinior the Brave as a surprise—but my mind is full, and I need to download.

Hello, all. I love you. I miss you. It's crazy. I've been away for a little over a week but my life as I knew it is forever changed...

Three days later, I stroll across the broad branch of a tree like I'm walking down a city sidewalk. Feline Finesse is my favorite new spell, and I'm strutting my stuff while smiling up at the dappled light breaking through the canopy. The energy of Granda's sacred grove feeds my connection and rough bark crackles under the soles of my shoes. I feel like Tarzana, Queen of the Jungle.

I breathe to the depths of my lungs and frown.

The crisp breeze from the east carries more important information than the scent of the O'Rourke's slurry spreader fertilizing their fields and the sound of fighting foxes getting frisky in the brush below.

It carries essential intel.

My lungful of nature's best brings me several vital tidbits at once: Gran's soda bread is out of the oven and cooling on the window ledge, Sloan Mackenzie is lurking somewhere close by, and—

Whack.

A branch hits my ass and knocks me tumbling.

"Oh, hell." I topple toward the forest floor, the wind pulling at my hair. During the thirty-foot freefall, I right my position, focus on slowing my descent, and land silently on the balls of my feet.

I absorb the impact and land in a crouch, my knee hovering inches over the forest floor. I laugh. "And the crowd goes wild as she nails the superhero landing! You'll have to try harder than that, surly."

Deep, eerie laughter echoes from all directions. Ha! Sloan casting his voice won't protect his hiding spot.

I adjust my stance and survey my surroundings. The rustle of bushes behind me brings on a second wave of attack. I spin as a dozen vines snake out of the scrub, scrabble across the forest floor and head straight for my ankles.

While springing backward, I flip into the air.

Yeah, baby. Feline Finesse for the freaking win!

My body arches and I strengthen my connection with the power of my natural surroundings. I've suffered the pranks of five brothers my whole life. I can take Sloan Mackenzie's best.

Reaching out with heightened senses, I smile. Not ten feet

from where he crouches behind a screen of bushes sleeps the perfect animal counterattack.

I send out a call, waking the creature curled in the pithy cavity of a hollow log. Establishing a connection with animals is now the work of a moment. I make my request and urge the little guy to abandon the warmth of its slumber.

Remind me not to get on yer bad side, Red.

And don't forget it, Bruinior the Brave. The bigger they are, the harder they fall.

To distract Sloan, I rub my ass where the branch hit me and put on a bit of a show. He is always so sure of himself, he'll never see the retaliation coming. "You've been a pain in my ass since I got here, surly. This is no different."

Sloan's laughter fills the air, then breaks into a sudden shriek. "Ow, *fuuuck!*" He launches into the clearing, stumbling over scrub and clutching his ass. "A hedgehog? Damn, Cumhaill, that was harsh."

If I wasn't doubled over laughing, I might feel bad for him.

Ahh...nope, not even.

"How's the training going, children?"

The two of us sober at Granda's greeting. He only started calling us *children* yesterday when we were fighting over who won our staff battle. I brush myself off and straighten.

"Granda, you're back." I flash my grandfather an innocent smile. "What did Wallace say?"

"He says I'm recovering nicely. Now, tell me what the two of ye were working on, exactly. It sounded like yer tormenting Sloan again, Fiona."

"*Me?*" I throw up my hands and blink at the gray-blue sky. "It was an even effort of torment, which he started."

My bear bursts free from my body and takes a playful swing at Sloan as he joins us.

Sloan grunts and dodges the mighty paw aimed at his head. "She's right, Lugh. It was an even battle. I'm far more committed to training when I get to attack Fi with hostile force. It hardly feels like work."

I chuckle and answer Granda's original question. "I've got Feline Finesse down pat and defended against Creeping Vine. We also covered Diminish Descent and Animal Messenger."

Bruinior lumbers over and rubs against my hip. I brace my stance to keep from stumbling forward. Big furball.

Granda nods. "So ye'll need time to get inked before the festival tomorrow, am I right?"

I groan. "Yeah, sure. Can't wait for the merit badge torture to begin."

"Well then," Granda says. "Yer in luck. TamLin stopped by to drop off the keys to our apartment for the festival. She brought her torture kit thinkin' ye might've mastered some new spells since Tuesday. She's in the kitchen waitin' on ye."

"Awesomesauce." With my triumphant mood ruined, I trudge toward the house. Little did I know when I agreed to train so hard, that for every spell I conquer, the symbol is etched into my skin. Ink magic eliminates the need to carry a grimoire like the witches.

Instead of ending up covered in tats, I'm keeping my spells on my back and adding them as the foliage of the tree of life tattoo already there.

Sloan says it hurts so much more than a regular tattoo because of the enchanted blood mixed into the ink. I asked him what creature donates its magical blood and he said that was a sacred secret, not even he knows.

So, here I go again to pay the price of magic.

To say that I have a better than average affinity for picking things up is the understatement of the century.

Then again, most beginner druids are ten.

Och, if ye don't mind, I'll pass on the needle torture and stretch my legs a bit longer.

Something in my bear's tone triggers my lie detector. I don't call him on it. I'm his companion, not his mother. One thing I've learned living with six men. If guys don't want to reveal every detail of their lives, it's better not to ask why.

"Not a problem. I'd skip the torture if it were an option."

Pain with a purpose. Isn't that what they say?

"That's childbirth."

Well then, almost the same thing. Enjoy.

"Yeah, you too."

CHAPTER FOURTEEN

The Rose of Tralee Festival is a fifty-year-old, five-day pageant originally started to draw people to the area to celebrate the life and ideals of Irish culture. It's not a beauty pageant, because the physical attributes of the Rose and her Escort aren't judged—thank goodness—but bringing together a collective of thirty-two inspiring Irish girls and their worthy escorts for fun, frivolity, parades, and parties does what it was intended to do.

It draws a crowd—a big crowd.

"If it's a street party and parade, why do I have to dress up in a formal gown?" I scowl at the selection of dresses Gran wants me to pick from. It's not that they aren't beautiful—they are—but I can't imagine myself in any of them.

"The festival is more than a party, luv." Gran holds up a yellow number to examine it. "Alongside the festivities, close to two hundred members of the Nine Families will converge for an annual druid gathering. Tonight is the reception dinner meet and greet. We need ye to impress the elders of the Order. Yer plans to return to yer life won't be met with any warmth. A good first impression is all we can hope for."

I chuckle. "That's comforting."

"Ye know what I mean."

"I do. And dressing me up like Cinderella will impress them how?" I hold up the ruched bodice of a blue silk gown and sigh at the accompanying white, opera-length gloves.

A peasant skirt and a pretty silk camisole I can pull off. This is well out of my wheelhouse.

"Just fer tonight. The rest of the event, ye can wear what ye want, and we'll have our fun."

I give the dress one last glare and give in. "It's a pageant, right? I suppose I can play along for one night of social pomp if the rest of the festival will be fun."

"It will be, I promise ye. Tons of craic. Tomorrow and Sunday there will be magical events and contests and the street carnival, and on Monday, while the Rose selection is being televised, the druids have our closing event that I think is quite spectacular."

"And Da used to go to this?"

"He loved it. Looked forward to it for months."

I let out a long-suffering breath and make peace with the baby-blue dress. "Bibbidy-bobbidy-boo, Faery Gran-mother. I guess it's time to get ready for the ball."

The trip to Tralee takes longer than it did when Sloan and I went to Ardfert Cathedral. Not surprisingly, the traffic in the area is one long stream of cars. I Google the festivities as we inch along, amazed to learn that while only five thousand people attend the Rose of Tralee crowning in the Rose Dome, many multiples of that flood the streets and pubs in droves throughout the five-day event.

That doubles the twenty-two thousand residents living there —and makes for a bustling town.

In the end, we make it to the apartment the Order reserved

for their Master Shrine-Keeper and are dressed and walking into the private banquet less than two hours later.

"Lugh, Lara." Wallace greets us inside the door. Like Granda, he's dressed in a formal black tux jacket with a leather kilt and a jewel-hilted sword at his hip. "Come, Evan and Iris were askin' about ye. They've been so worried."

Gran turns to grab my wrist but spots Sloan and nods. "Make sure she meets some younger folks and stays out of trouble, would ye dear?"

"I will, Lara." He slides in beside me. "And let me say, ye look the part of a vision tonight."

Gran smiles and waves that away, and hurries to join Granda and Wallace by the champagne fountain.

"Wow, druids know how to party. This place is lit." And it is, from the fireflies glowing and blinking above our heads to the ceiling resembling the hanging gardens of Babylon, to the swags of lace and linens decorating the tables.

"Ohmygoodness, baby bunnies." The centerpiece on every table is a terrarium scene with little bunnies hopping around. "They don't get near the plates, do they?"

Sloan smirks. "No. There's an invisible boundary that keeps them penned in the center.

It's amazing.

"Can we keep our centerpiece bunny?"

"No. They're wild creatures. We set them free."

Oh, right. I'm a little deflated that I don't get to keep my bunny, but I see his point. Druids are supposed to protect nature and her inhabitants, not cage them.

Maybe that's why Da was so strict on pets when we were kids. Oh, and why we live in the house right beside the ravine. Even if Da were exiled, I'd bet he still lived true to the beliefs he was raised on. Things make so much sense now.

And yes, Gran was right.

I needed the formal gown to at least appear to fit in. After admiring the room, I shift my appreciation to Sloan. Yep, he makes formal look super sexy.

And hell…a man in a kilt. It's a weakness.

"Why are you looking at me like I'm a prize cow being displayed at the fair?" I brush a hand down the front of my gown. Everything seems in place. Have I busted a button or something?

He chuckles at my sudden panic and catches my hand as I check my hair. "Sorry. It's rude to stare. I confess that earlier tonight I was wonderin' if ye had any lady in ye, at all. I see now that ye do."

I snort. "Yes, I have all the required parts, if that's what you wondered. Still, don't count on me being much of a lady. This is all for my grandparents' benefit."

"I promise not to out ye fer puttin' on airs. And it's good of ye to hide yer rough and tumble for their sakes."

"Are you implying I'm an embarrassment?"

"I wouldn't go that far. Yer demeanor suits ye well while we train but tonight is about the gatherin' of our ilk. It may seem like a friendly feast and dance, but many a strategic alliance will be made here tonight."

"Hands promised, women scorned, the whole shebang."

I blink at the leggy brunette who said that, and she stops to join us. Her scarlet dress leaves little to the imagination, the slit up to her hip exposing even that.

"Ciara Doyle," Sloan gestures between us. "This is Fiona Cumhaill. Lugh's and Lara's granddaughter."

She eyes me up and down with freaky golden eyes that slit vertically like a cat. I'm not sure if it's a spell or specialty contacts, but if the intention is to unnerve people, done deal.

She leans close and runs her tongue along her shiny red lips. "Fresh blood to chum the pool of sharks. Let me offer ye a bit of free advice. If yer hopin' to catch the eye of a young sword master fer a bit of fun, look past junior here. He's a dullard in the sack and not much better out of it."

I smile. "Not to worry, hon. Sloan's helping my grandfather with my training. You don't have to feel threatened by little ole me."

Her gaze narrows. "Oh, I'm not threatened by anyone, girlie. And while he might spend time trainin' ye up, he's most definitely hopin' yer up to blow his flute—and when I say flute, I mean—"

I raise my hand, that image now burned into my mind's eye, evermore. "No explanation necessary."

"You have to excuse Ciara." Sloan's eyes churn with a storm. "She was a late bloomer as a girl and is compensating. Now that her tits are full-grown, she thinks everyone should admire them. Pay no attention. Her soap opera drama should come to an intermission soon."

I chuckle and give Sloan a point for that one.

Ciara pegs him with a seething glare but catches herself and smiles at me. "I know yer new to Kerry, so let me save ye the trouble of an embarrassing regret. Sloan here isn't nearly as impressive beneath the kilt as his ruggedly impressive façade. In fact, little Sloan is as small as a mouse's wee diddy. Ye'll be disappointed. We all were."

"Careful, Ciara. Yer claws are showing."

I chuckle and offer her the sweetest smile I can muster. "Thanks for your concern, but Sloan's male bits and I are well acquainted. Now, if you're done with your Welcome Wagon routine, you should make other people miserable. We'd hate to hog you."

Seeing she isn't getting anywhere, Ciara lifts her shoulder and shoots me a withering look. "Suit yerself. Can't say I didn't warn ye."

Sloan's deep-throated laughter makes me smile. "Well done, Cumhaill. Ciara has melted more than her share of steel-spined women and ye don't even seem fazed."

I laugh and capture two glasses of bubbly from a server's tray as he passes. "She didn't even tinkle my chimes. Toronto girls would rip her to shreds and leave her in the gutter."

Sloan accepts his flute of champagne and taps my glass. "Then here's to Toronto girls."

The next morning, I take advantage of Gran's and Granda's plans with the heads of the Nine Families and sleep in. By the time I'm up and dressed, they've been out of the apartment for hours and all is quiet. I grab one of Gran's honey pastries out of the sealed container we brought, pour myself a cup of coffee, and take the opportunity to call home.

"Fi," Emmet says, on the second ring. "Geez, I'm glad you called." There's a tussle on the other end of the line and a fair bit of cursing before Dillan comes on. "Fi, how's Ireland? What do you mean magic? What kind of powers do we have?"

The echo of male grunts and punches increases. I can't help but laugh. "Instead of fighting over the phone, put me on speaker, you goons."

A burst of laughter precedes Callum joining in the fun. "Yeah, they didn't think of that. Meatheads."

"Tell us about our powers," Emmet pleads.

"Ignore Frick and Frack. How are you, Fi? Da says you're staying a couple more weeks. Any chance you'll cut that short and come home?"

"Why? Has something happened? Any news on Brenny?"

"No. Nothing happened and no news. We miss our little sister. Is there any crime in that?"

"You're the cops. Why ask me? Hey, speaking of being a cop. Emmet, how was your first week on the job?"

"I chased down a burglar and got my first arrest."

"That's amazing." I take a big bite of Danish and lick the icing off my lips. "I'll buy a round when I get home, and you can tell me all about it."

Dillan and Callum are laughing in the background, and I can picture them all in the kitchen fussing and fighting around the phone.

"It wasn't a burglar," Dillan shouts.

"Was so."

"It was a kid stealing neighborhood bikes," Callum says.

"It was still a collar, and he was eighteen, so it counts as an arrest. Besides, he ran like a freaking gazelle."

"I'm with Emmet," I say. "It totally counts. Great job."

"Thank you. At least there's one person in this family who appreciates me."

"I do, Em. I love you to bits. How are Aiden and the fam?"

The three of them go on to tell me about the family barbeque I missed last weekend and setting up a new climbing fort and swing set for Jackson and Meg. "Kinu wants a family day at the zoo. Da convinced her to wait a few weeks until you get home. He said you'd hate to miss their first experience with the animals."

"He's right. I would. Yes, please wait for me."

A knock at the door has me jumping out of my seat. I shuffle over and lean close to view out the peephole. Opening things up, I step back and wave Sloan in.

"Okay, guys, I've got to get back to things here."

"But you haven't told us about our powers yet."

"I will. I promise. When we have time to really sit and talk." There's a united groan, and it breaks my heart. "I love you too. Kiss the kids from Auntie Fi and let me know if we get any word on Brendan."

"Will do," Dillan says. "Da's talking to Brenny's captain today. Maybe we'll hear some good news."

I knock on the table. "Safe home, Brendan."

"Safe home to you too, Fi," Emmet says.

"Yeah, get home soon, Fi," Callum says. "We're a sinking ship without you, sista."

"Then keep bailing a little longer. I'll be there soon." I end the call and can't help the silent tears. I make a quick dash for my bedroom, but Sloan appears in my path before I get there.

"I've got broad shoulders, Cumhaill. Use them if ye need them. No catch."

I blink up at his stupidly handsome face and smile. "I'm okay. Thanks, though. I'm just homesick, you know?"

"Not really." He shrugs and heads into the kitchen to raid the sweets bin. After taking a bite of a pastry, he grabs a beer from the fridge.

"Beer and pastry?"

He shrugs. "It's Tralee week. There are no rules. Besides, after all that family affection, I need a drink."

"Hey, I'll let you get away with dissing a lot of things about me but if you take a shot at my family—"

He waves me off. "Wouldn't dream of it. In truth, I envy everything about what I heard. I've never known that kind of connection with family or friends. When ye first got here, I thought it made ye weak. I see now yer love fer family is the flame that stokes yer inner fire."

Sloan's an only child to two people who are exceptional druids and professionals, but I wonder how good they were at being parents. Maybe that's why he's so attached to my gran and granda.

"So, what brings you to my door today, surly?"

He finishes his breakfast and washes it down. "I signed you up for the junior trials druid competition this afternoon. It's a rite of passage."

"*What?* Why in the world would I want to compete? I've been a druid for two weeks."

He finishes his beer and grabs two more for the road. "Lugh told me to sign ye up. So, I did. Grab yer jacket. I want to give ye the lay of the land before the games begin. Lots to do and little time to do it."

Och, no! Let me off this ship. My bear bursts free and materializes in the space between the kitchen and living room. "I'll pass on a day of junior druids thanks. Hey, Red, how about a beer for the bear before you go?"

I laugh and pour two beers into a stainless-steel bowl and put it down on the kitchen floor. "Stay out of sight and out of trouble. Not only are you extinct, but you're also in a town with forty thousand humans."

"Thanks, Ma." He laps up beer with his long, pink tongue. "Have fun. Call me if ye need me."

I ruffle the fur on his muscled shoulder and meet Sloan at the door. He's looking at me like I've gone hydra and grown two extra heads. "What now?"

"Ye set down a bowl of ale for yer ancient bear spirit. Do ye honestly think that's a good idea?"

"He's old enough. How old are you, Bear?"

He lifts his face out of the bowl and twists his mouth. "Maybe two hundred? Can't say. It's all a bit of a boring blur."

I shrug and grab my keys. "See, two hundred. Where's the problem?"

Sloan shakes his head and mumbles something about crazy women under his breath as he steps into the hall. I follow, close the door, and lift the keys to lock up.

"Silly girl." He hands me one of the beer cans and passes his free hand over the lock. The click of the knob and slide of the deadbolt signal we're set to go. "Get yer head in the game."

Right. Magic.

"So, these junior trials. I'm not going to be competing against ten-year-olds or anything am I?"

He snorts. "Och, now ye've gone and ruined the surprise."

CHAPTER FIFTEEN

Sloan helps me maneuver the seven events of the junior trials, and I'm proud of my final score. Each was a test in one of the seven disciplines. I placed well in five and did okay in the last two. It wasn't a standard head-to-head competition. We all earned a medal. Well, in truth, Seamus Scott was named the grand champion, but he was twelve so had two years on me.

"Yer not seriously gonna wear that at the pub?"

We step into the crush of festival revelry, and I swing my medal in the air between us. "Why shouldn't I? As you said, it was a rite of passage." He's about to argue when I laugh and put on my best impression of my da. "I'm coddin' ye, boyo. Where's yer sense of humor?"

He looks genuinely relieved.

Did he think I would embarrass him, my grandparents, or myself by highlighting that I'm a noob? I slide the award into the pocket of my jacket and zip it up to avoid it getting lifted. Does that happen in Kerry? Would a pickpocket want my junior trials medal? Likely not. That doesn't mean *I* don't want it as a keepsake.

"Wow, look at this."

The street is packed with people laughing and dancing and making new friends, for as far as I can see in both directions. Along the sides of the street, strings of yellow and pink lights connect each lamppost. Over the road, strung from the same streetlamps high above the crowd, four huge lit-up roses and ribbons blink and light the night sky.

"This whole celebration is much bigger than I expected."

Sloan casts a glance around and shrugs. "The Rose of Tralee coronation is the most widely-watched program on television in Ireland each year. It's a beloved part of Kerry tradition."

It's funny. I see dozens of people stuck in the crowd unable to move forward, but we cut through the congestion like a warm knife through butter.

Like magic.

"Tell me about these friends of yours we're meeting."

Sloan lets a rowdy group of drunkards pass and arches a brow. "Friends is too generous a word. The heirs' apparent for the elder positions of the Nine Families are acquaintances. We were born into a group that not one of us chose. It's a snooty, self-entitled bunch."

"Oh, I see how you fit in now."

He scratches the side of his cheek with his middle finger. "Under it all, they aren't half as bad as they seem—well, most of them. Still, ye'll have to stay on yer toes."

"And will Ciara be there?"

"She will."

I turn sideways to squeeze through the crowd and not get left behind. "What did you see in her?"

"I told ye. She has great tits and likes men to pay attention to them. It's as simple as that."

I burst out laughing. "Your depth of character never ceases to amaze me."

"Och, don't judge. She was into me fer much the same reason. Ye may notice, I have certain attractive qualities women gravitate to."

"You mean Manx?"

"Funny girl."

We get free of the press of bodies lining the streets and duck down a side lane. It's amazing how much quieter it is as we distance ourselves from the buzz of the crowd. "And where is this meeting of the minds being held?"

"A druid pub up here. It's warded to repel normal folk, so we'll be able to get our drink on and not be crowded out."

Cool. Pubs I can do without feeling like a sad little tadpole in a mercury infected lake.

"Forewarned is forearmed, McCool," Sloan says. "Ciara's not the biggest asshole in the bunch. Watch yerself around Tad McNiff. He's a wayfarer like me, and ye can't trust him as far as ye can—"

A glowing orange ball of magic whips in front of our faces and explodes against the building on my right. The instant it bursts, my tingling skin falls silent.

"Fucking hell—" Sloan turns back but a fraction of a second too late.

A figure wearing all black hurtles into him. Ducking low to grab him around the waist, he collides with Sloan's chest, and *poof* they're both gone.

Someone grabs me from behind, and I scream. I try to call on my connection and defend, but there's no magic. It's like the ambient mist of magic always in the air suddenly dried up.

Plan B. I'm a Cumhaill. I can fight.

Red? Are ye all right? Yer heartrate's racing like mad.

Busy... I flail behind my head but can't get free from the hold. *Being attacked in an alley.*

I thrust my elbow back with all my strength, and the crack of cartilage gives me a warm, fuzzy feeling.

"Fuuuuck."

Bile burns the back of my throat as my captor spins me toward the wall. I push my palms flat against the brick and lock my elbows. Resisting his strength, I throw my shoulders and my head back.

"Would ye grab her fucking arms?"

Hands flail to secure my flying fists, but before they do, a furious growl erupts behind me, and the hold on me is gone. I stumble back from the sudden loss of force and land on my ass. Hard.

Oh, thank gawd. My bear is here.

With a violent swing of his paw, men go flying. One hits a dumpster and crumples while a second is lifted off the sticky concrete ground and hits the brick wall five feet in the air. He collides with the brick and drops in a mangled heap.

"Shite, *stop*," a woman shouts. "Fiona, stop him. You win. We were fucking with ye."

I win? With the adrenaline pumping inside me, it takes a minute for the message to travel from my cranium to my fists.

Fight or flight is real.

I'll always fight.

Ciara pulls her hood back and runs to one of my crumpled attackers. She's pissed. "Yer a feckin' menace, Cumhaill. What's wrong with you?"

"Me?" I move closer to my bear and sag into the strength of his broad shoulder.

A flash brings Sloan back into the mix, looking wild. His scattered gaze finds me first, then assesses the two downed men. "Ye fuckin' eejits. I suppose ye thought attackin' her would be a laugh, did ye? Haze the noob?"

Ciara pulls out her phone and calls for someone to join the bedlam. "She's had her power for two weeks. It should've been a harmless prank."

I assume the man who flashed in when Sloan did is Tad

McNiff. He shakes his head while staring at my bear. "How were we supposed to know she's bound a fucking battle beast? It's impossible. None of this should have happened."

"No. It shouldn't," Sloan spits, shaking with rage. "But ye couldn't just welcome her and raise a pint. Ye had to try to show her who's boss. I'd say her and the bear turnin' the tables serves ye right, except Flanagan and Perry got caught in the crossfire."

I bend over and prop my hands on my knees. With the adrenaline of the attack cutting off, all the fire and fury sucks out of me. "If that was your idea of a joke, it wasn't funny."

"It might have been if ye weren't some kind of Tazmanian Devil. We cut off magic so no one would get hurt."

The one who hit the dumpster, Flanagan I think, rolls to sit up. His nose is busted and bleeding like a scarlet fountain, but I'm more worried about what's broken inside.

"Should you call your dad?" I ask Sloan.

Ciara waves that off. "Ye'd like that, would ye? Call in a senior member of the Order and get us put on notice? No. Ye've done enough fer one night, ye wee bitch. Run along. We'll clean up yer mess."

"*My* mess?"

Sloan is still cursing under his breath when my bear puts himself between my fellow druid heirs and me. As he checks that I'm unharmed, his concern morphs into protective fury. *I'm sorry about this, Red.*

I scrub one of his velvety oval ears and draw a deep, steadying breath. "No need to apologize, buddy. You were spectacular."

Good of you to notice.

I chuckle and run an unsteady hand through my hair. "I'm sorry you boys got hurt. I truly am. I hope you're all right, and that the next time these bullies decide to rope you into something, you think it through. My da always says, 'There is *always* someone bigger and better prepared for the fight.'"

"They'll be fine," Sloan says. "And don't ye dare feel bad fer them. Ye reap what ye sow."

"Well said, young man." I follow the woman's voice into the shadowed darkness of the lane. She steps into the light, and I grab Sloan's arm. It's the ebony angel from the airport luggage desk. How did she find me here? "Hello, Fiona Cumhaill of Toronto, Canada. We need to speak."

Sloan stiffens, and I don't think it's from my nails digging into his forearm. The guy has a quick wit and probably put two and two together. He steps forward and tugs me in behind his tall frame. "It's been a night already. Maybe another—"

The ebony angel flicks a manicured finger and the world around me freezes. The buzz of the festival crowd stops. Sloan is locked in time. The only two people seemingly unaffected by the spell are her and me.

She stalks closer. Whatever spell sucked the ambient magic from the air is broken. My skin tingles back to life, and my Spidey-senses are ringing off the hook.

"Come, we have matters to discuss." She waves her fingers, and I'm transported away.

In the space between two racing heartbeats, I go from an alley brawl to standing on the top edge of a cliff looking seven hundred feet down to the blackness of crashing water below. The salty sea air whips my hair into my face as wind buffets against me, forcing me toward the edge. I lock my footing, my legs still trembling from being attacked in the alley.

Connecting with my power, I search for my bear and come up empty. "What have you done?" I shout over the thunder of wind and waves. "What did you do to them?"

"Relax. Yer friends are fine, but they won't find you."

"Who are you?"

"Ye haven't figured that out yet?"

There's nowhere for me to go, and based on the power coming off her, I won't get far if I try. "I take it you're more than a creepy luggage lady."

Her smile smooths out my panic, and I fight the influence. "Da, more." Her Irish accent slips away. "My two sisters and I are called dark lady of magic."

What's that accent? Russian? Romanian?

The glamour of her beauty glimmers in the moonlight and I understand that the woman I see isn't the real woman at all. Who the hell is she?

"All three of you are known as *the* dark lady? That's not confusing at all."

"You call me Stacey."

Weird. But whatevs. I've got bigger problems.

Stacey tilts her head. Although the wind whips my hair wildly in every direction, she looks like a supermodel in front of a photographer's fan. "My sisters and I are one but three at same time. Until recent. Which is why we stand here."

"Care to expand on that?"

She flicks her fingers, and the moonlight brightens. Maybe it's a trick of the light or reflection off the water or perhaps she has the juice to crank up the moon's wattage. I have no clue. It's freaky no matter how she does it.

"You see cave opening down there?"

I follow the point of her manicured fingernail and squint into the night. About halfway down the cliffside, there is a spot where the darkness seems denser and darker than the stone wall. "I think so."

"I bring you for important task. You enter cave and make deal with dragon who sleeps deep within."

Hubba-wha? "While I'm pretty sure that even with Animal Communication, I don't speak dragon, I am *really* sure that if a dragon sleeps in that cave, I don't want to wake him up."

"Her. Lady dragon in cave."

"Okay, her. Why ask me?"

"Druids are attuned to land and dragons influence land. Your people build sacred stone circles on power nodes on what called ley lines. Dragons and Irish druids share long history. What is traditional meaning of word *ley* in Celtic tongue?"

I swallow. "Dragon."

"Da. In this part of world, 'ley of land' was not about geographical nature. It holds much more powerful meaning."

"Which is?"

"It describes how cosmic forces flow through land and influence area and how area influence cosmic forces in return. Is nature symbiotics. Druids are protectors of nature. You are druid, no?"

I draw a deep breath. "Yes, but I'm a very new druid. There are many others here in Ireland and abroad who have more power and would be a better choice."

"Is you. I wait many moons filling tickets in stupid airport. Prophecy says,

Daughter of son of long ago,
Hark back to home from land of snow.
Grant abeyant drakaina hearts true thirst,
Speak your plea for the one who's cursed.

I run a hand through my hair and hope I don't pass out and topple over the cliff. "Hey, I super love riddles, but although the first part does sorta sound like me, I don't think waking a dragon is a good idea."

She holds out a carnival glass bottle that glitters in the moonlight. It's about the size of a bottle of wine, but the glass blooms out to a bulbous bottom from the narrow neck. It's like a giant teardrop with a cork.

"For drakaina. She needs."

"And what is the dragon doing in the cave?"

"She sleeps."

"Right. We covered that. But is she hibernating or entombed or taking a nap?"

"What you know of dragons?"

I grab a wild rope of hair smacking me in the face and tuck it behind my ear. "Not much."

"Tell me, not much."

I search my memory. "Ancient Celts thought dragons were gods who brought Earthly and heavenly forces together. They were thought of as guardian spirits and are depicted as the most powerful of all the Celtic symbols."

"And guard gate to Underworld—to my sisters."

"Okay, so you want me to wake up the scary giant magical serpent for an offer of refreshments, then ask her for a favor for you?"

"Da. Then you give her this for dark lady."

A jeweled box the size of a glasses case appears in my empty hand, and I frown. "Why would I agree to this?"

"I kill you if you don't."

"And I'm dragon kibble if I do."

"She no eat you. You bring elixir. She be happy."

I tip the glittering bottle in the moonlight and watch the creamy glop sludge its way along the inside of the glass. "Are you sure she wouldn't prefer a Guinness?"

"Stop talking now. Give elixir to drakaina and tell her box is for dark lady."

I look at the jeweled box. "I'm sure there are more than your two dark ladies in the Underworld. Assuming I'm not a dragon snack, what if she doesn't know who I mean?"

"Baba Yaga dark lady. That is us."

Baba Yaga? *Oh, crap.* Okay, that name I know. I stare at the stunning ebony-haired angel, and her glamour fades away. The weathered woman left behind is more terrifying and bleeds more toxic power than I can take. I step back, perilously close to the edge of the cliff. "And if I say no?"

Stacey flicks her fingers, and I feel the rush of her tainted powers hit me like a physical force. It knocks me off the edge of the cliff, and I plummet, screaming toward the water.

CHAPTER SIXTEEN

My fall is short-lived—thank you, baby Yoda—and a moment after I plummet off the edge of a seven-hundred-foot cliff drop, I'm standing in pitch dark. By the stink, I'm in the dragon's lair. Or it could be the garbage compactor scene in Star Wars, but Luke and Han aren't with me, so I'm going with dragon lair.

Damn, where's Sloan Mackenzie in the clutch? He could wayfarer me right outta here. Men, never around when you need them. Always around when you don't.

Yes, I'm stalling.

To be fair, I think I get to take a minute in this situation. Baba Yaga, a.k.a. Stacey kidnapped me and sent me into a dragon's lair to wake her from her sleep and ask a favor. "And in exchange, I have this yummy bottle of spuge to whet your whistle."

I stand there a few more seconds, but the humid, stench-laden air is making me gag. If I don't hurry this up, it'll be the sound of me hurling that wakes up the lady dragon.

Closing my eyes, I try again to connect with Bruinior. Man, I hate the name Bruinior. We need to do better. Regardless, there's still nothing.

Baba Yaga is arguably the most powerful or one of the most powerful, preternatural beings alive. I suppose if she doesn't want me to phone a friend, I won't be able to.

On the off chance... I pull my cell from my pocket but have no signal. Instead, I turn on my torchlight. The moment the brilliant pool illuminates the cave interior, I cringe.

Ew. File this place under things you can't unsee.

Human corpses and animal carcasses lay slung and littered along the jagged stone walls of the cave, slumped seven and eight high. Throats are torn out. Blood is dried black and caked thick with flies. My eyes burn from the stench.

Everywhere my light pans, it's more of the same horror, and I realize I'm likely about to join the pile. I turn back to the opening. There's nowhere to go. I can't portal out. Maybe I could wait and see if Sloan or Granda find me.

As the flicker of hope sparks, it extinguishes.

If Stacey is as powerful as I think she is, I'll die here long before anyone ever figures out where I am. I grimace at the crunch and munch landscape and wish with everything in me that I knew what I was doing.

"I'm the Skip-the-Dishes bitch for a witch."

Going back and staying put are both no good. That only leaves one option—dragon dinner. The suction of my footsteps in the half-clotted aftermath is *soooo* gross. I move deeper into the cave, and gore squishes and squelches under the tread of my sneakers.

I make a face, focus straight ahead, and try my best not to think about it. It doesn't take long before the long, rounded tunnel opens into a massive, torchlit cavern that stretches beyond and above where the light travels.

"Ah, Miss Cumhaill, I've been expectin' ye. Welcome." It takes a second for my hamster to get back in its wheel, but I smile at the Man o' Green I met outside the airport that first day I arrived. "I'm Patty, by the by. And it's Patty with two t's not

Paddy with two d's. Ye wouldn't believe how often yer people from across the pond get that wrong."

He's lying in a La-Z-Boy recliner set on a huge area rug. His lounge area is furnished with a couple of lamps, an old-fashioned gramophone, and a stand-up wet bar. When I step farther into the cavern, he sits up and waves with the videogame controller in his hand.

I turn off my light and slide my phone back into my pocket. "Are you playing Animal Crossing?"

"That I am. It's an addictive pleasure, I tell ye. I'll be with ye in one second." His mischievous blue eyes sparkle as he focuses on his screen. "I need to sell my turnips while the price is right. Makin' a small fortune."

The snowy-haired leprechaun goes back to finishing the stage of his game, and I glance around the cavern. My eyes adjust to the low light and fifty feet from where I stand, lays a sleeping dragon coiled up with her tail, her scales glimmering in shades of red from burnt umber to scarlet.

Wow. This is happening.

Beyond the dragon, the cavern glows gold. What I initially thought was torchlight is a magical glow coming off more treasure than could be held in a thousand druid shrines.

"I didn't know dragons collect gold."

"Och, she doesn't," Patty says. "She collects Elvis paraphernalia. It was a bitch gettin' that beast in here." He points to my left where a pink Cadillac sits spotlighted on a red carpet. "The treasure be mine. Her Magnificence helps me guard it. A last line of defense, one might say."

It's hard to soak up how much treasure there is in this cavern. It's incredible. Mounds and mountains glisten as far as I can see. "I guess you've never been caught and forced to give any up."

Patty chuckles and pushes his glasses further up his nose. "Och, I've been caught a time or two, but when I bring them here to claim their prize, Her Exaltedness ends my obligation with a quick snap of her mighty maw."

"She gets a snack, and you get to keep your gold."

Patty nods. "A grand union fer near a millennium."

"And the bodies in the tunnel? They're the people who bested you?"

"Some. Others came in search of Her Eminence to satisfy curiosity. Most were stupid enough to try to force her favor."

My bowels twist, and I wonder if there's a bathroom around here if I need it. "She's not fond of the favor seekers?"

Patty chuckled. "Not a bit, but they keep her fed. So, Miss Cumhaill, what brings ye by?"

I swallow against the bile rising in my throat.

Before I answer, he bursts out laughing. "I'm coddin' ye. Are ye ready to give it a go?"

"You know why I'm here?"

"Och, of course. I keep an eye on the dark lady fer just such things. She's singularly focused on solving the prophecy, that one. A stubborn being, but Her Illustriousness and I do enjoy her offerings to break the monotony."

"Awesome. It's good to know that when she grinds my bones to dust, at least I've provided a distraction."

"That's the spirit," he says. After shuffling over to the dragon, he strokes a section of her scaly tail. "My Ladyship, we have a guest. It's Fiona of the Clan Cumhaill. She brings you a gift from the dark lady."

I swallow, once again hearing Da's warning. *"Forget hoppin' the pond fer a grand family reunion. It won't be like that. What he offers, yer best without."*

Getting munched by an angry she-dragon applies. I cling to the glittery glass bottle and wish with everything in me that I am safely home in my bedroom in Toronto. As I suffer my mental meltdown, the dragon's eye slowly peeks open.

Against the shadowed, blood-red wall of wound serpent, a

glimmering gold oval widens. Her eye shimmers in the dim light and seems almost backlit.

Patty gestures to where I stand, and I fight not to pee my pants. "Greetings, Your Awesomeness." I offer an awkward bow. "I'm sorry to disturb you."

"Yet you do."

"It wasn't my choice, I'm afraid."

"Lies. It was the choice you made. Three of those who came before you dove to the water below rather than face me or the witch's retaliation. Lie to me again, and our conversation ends with your blood-curdling screams."

Oh, great start. "I'm sorry. That is true."

"And why do you bother us?"

I hold up the bottle of creamy goop in both hands and drop my gaze. I'm going for the Lion King presentation stance, but I'm not sure I pull it off. "Baba Yaga sent you this to quench your thirst. I hope you like it."

I really, really hope you like it.

"I doubt I will." She sighs as she lumbers to uncoil. "Give Patty the elixir and go through the prophecy."

I hand the bottle to the spry old leprechaun and try to remember what Baba Yaga said. "'Daughter of son of long ago, Hark back to home from land of snow.' My da left the Order years ago to move to Toronto, Canada, and start a family. I'm the daughter of the son, and we get buried in snow in the winter, so I think that part is a slam-dunk."

She unwinds enough to sit up, her muscles clenching and sliding with the shuffling sound of scales on stone. "I'm listening."

"'Grant abeyant drakaina hearts true thirst.'" I have no idea what abeyant means, but don't think it's in my best interest to mention that. Hopefully, Baba Yaga does. "She seemed sure the bottle of elixir would be to your liking."

Although how a bottle smaller than her pinkie toenail is

supposed to quench her thirst, I have no idea. I should've brought a tanker truck.

"'Speak your plea for the one who's cursed.' When you're happy with the offering, I'm supposed to give you this box and ask that it get delivered to her dark lady sisters on the other side."

The ground rumbles beneath my soggy sneakers, as the dragon's laughter fills the cavern. "I am well aware of what the dark lady wants." She swings her serpent head and lifts her horned nostrils toward a ten-foot mound of gemmed boxes the same as the one I hold in my hand.

How many people has she sacrificed for this?

I stare at the mountain of failed offerings, and my chest constricts. The box in my hand will soon be tossed into that pile as I'm claimed as dragon chum.

The cheery whistle of Patty behind me has me turning. He's emptying the creamy contents of the bottle I brought into a Nerf Super-Soaker Scatter Blaster.

Is that how she likes to drink? No wonder her thirst never gets quenched. I'm thinking of how I can word that diplomatically when he shuffles off past his lounge area and waves me to follow. "Ye might as well watch. Yer fate depends on this."

The dragon shifts and the lengths of her body writhe in opposite directions as she uncoils to follow.

What's going on?

I hustle to keep up and stop when we round a rocky jut in the cave wall. Patty takes a torch from its housing and touches it to a stone trough built along the floor.

Whoosh. The liquid in the trough ignites, carrying the flame around the perimeter of a hundred-foot chamber.

"Eggs." I stare at the dozens of watermelon-sized, teardrop-shaped mounds nestled in moss.

"My children," the dragon says. "Now is the moment for you to pray to your druid goddess that what you brought me is truly the viable seed of a basilisk."

It *is* spunk. "Your heart's thirst is to be a mother."

She dips her chin. "I was once the queen of incredible worms, respected and revered by all who set eyes upon them."

"Um, sure. I guess that with the right leadership, worms could be incredible."

Patty raises the nozzle of the water gun and sprays an arcing stream over the shells. "Not worms—w-o-r-m-s. It's wyrms—w-y-r-m-s. Her Ladyship is Queen of Wyrms."

I nod but have no idea what that means.

Patty chuckles. "Wingless, legless dragons. Great serpentine beasts found deep in the Earth's core and waterways. Ye've heard of the Loch Ness Monster, have ye?"

"Yes," I say, glad to be catching up. "So, Nessie was a wyrm dragon?"

"That's right." Patty finishes with the basilisk sperm shower. "All right, now. Do yer druid thing as if yer life depends on it. Fertilize these eggs."

Do my druid thing? He has to know I'm only two weeks into learning spells. The scary queen swings her open mouth toward me, and I wither under the stench of rotten breath. She must have a favor-seeker stuck in her back fangs somewhere.

Um, gross.

"Make them grow, Lady Cumhaill, and become Mother of Dragons."

I bite my tongue. It almost kills the smartass in me not to mention that position was claimed, and it didn't work out well for Khaleesi. "I would be honored, Your Graciousness."

Dammit, I haven't taken egg fertilization 101. I search through my mind for the spells I've learned, suddenly very aware that I've focused heavily on the physical magic of offense and defensive fighting.

Feline Finesse won't help me here.

The only spell I know about growing is my beanstalk lesson. Can I modify it to work? I slide my hand into my front pocket and pull out my little pouch of casting stones. After knocking everyone on their asses in the training rings, I'm only allowed to carry three at a time.

I choose the moonstone for fertility, hormone balance, and conception. The malachite is to amplify my power to influence. I stuff the jasper back into my pocket and squeeze a stone in each of my palms.

Eyes closed, I call on the energy of my casting stones, set my intention, and ask nature to comply. Projecting my casting energy onto the objects, I modify the spell on the fly.

I envision the shells of the eggs being sprinkled with the magical nutrients donated by the basilisk daddy. How Baba Yaga collected it, I have no idea and no time to think about it.

I focus my intention, rub my thumbs over the globes in my hands, and call on the spell inked on my back.

Up shit's creek, so here we go,
Sprayed and fed and time to grow.
Your dragon queen awaits your birth,
Quench her thirst and bring her mirth.
Eggs fertilize to mighty beasts,
Hope and pray I'll be released.

I call my powers to the fore and push out with more strength and determination than ever. Hell, if I'd been this keyed up, I would've crushed Seamus Scott and taken the grand championship of the junior trials.

I repeat the spell until my energy is spent. When I open my eyes, I meet the expectant gazes of the dragon queen and her leprechaun. "I've done what I can."

Patty shrugs and glances over the mossy garden of eggs. "Then we shall wait and see the outcome. May the luck of the Irish be with ye, dearie."

CHAPTER SEVENTEEN

And wait I must. Days and days and days. I try not to complain. I figure an ungrateful guest—*cough* captive—is a tasty guest, so I suck it up and work on becoming besties. Snacking on your friend can't be as palatable as chomping some stranger who invaded your cave to ask a favor for a scary witch, amirite?

Patty does his best to make me comfortable. At the snap of his finger, I get a recliner to match his for gaming. Then, he *poofs* me a three-inch memory foam to soften the frame of the guest cot they keep for such occasions.

Now and then, I glance at the mountain of abandoned Baba Yaga boxes from failed favor-seekers. The witch might be scary-powerful, but she sucks at solving prophesy riddles.

That isn't comforting.

I wonder how many people died to send her sisters whatever she needs to send them? And how did she get the basilisk seed? And how many people have slept on my cot?

I don't want to know the answers to any of those...except maybe...no, ew, not even the spunk question.

"Fiona, get that present flying over yer head. Ye need yer slingshot. We're lookin' fer the ironwood dresser recipe."

I look from the screen to Patty and frown. "Why do we want that? Are we making the ironwood kitchenette?"

"Och, we could, or we could sell the recipe fer a fortune on Nookazon."

"Really? That's a thing? You're codding me."

"Och, I never joke about money."

I go back to the game, bopping to the beat of the current Elvis song playing. Her Illustrious Wyrm Queen is right. Elvis is the King of Rock and Roll for a good reason.

I fire my slingshot and the present drops to the ground beside me. "Oh, damn. It's a lump of four clay?"

Patty sighs and falls into his chair. "That recipe is harder to find than a black cat in the coal cellar."

I'm in the middle of putting away my virtual slingshot when my serpentine hostess with the most-ess uncoils in a scaly hiss and lifts her head. "Did you hear that?"

Patty waves a hand, and the gramophone needle lifts off the record. Suddenly there is literally *A Little Less Conversation*. Sad. We were just getting to the part that makes me want to rob a casino.

I pause and save our game and the three of us stand silent and still. We all know what we're hoping for. There have been four other such moments of active listening.

Her Mighty Slitheryness is getting anxious.

She senses growth in the eggs but doesn't want to get too excited until they start to hatch. I won't be free to leave until they do. I'm not panicked now, though. I sense the growth within those eggs. It's a matter of time before twenty-three new dragons are born into the world.

Yay me. Mother of Wyrms, here I come.

If given a choice, I'd rather be the Mother of Jaguars or

Mother of Koalas, but hey, if these slimy little suckers ever hatch, I'm free to go. So, yay team!

Patty stiffens, and a smile rounds his cheeks and lifts his glasses. "Och, I did hear that, Mistress. It can't be long now. Come, we don't want to miss the grand arrival."

It takes another twenty minutes before the first little horned snout pushes through a shell. "A blue one." I admire the shimmering sheen of its damp scales. The thing is the size of a ferret but skinny and slick with a mucusy goop. "Can you tell if it's a boy or a girl?"

"It's a boy," the she-dragon gushes. "Males have a three-pronged spike at the tip of their tail."

I'm neither close enough nor tall enough to see it, so I take her word.

The queen lowers her face to the little squirmer and with a quick flick of her tongue snatches him up and pops him into her mouth.

"*Oh!*" I shout, horror making me forget my dedication to good behavior. "You're going to *eat* him?"

Patty laughs. "Of course not. Mother dragons carry their young in a pocket in their mouth. They're safe and warm, and when she feeds, they'll get scraps."

Gross. "Oh, awesome."

The second baby wyrm frees—I note the single-spike tail —*her*self from her egg, and the queen scoops her up too.

And so it goes.

An hour later, there's a break in the action, and the queen rises on her tail and faces me. "Thank you, Fiona Cumhaill," she says, her words garbled from gargling seventeen baby dragons. "You are free to go. You have earned my undying affection."

The end of her tail wraps around me and gives me what I imagine is a hug similar to that of a boa constrictor. Where the spiked tip of her tail touches my bicep, my skin ignites with a skin-melting burn.

"Holy hell," I gasp. I look down expecting to see singed and bubbling flesh, but instead, there's another tattoo rising as an armband. What is with fae creatures and inking people?

"And what about Baba Yaga?" I ask.

Patty reaches up to link his arm with mine, and we turn toward the main cavern. "After Her Mothership finishes welcoming her wyrmlets, she'll deliver the dark lady's box. I'll send the oul witch confirmation, and make it clear yer to be left alone from here on."

"Thanks, Patty."

He nods. "It'll not be the same here without ye, Fi. We had some good craic, eh?"

"Yeah, it was fun. And hey, if our futures turn on us, we can always polish off our dance routine. I bet we could make a fortune as an Elvis tribute roadshow."

Patty laughs and points toward the main cavern. "I have all the fortune I need. But if yer future turns on ye, speak the word, and together we'll make it right. Come to me now. I have something to give ye before ye go."

―――――――――

The scent of Gran's cooking breaks through the singe of dragon lair stink and stirs my emotions more than I like. I won't cry. I refuse. The terror of being kidnapped by Baba Yaga and the annoyance of imprisonment by a mythological Wyrm Queen is over. I didn't cry then, so why would I open the waterworks over the succulent aroma of steak boxty?

"Howeyah, Gran."

"*Och!* Thank the Sweet Goddess yer home." Gran rushes from the stove and envelopes me in one of her WWE bone-crusher hugs. I'm not sure who's shaking more, but neither of us is steady. She pulls back and grips my shoulders with her cushy oven mitt hands. "Let me look at ye. Are ye all right?"

"Fine. Just *really* glad to be back."

"Och, we need to call Lugh home. Everyone's been beside themselves with worry."

She rushes to the bird platform and holds out her hands. A blackbird lands in her palms, and she speaks her message. "She's safe home. Stop the search."

Tossing the bird into the air, it disappears into nothing, her magic sending it off to deliver her message. "Come, luv. Ye must be famished."

She takes my wrist and presses her fingers to her nose.

"I know. I stink. Sorry."

"Och, don't worry about that. Lugh's come home reeking awful more times than—"

"Fiona, *mo chroi*." Granda is portaled into the kitchen by Sloan and grabs me up in his arms. His hug is nearly as tight as Gran's, although it doesn't last as long. He quickly regroups and steps back to check me over. "We've been out of our heads not knowin'—"

Granda staggers to the side, knocked by the furry shoulder of my bear as he materializes into the group. *Och, I'm glad to see yer face, Red. Ye scared me somethin' terrible.*

"I missed your face too, big guy." I wrap my arms around his burly neck and burrow into the decadence of his fur. "I tried to contact you a million times. Sorry you missed the adventure."

I'm sorry ye went it alone. He swipes his tongue up the length of my cheek and vanishes. The flutter of him settling inside my chest rights the tilt of my world.

"What the hell happened?" Sloan asks. He's not looking like his usual GQ hottie self. He's disheveled. It's like he picked up yesterday's clothes off the floor and didn't bother with his shower and shave regimen. "Where'd she take ye? Are ye hurt? Should I get my Da?"

I lay my hand against my sternum, stronger now that my bear

and I are reunited. "No, I really am fine. All I need is some of Gran's cooking, a shower, and some fresh clothes."

Sloan's gaze locks on the new armband tattoo that encircles my bicep. It's a wyrm dragon in stunning detail, the head of the beast biting the tail to create an unending circle.

Brushing a finger over the dragon's eye, I shrug. "It's a long story involving Baba Yaga, a leprechaun, wyrm dragons, Elvis, and a lot of Animal Crossing."

"I'll send word to Niall." Granda heads toward the office. "I'll tell him yer safe home, and ye'll call him the moment yer settled and fed. Ye best wash off. Ye stink of dark magic and death. Ye don't want that energy on ye any longer than necessary."

"Da has an enchanted body wash with rejuvenating properties," Sloan says. "I'll be right back. Don't start the tale without me."

It takes three cycles of rinse and repeats with Wallace's enchanted shampoo to get the ode to dragon's dead out of my hair. Tucked in my towel, I pad barefoot to my bedroom, check that my phone is charging, and pass on my shirts in favor of one of Da's threadbare concert t-shirts.

Fresh clothes feel like an insane luxury, and one I'll never take for granted again. I lost track of how many days I was gone—hanging out in an underground cavern will do that to you—but I'm guessing ten or eleven.

I finish brushing out the tangles and head to the kitchen to fill my tummy and catch everyone up on my adventure.

It's weird. Even with the dark juju washed off, I feel a little floaty and lost. There were times, including those moments at the edge of the cliff with Baba Yaga when I thought I'd never get back here alive.

"*Seven weeks?*" I stare at the three of them, my forkful of boxty hanging in the air. "How is that possible?"

"Time passes differently when in the presence of powerful fae creatures fer extended periods," Granda says.

"And with Baba Yaga, a dragon queen, and a Man o' Green, ye certainly had that," Sloan adds, shaking his head. "Damn, Cumhaill. Only you could trip into a hape of manure and come out smelling like a rose."

I laugh. "No. I stunk like death, remember? The floral aroma is not me. That's your dad's soap."

"Nonsense," Granda says. "Yer a Cumhaill, *mo chroi*. Sloan said from the start ye had remarkable potential. Right as usual, son."

I arc a brow. "A compliment? Potential, eh? I can't wrap my head around that."

"Hey, I can be objective." It's good to see some of the haunted panic in Sloan's eyes replaced by his usual haughty arrogance. I got snatched on his watch. With a guy like him, that probably cleaved his pride and self-image in two.

"Oh, and Patty gave me this." I hold up the chunk of green gemstone, and Gran's eyes go wide. "Ye have yer first casting stone, luv, and she's a beauty."

"Really? I thought casting stones were round and shiny."

"Yer Da's are, but that's not necessarily the case. If a Man o' Green favors ye with a bit of his treasure, that stone will be invaluable to ye as ye grow into yer powers."

"Cool. What is it?"

"A peridot." Sloan holds out his hand. I let him take a closer look, and he seems genuinely impressed. "Peridot and diamond are the only gemstones not formed in the Earth's crust, but instead fire-forged in the molten mantle below."

Gran holds her hand out next and smiles as she closes her palm around my green rock. "It's called a money stone but is used to clarify the mind, and increase willpower, well-being, and vitality."

Sloan snorts. "Not that ye need increased willpower. Yer as stubborn as rocks."

I laugh. "It's a family trait."

Granda looks pleased about the whole thing. "There is great power in the fact that Patty gifted it to ye, Fi. Ye didn't thank him when he gave it to ye, did ye?"

"Of course, I did." All three of them stiffened. "Why? What's wrong with that? Why wouldn't I?"

"Words have great meaning with the fae, luv," Gran says, "and with the greater fae especially. To thank a fae is to imply that you recognize an indebtedness. It forms a bond ye may or may not want to form."

Granda nods. "Most are a good lot, but even they might take advantage of a bond of gratitude if they find themselves in a situation when it gives them a leg up. Patty may well have given ye the stone for that purpose. If he realized yer special, he might want to have a tie to ye."

"Okay, well that sucks. Here I thought we were friends."

Gran pours herself another cup of tea and adds a squeeze of honey. "Ye may be right, and it was a heartfelt offering. Ye simply can never be too careful is all."

Granda takes the teapot next and refills his cup. "Next time say somethin' like, 'Your gift is kind. I will treasure it,' or 'The honor of your gesture won't be forgotten.' Ye see how that's expressing yer appreciation without opening the door to being in their debt?"

"Okay, yeah, but 'thank you' and 'sorry' are a reflex. I'm Canadian. We're known for being overly nice."

"So you keep sayin'." Sloan rises to take his plate to the sink. "I'm waitin' to see it myself."

Gran sips from the edge of her delicate, flowered teacup and sets it gently on the saucer. "What did ye say to him exactly, luv? Do ye remember?"

I run it back in my mind. "I said, 'Thank you, very much,' then I hugged him. Was that wrong, too?"

Sloan drops his plate in the sink and sends up a plume of bubbles. "He let ye touch him?"

His wide eyes make me giggle. "A quick hug to say thank you and goodbye, yeah."

"Och," Granda says. "Then maybe yer all right. I've never known a Man o' Green to allow such a thing. He obviously trusts ye not to hold him ransom fer his gold."

I chuckle. "Or he knew I'm not stupid enough to try. That's why he lives with the dragon queen. She eats anyone who catches him when he leads them to his stash."

"A canny and dangerous lot, them."

I think about the time spent with Patty and the dragon waiting for the eggs to mature. We played a lot on his game console, but could it have been seven weeks?

"How long does it take for dragon eggs to hatch?"

I look at Granda because his discipline is being a walking encyclopedia. "Somewhere between fifty-two and sixty-eight days, I believe."

It was only after the majority hatched that the she-dragon said I could go. Wow. Seven weeks. "I'm surprised Da isn't here. He must've been out of his mind."

The room falls eerily silent.

Sloan is finished with his plate but remains facing the sink. His shoulders are rigid, the muscles in his back tense. Granda clenches his jaw so tight that I'd bet he's grinding his molars to dust. And my sweet gran looks at me and her chin starts to quiver. Is she tearing up?

"What happened? Did something happen to Da?"

Granda shakes his head. "Niall did come when ye first went missing—and yer right, he was in a state. We searched every avenue we could think of. The Order called in favors as we combed the countryside. But then yer father was called home on another matter."

A hot flush ignites my whole body in a rush. Da would never abandon his search for me unless another one of his kids needed him more. "Who is it, and how bad?"

"It's yer brother Brendan," Gran says, her voice soft. She reaches over and squeezes my arm. "He was admitted to the hospital after being shot. The doctors did everything they could. I'm sorry, Fi. He passed a few weeks ago."

I swallow. My hearing *whooshes* as blood thunders in my head. *Brenny?* "But... He can't... I wasn't there."

"It's not yer fault ye weren't there, luv. Ye were missing. Yer family understands that. Yer brother would under—"

I press my hands flat on the table and stare at them, trying to hold back the shakes. "What happened? Was his cover blown? Did they find out he's a cop?"

"Not as far as anyone can tell," Gran says. "From what yer father said, the men he was investigating accosted a woman and her daughter on the street. Things got out of hand, and a fight ensued. When the man drew a gun in anger, yer brother stepped in front of the bullets."

"Of course, he did."

"He met his end with honor and bravery," Granda says. "He saved the woman and her girl. A true hero."

The scrape of wooden chair legs echoes in my skull as I rise from the table. The last time I saw Brendan, I pretended I didn't know him and walked the other way. If I knew...

What? Would I have broken his cover? Would I knowingly put him in more danger?

I wander back to my room but can't decide what to do with myself. I stop, locked in a whirl of indecision. My fractured attention bounces around the room. It's not my room.

Not really. Why am I here when...

I'm sorry, Red.

I crawl onto my bed and pull the quilt over my head.

"Yeah," I whisper. "Me, too."

It's my biggest fear come to life. I've worried about each of them for years—known this could happen. Still, I don't know how to dislodge the blade piercing my heart.

The mattress dips beside me, and a hand presses on the quilt tented over my head. A rush of healing energy takes the edge off the pain but doesn't ease the loss. "I'm sorry, luv. With all the magic in our lives, ye'd think we could fix something like this. Alas, there was nothing to be done."

I pull the blanket down and wipe my eyes. "I have to go home, Gran. They need me, and I need them."

She nods. "We knew that would be yer first thought. Sloan's agreed to see ye safe home. That distance will take a lot out of him. Since he won't be able to return straight away, Lugh asked him to keep up yer trainin' fer a few days until he's strong enough to make his way back."

"Thank you." I hug my gran and look around the room. "I guess I should pack."

CHAPTER EIGHTEEN

S loan portals us onto the back porch of my beloved Victorian house. It's mid-morning, and the city is alive and bustling in the hum of the air around us. Our backyard is fairly private, but I check to see if our neighbors or anyone driving down the back lane saw us arrive. "You should've *poofed* us straight inside."

"I've never been inside," Sloan says. "I can only portal places I've been."

That reminds me that he had likely been in my backyard when he was spying on us for Granda. "How'd you get here when you came to test our powers in the beginning?"

"I flew economy here and portaled home after ye laid yer beatin' on me. Da thought I'd been mugged in the big city. I didn't have the stones to tell him I got whipped by a wee girl."

I know he's trying to cheer me up, but it doesn't touch the heaviness in my chest. "Come inside. Then you won't have to spook the townsfolk next time."

I set my computer bag on the table against the stairs and find Da, Calum, and Aiden in the front room. They're sitting together, each of them with a longneck bottle in their hands but a million miles away in their minds.

"Hey," I say. "How about a hug?"

The three are on their feet in the next instant, and love swallows me. "Fiona Kacee Cumhaill," Da says, refusing to let me ease back from his embrace. "Let me hold ye a bit longer before the world crashes in. I need to convince myself yer real."

I don't argue. I'm exactly where I want to be.

I'm home.

When I'm set free from my dad's embrace, Aiden takes his turn. "Hey, baby girl. Howeyah?"

"Sad. You?"

"Same." He kisses the side of my head, then eases back to look at me. "Sorry your grand return from adventure is shrouded with shadow."

I shrug. "It's okay. Brenny's the hero. Granda said he saved a woman and her daughter?"

"That he did," Da says. "I spoke to the ladies myself and read the report. Yer brother is the only reason they live today. We need to keep that foremost in our minds."

"Nothing makes it better," I say, "but that helps."

Da sees me tearing up and opens his arms again.

Yeah. It's good to be home.

"Is this *him?*" Dillan flies in from the front door and goes directly for Sloan. "You're the bastard who took Fi down in the alley and scared the shit outta Kady, yeah? You filthy piece of shit."

Oh, crap. I rush to stand block between them, both hands flat on my brother's chest. "It was a test, D. Remember I said how he never hurt me or took a swing or anything? He wasn't here to do harm."

Dillan scowls at me, his dark hair much longer than when I left. "Tell that to Kady. She's fucking traumatized. She can't even walk to her car at night by herself. Whether or not Granda's little messenger man meant to do no harm, he *did.*"

"I'm sorry," Sloan says. "I was singularly focused on saving yer grandfather's life. If ye let me apologize to the woman for the misunderstanding, I'll fix it."

"Yeah, no. I don't bloody think so. There was no misunderstanding. You assaulted her, plain and simple. I'm gonna run you in." Dillan lunges around me and grabs Sloan's wrist. "You're under arrest, asshole."

Sloan disappears and reappears across the room. "No. I'm not."

"What the fuck?" Dillan closes the distance and grabs at him again.

Sloan flashes back to the hall. "I'm sorry—truly, I am—but your choices here are to either let me fix it or forget it. There's no scenario where you arrest me for doing my duty."

Dillan goes for him a third time, and once again, Sloan slips his hold by using his wayfarer gift. He reappears in an empty corner of the room right as Shannon and Liam arrive.

"How the... What just happened there?" Shannon steps in from the front hall. "And why is Dillan trying to kill that man?"

"He's the guy who assaulted Fi and Kady in the alley."

Okay, now Shannon looks like she might try to kill him.

"Everyone, calm down," I shout. "Can we not fight tonight, please? Yes, Sloan is the guy from the alley. No, he wasn't mugging or assaulting us. He was testing the potential strength of my powers."

Shannon looks at Da and frowns. "And why aren't ye tryin' to kill him yerself? The man roughed up Fi and took her to ground."

Da, bless him, is calm as ever. "Sloan and I made our peace in Ireland while we looked fer Fi together."

I meet Sloan's gaze and wonder why he never mentioned it. A head-to-head with Da couldn't have gone well.

"My father is a persuasive bastard, and Sloan was duty-bound to find which of my children held the most potential to save his life. Fi fit the bill, and he did what he did."

"Potential fer what?" Shannon asks.

I search the faces of the men in the room and realize Shannon is the only one still in the dark. "Da, would you like to do the honors?"

He laughs and waves that away. "Och, no. This is yer shite-show, Fiona. You opened this particular kettle of worms, so have at it."

I do my best. I start with the tattoo appearing on my back the morning after the alley incident, then explain how the letter arrived by courier with the same seal, then go into all the Ireland stuff, and end up right where we are.

Da and my brothers hadn't heard the last part about being held captive by a leprechaun and a dragon, so that threw them a bit, but in the end, everything is out in the open.

Liam goes to the kitchen and grabs an armful of beer. Emmet, who came in halfway through the recap, helps him pass them around.

"Sloan is my friend," I say, surprised that I think so after all the crap he's put me through. "And yes, he's too serious, quite conceited, and awkward to get to know, but if you take the time, he's worth it."

"If you say he's an acquired taste, I'm going to hurt you," Dillan says.

"No. He's more like a fungus that grows on you."

Sloan rolls his eyes. "Maybe it's best I leave."

"Best idea I've heard all day," Dillan snaps.

"Ye'll take the pullout in the basement," Da says, pegging Dillan with a look. "And Dillan, ye'll leave him in peace and bring Kady by in the morning. Give Sloan the chance to apologize and make it right with her."

"But Da—"

My father lifts his hand. "If ye do somebody wrong, ye make it right. Sloan is offering to do that. It's not yer place to deny it fer either him or Kady."

Shannon's sitting in my armchair in the corner, her arms crossed as tightly as her lips are pursed.

"You don't believe me, do you?"

She sighs. "I think ye've suffered an ordeal and what ye think is true and what is actually true is night and day different. All this craziness about magic and druids and dragons is a tale yer mind has told ye to help ye through. A coping mechanism, of sorts."

I look at my brothers lounging around the room and shrug. "Let me prove it to you. I want you to meet someone. *Ready for your big family debut, Bear?*

Ready and waitin', Red.

"He's what the druid's call an animal companion."

Sloan snorts. "Still not."

"Oh, shut up." I wave at Sloan, and his smirk is all censure. Ha! Too bad. I've been waiting for this moment for months. "Now, he's a little shy, so lean in and stay very still."

They humor me. It strikes me then... Brendan would've loved this. He was the king of Cumhaill pranks. *This one's for you, Brenny. Watch this.*

"Okay. Come on out, baby."

The flutter in my chest precedes the manifestation of my massive brown bear in the living room. Emmet, Calum, Dillan, and Aiden jump back with a shout. Shannon pulls her knees up and screams. Liam yips and jumps behind the chair.

Da takes it all in with a chuckle. "Hello again, bear." He walks over and gives his shoulder a scratch. "Looks like ye get yer city adventure after all. Welcome home to ye both."

"What the fuck, Fi?" Calum shouts from his perch on the back of the couch. His eyes are bugged. "You have a pet bear?"

"Not a pet." I drape my arm over Bruinior's broad neck. "He's my druid animal companion."

"Again, no," Sloan says. "Yer sister's cracked. Her bear is a bound spirit meant to be a beast to cast in battle."

"Fuck me." Aiden takes a long draw on his beer and comes

over to meet him. "Can you imagine having backup like this in the thick of a takedown?"

Emmet snorts. "The perps would scream and run faster."

"Nah, they'd piss themselves and crumble. Most criminals are only brave in their wheelhouse. The rest of the shit you see on the street is machismo."

Liam leaves his position of human shield between Bruinior and Shannon and flops onto the couch. "Holy shit, Fi. A little heads-up would've been nice."

I'm still laughing. There's no helping it. Their reactions were as good as I hoped. "Not on your life. The past two months emptied my heart of joy. That filled me right back up. Thanks, guys."

"You're demented." Emmet brushes his shirt where beer sloshed down the front. "But damn, you deserve an Oh Henry! for that."

I raise my hands in triumph. "*Yessss!*"

Aiden nods and holds up his palm for my bear to sniff. "Yeah, Brenny would've loved that one. Definitely chocolate bar-worthy."

Sloan looks lost, so I fill him in. "Brendan was our trickster. When we were kids, he created a scoring system for how well your prank ranked in the hierarchy. You get points in four categories: originality, reaction, fallout, and reach. If you kill it in all four categories, the prize is an Oh Henry! bar. To be awarded one is a grand family honor."

His gaze skitters around the room. "Ye come by it honestly, then. Yer all cracked."

Emmet's grin warms me. "Now you're suckin' diesel."

Da holds up his beer and smiles. "That one was all craic, Fi. Good on ye. Brenny would be proud."

"To Brenny." Calum holds up his beer in salute.

"To Brenny," we all repeat.

"I've never seen so many men in uniform."

I cast Sloan a sideways glance and smile. "Is it doing something for you, big boy? Is it only cops that crank your gears, or do sailors do it for you, too?"

Sloan rolls his eyes, but before he can throw a remark back at me, I grab two whiskey bombs from a passing tray filled with courtesy libations and give one to him. "Thanks for coming. I know you're not the most popular guest in the room, but I appreciate you being here."

"When has popularity been a concern, right?"

"With your winning personality, likely never."

"Exactly." He lifts his gaze and scans the crush of cops, friends, and neighbors. "He must have been one helluva guy, yer brother."

I slug back my whiskey and track the burn as it slides down to the icy pit in my belly. "He was. Brenny had a big heart and a wicked sense of humor. Most of the scolding we got as kids was because of him or something he thought up. Da always said, 'Never listen to Brendan once he gets that look in his eye. It'll only lead ye back here to me.'"

"I'm glad ye didn't miss it."

I smile at all the familiar faces, thankful that Da held the wake until they knew for sure if I was lost or not. It would've broken my heart to miss Brenny's celebration, and he knew it. "Yeah, me too."

"Hey." Emmet joins us as we ease around the perimeter of our guests toward the bar. He kisses my cheek and lifts his chin in greeting to Sloan. "The band is going to start in a few. Before things get too loud, do you guys want that minute with Kady?"

"Did she agree to talk to Sloan?" I ask.

"Dillan's not happy about it, but yeah. Da explained what happened to her, and she's game."

"He what?" Sloan says.

Emmet tilts his head. "Well, not the real reason, of course. Who in their right mind would believe it was a druid testing the magic of Fiona's heritage power? No, he said you were a misguided fool who tested Fiona's defensive skills on his request. He asked you to make the attack realistic, but you were too good at your job, and now that you're back in town, you'd like the chance to apologize. Come on. She's wrapping more cutlery. You can do your thing and be done with it."

We follow Emmet into the kitchen, and the noise of the gathered crowd dulls to a constant hum in the background. I point to the server prep station, and we head over to where Dillan is standing guard over his girlfriend as she wraps napkins around cutlery.

Dillan glares. "I don't like this."

"Noted." I lean past him to hug Kady. "Trust me. Sloan's not a bad guy. And if a quick apology can help smooth out Kady's troubles, it's best to get it out of the way."

Kady doesn't look so sure. She's eyeing Sloan like he's the evil nastiness of her worst nightmares. In turn, Sloan seems to be trying to make himself smaller and less threatening and failing miserably.

"Kady." Sloan meets her gaze. The tingle of my skin tells me he's working his magic. The tension draining from Kady's body tells me it's working. "It's nice to meet ye. I'm ever so sorry fer yer scare. It's not as ye thought it was. It was an unfortunate misunderstanding, but ye handled it with grace and strength. Ye can feel better about it now."

Her smile is warm and easy as she reaches past Dillan to extend her hand. "It's nice to meet you too. Niall says you're visiting from Ireland?"

"I am." The energy in the air dials back. "Only fer a day or two more. I wanted to apologize fer givin' ye a fright last time. It wasn't my intention."

Kady shrugs. "Niall explained everything to me. No harm done."

Dillan scowls and looks from Kady to Sloan to me. "Fine, he's done what he came to do. How about he leaves now?" Dillan is a cop, protective of women, and involved with Kady. I don't blame him for his hostility.

"Cool," I say, turning back the way we came. "Good to see you, Kady."

"You too, Fi. Glad you're back safe. I'm so sorry you came home to heartache."

I nod, my heart heavy. The next hours are going to hurt like hell. "Yeah, me too."

With Kady taken care of, we head back out to the party going on in the pub proper. Dillan's still put out, but he's quick to forgive once things are sorted, so I'm not worried he'll hold it against Sloan for long.

"Good, yer back." Da finishes a shot and slams the glass on the bar. "It's time to send yer brother off with flair." He looks at Liam and nods. "Maestro. If ye please."

"What are you two up to?" I ask.

Da smiles and gestures toward the dance floor. "Brenny always loved to dance. I think it's only right that we give him a final show in his honor."

"Da, I just got back. I haven't danced in donkey's years."

"And we're three sheets, Da." Emmet gestures at himself and Calum.

I give in the moment the music comes up and the beat of the reel hits me. "For Brenny, then." I nod at the boys. "If I'm doing this, I'm not doing it alone."

I toss my sweater onto the bar and pull up my socks. My dress shoes have a square heel on them, so they should work. Dillan takes off his blazer, and Emmet rolls up the sleeves of his dress shirt. I press my finger and thumb together and let out a whistle. "Clan Cumhaill, report to the dance floor."

Aiden waves at me from the other side of the bar and hands his drink to Kinu.

The crowd opens as we gather on the dance floor and pushes out to give us a wide berth. The six of us had years of lessons. Ma loved it. I think Da loved having the house to themselves for an hour and a half every Saturday.

Whatever the motives, the six of us became fleet-footed.

Together we face the audience, turn our feet, and settle into our beginning pose. Hands on our hips, I count us off. "On my mark, ladies. One. Two. Three."

The night drums on, the band is great, the liquor goes down easier by the hour. By the wee hours, most of the polite, "pay their respects people" have cleared out and we're left with those here to celebrate Brendan or console one of us. Sloan returned to the house a couple of hours ago to rest. If he's going to portal back to Ireland in the next couple of days, he needs to recharge.

Do you feel that? Someone is watching us.

Lost in the fog of drink and hilarious family memories, I have to fight to focus on what Bruinior is saying. He's right. The hair on the nape of my neck sparks with the knowledge that I'm being observed. I lift my tumbler to my lips with a feigned smile and pivot my bar stool.

I scan the crowd and know or recognize pretty much everyone in and out of uniform—except.

My early warning system fires to life as I pan past a stocky dude in a black blazer and jeans. "Hey, Liam. Who is the skull-trimmed guy over by the back hall?"

Liam scans the crowd and frowns. "What skull-trim guy by the back hall?"

I set my glass onto the bar and reach over for the chrome

napkin dispenser. Angling it toward the back hall, I find him. "To the right of the *V. I. Pee* sign for the loo."

Liam finishes pulling a couple of draughts and sends Kady on her way. "Either I'm blind, or you're hallucinating. There's no one there."

"Why can't he see him?"

Liam frowns. "Are you talking to me?"

"No. That was for Bruinior."

He nods to a regular and goes to the register to close out a tab. When the printer spits out the bill, he comes back and sets the plastic tray on the bar. "A bit of friendly advice, Fi. First, people are gonna think you've lost your mind if you start talking to your invisible bear in public. Second, Bruinior the Brave is a mouthful and unhip. You said he came to start a new life. Why not give him a snazzy new city name?"

"We've talked about it."

Ask him what that should be?

I frown. "Can we focus on the creepy peeper in the back and worry about the name game later?"

Liam takes another look and shrugs. "I got nothin'."

Seeing that Liam is no help, I take my half-eaten basket of wings down the bar and hop onto the stool next to my father. Tonight has been cathartic. I still miss Brenny like crazy, but if anyone would want us to think of him fondly, raise a glass, and laugh, it was Brendan.

Da seems a little lighter too. I'm relieved. "Hey, Da? Quick question. In the magic world, you know how you and I can hear Bruinior speak, but the others don't?"

"Uh-huh." He snags a wing from my basket.

"Can that happen with people? Could I see a creepy stalker near the back hall and Liam not?"

Da drops the wing and frowns. "Where?"

"Under the Pee sign."

Da looks, and the crease in his brow deepens. "Do ye still see him now?"

I look and sigh. Whoever he was, he's not there now. "I guess he bugged out."

Want me to have a covert look around?

I snort. "I don't think a bear in a bar in the middle of the city will be considered covert."

The rumble of his deep laughter feels funny in my chest. *I meant as a spirit ye eejit.*

"Oh, okay. Good idea. Don't get into any trouble and don't be long. Jetlag is real. I'm ready to head home to bed."

If I'm not back by the time ye leave, don't wait up.

"What? No. Bear—" I turn and scowl as the pop of pressure in my chest signals his departure. "Dammit. Why do I get the feeling I'm going to regret this?"

CHAPTER NINETEEN

I'm sitting at the kitchen table nursing my coffee when Calum and Emmet come down dressed for work. I'm not sure how they're upright and looking so chipper. Did I drink that much more than them?

"Is your other half back yet?" Calum asks.

"No. Not yet."

"I'm sure he's fine." Emmet heads over to the dishrack. He grabs two bowls and two spoons and joins me. "He's a bear loose in the city streets of Toronto. How bad could it be?"

I snort at his attempt to cheer me up. "Now I have Godzilla scenes flashing in my head."

"Nah." Calum pours two coffees and joins us. "Godzilla was mindless. Bruinior the Beast is smart."

"Don't indulge him by calling him that. I'll think of something better."

Emmet fills a bowl with Honey Shreddies and slides it over to Calum. "Whatever his name, he's new in town. Maybe he got turned around and is lost."

"I don't think he can get lost. He's bound to me."

"Well, he's only been gone for eight hours. You've got a long wait before he's officially missing."

"And what? Am I putting out a missing person's report? I'd love to see how that goes over."

Calum pours milk into his coffee and stirs things up. "If he's bound to you, can you find him by tracing that connection back to its source?"

"I don't know."

"Does he need to, like, recharge or something if he's out too long? Any chance he gets weak or sick?"

"I don't think so. I was in the dragon's cave for seven weeks, and he was fine."

The boys grow horribly still.

"Don't remind us," Calum says.

Emmet sets his spoon down and pegs me with a look. "We were out of our heads, Fi. And Da... He's not been right since ye went over there. Now, with Brenny's death...I'm worried about the old man."

"Worried how?"

Calum leans back to look up the hall toward the stairs. "He's been drinking more and more. And not just with friends or at the pub. He's been drinking alone, too."

Emmet leans in. "I rarely see him without a drink in his hand now. It's not good."

No. It's not. "He got like this for a while when Ma died."

"Yeah, but he had six kids to raise then. Now, his time and his money are pretty much his own."

"Well, I'm home now, and I'll watch him. Maybe now that the wake is behind him, he'll slow down. Maybe it'll help if we all slow down. You know, out of sight out of mind."

There's a noise in the back alley, and I stand to look out the kitchen window.

"Is it your bear?"

"No. It's the Navar kids setting up hockey nets with their friends. If he does come back, he probably won't be clunking around behind the house. He'll wisp in like a breeze."

"How does the whole spirit thing work anyway?"

"I don't know. He came to me. He's a spirit. He saved my life. That's all I know."

"That's it, is it, Cumhaill?" Sloan tops the last of the basement steps. "I thought ye'd be further along unraveling the mystery by now." He flashes me a GQ smile. He's way too cocky for his good.

"Tell me, Sloan. What has my inferior intellect failed to realize about my bear?"

"That he's not a spirit bear, he's THE spirit BEAR."

Emmet's eyes widen, and he laughs. "Do you think if you say it louder and with more drama, we'll hear a difference? Is that a druid thing?"

Calum finishes chewing a mouthful of cereal. "You're aren't only my brother, Emmet. You're MY brother, EMMET. Did that change anything?"

"NOPE," Emmet shouts.

I crack up. "Man, it's good to be home. I missed you, boys." They both smile up at me, lost in their crunching and chewing. I sweep a hand toward the counter. "Sloan, help yourself to cereal, toast, or the buffet of leftovers from last night. While you fend, you can explain what you mean."

Sloan makes himself a plate and sits—in Brendan's chair. I stiffen and start to protest but catch myself. The boys have the same reaction, but none of us says anything.

What is there to say?

Sloan doesn't seem to notice. Then again, he's an only child, so he doesn't always pick up on the subtext telepathy between my siblings and me. "Despite what your sister says, or maybe even believes, bonding with a spirit animal is rare."

I swallow my coffee and squint at him. "I thought physical

druids got a battle beast as one of their skills. You said druids use spirit animals as weapons when fighting."

"Och, they do. Did ye see how yer bear responded to that notion when I mentioned that fact in front of him? He's more than that."

"More, like how?"

"Do ye remember what he said when ye asked how old he is?"

I think back. "He said it was a blur but maybe a century or two."

Sloan takes a bite of his raspberry Danish and chuckles. "Try nine hundred."

"Whoa," Emmet interjects. "Your bear is a geezer."

"Is not," I snap. "Sloan's full of shit."

"What is my discipline, Cumhaill?"

"Health and Spiritual."

"And he's a what kind of bear?" He waits for me to fill in the blank.

"Spirit. Okay, I'll give you that." I make a quick trip to the counter to grab my Danish. "What does that matter?"

Sloan takes a long drink of water. "As ye might remember, part of my discipline is gauging the power and potential of magical beings. From the first time I came in contact with yer walking rug, it was clear as an Irish sky. He is BEAR, the spirit king of all bears."

"Ooo, royalty." Calum points at me with his spoon. "You're stepping up in the company you keep, Fi."

I open my mouth and show Calum my half-chewed Danish, and he snorts and goes back to his breakfast. "What do you mean, spirit king?"

"Are ye familiar with the stories indigenous people tell about their totem animals?"

"You mean like Thunderbird and Coyote?"

He nods. "The same. In folklore, Bear is considered a

powerful enforcer who punishes the disrespectful and protects the clans with his godlike powers."

"I don't buy it. If he's a spirit god, why was he hanging around Granda's place looking for something to do?"

"If I had to guess, I'd say that when the bears living in Ireland died out and disappeared, he lost focus. Maybe he doesn't remember being a god, or maybe he does, and he wants a demotion."

"Rude. Why are you considering me a demotion?"

He scowls. "My point is, I can't be sure of exactly what he is, but his potential power isn't like anything I've ever felt before."

"Maybe that's why he picked you, Fi," Emmet points out. "Da said you're super-jacked with druid potential or some shit, yeah?"

"That's what they say."

"She is," Sloan agrees. "And it pains me to admit it, but she has a natural skill I've rarely seen before to go with it. She'll be one helluva druid once she goes back to finish her training with yer Granda."

My brothers hit me with matching dirty looks. "You're going back?"

"Not for a very long time—years from now. In the meantime, I'll prove to Granda and the stuffed shirts of the Ancient Order of Druids that their snobby ideas about the world beyond the Emerald Isle holding no power is bullshit."

"Yeah, you will." Calum rises to take his bowl to the sink. "You show them, sista. They don't know what they're in for."

Emmet hands off his empty bowl and grabs their mugs. "My only question is when do we get our power sparks? 'Cause dayam, I want a pet tiger."

I snort. "Emmet, every pet you ever had fell to the fate of a shoebox under the tree or flushed."

"Hey! Those hamsters were duds. I told you all that. Everyone knows that small rodents are hard to keep alive. And fish? Please.

I need something more substantial to call out my latent Doolittle genes."

Calum laughs and closes the dishwasher. "You've been a 'do little' guy your whole life. Nothing to call out."

There's a quick exchange of fists and slaps, then they laugh and break it up. Both of them kiss my cheek and grab the sack lunches I made them from the leftover catering.

"Safe home, boys." I knock on the wooden table. "I love you like crazy."

"All the ladies do." Emmet waves over his head as he bounds off the back steps and heads toward the gate.

I watch them out the kitchen window until Emmet starts the car and they pull away. "Safe home, boys."

Sloan watches me watch them, and I shrug.

"It was hard letting them go every day before. Now that Brenny is gone, I don't know how I'll sit here day and night without going squirrely."

He moves to the counter and grabs another Danish. "Well, if there's one thing I've learned since knowing ye, Cumhaill, it's that whatever comes yer way, ye handle it."

I chuff. "You getting soft on me, surly?"

"Hardly. Get your training clothes on and meet me in the basement. We've got work to do and a short time to do it."

"Eyes front, Cumhaill," Sloan snaps. I throw my head back and narrowly evade the end of the fighting staff he swings at my face. We finished with the weights downstairs and moved outside to have room for melee fighting. "Come on. Where's that fighting spirit? Don't ye want to clip me one in the head?"

"More than you could imagine," I grunt.

The muscles in my arms are burning, my back is sore, and

there are runnels of sweat seeping into cracks and crevices I didn't know about.

I adjust my footing on my back lawn, anticipating the forward jab before he throws it. My timing is a little late, but I manage to strike the attempt away with only a grazing blow to my hip as I step to the side.

Sloan growls. "Believe it or not, Cumhaill. I don't want to hit ye, but if yer Granda's enemies come fer ye, they won't have the same concern."

My hands are sore, and I've had enough staff practice for one day. When he arcs a swing to come down at my head, I drop my staff and shift to hand-to-hand. He's stronger than me, but I capitalize on his forward momentum. I duck his staff, grab his arm, and pull him to the ground.

My back roll doesn't execute as well in reality as it did in my head, but I get the job done. He's down, the staff isn't chafing my hands, and I'm close enough to the hose to grab it and spray him before he has a chance to recover.

"What the hell?" he sputters and holds up his hands as shields. "Shite, that's cold."

I laugh while jockeying my position to keep him back. Except, I step on an abandoned staff, and when my footing falters, he turns the tables.

I scream and turn my back on the dousing. "Okay, I'm sorry. I'm sorry." I try to run, but there's no escape. My hair is stuck to my face in wet strands, and thanks to me slipping and going down on one knee, I'm muddy and gross.

"Say it, Cumhaill." Sloan laughs. "Forfeit the fight. Tell me I win."

"In your dreams." I hold up my hands to block the attack. Water sprays up my nose, and I try not to choke. "No one gets a forfeit from me."

"Technically, that's not true," Liam calls from behind the back gate. "You surrendered to me that summer when we all went to Center Island."

The interruption in our mayhem halts the hosing on the spot. Sloan's laughter stops and the first truly unguarded moment with him comes to a crashing halt. It's a shame.

Waterlogged, I wave Liam inside the gate. "Hey, come on in. You're safe."

"Am I interrupting?" Liam casts a disapproving glance at Sloan and me.

I hold my hands out to Sloan, and he sprays off the mud and grass. "I was overheating during training and decided to cool Sloan off."

Sloan wraps the hose back into its coils and then goes back to pick up the staffs. "I assure you, she got the worst of it." He steps toward the house and looks down at himself.

"Yeah, don't even think about traipsing that mess into my house."

"Wouldn't dream of it. Who needs to traipse when they can portal?" Then he's gone.

"Show off," I shout at the house. Honestly, I wish I could portal myself into my shower and peel off these clothes without making a mess through the house.

I stomp into the back mudroom, toe off my shoes, and grab a beach towel from the cabinet above the dryer. Growing up, Ma never let us come inside soaking wet, so I'm a pro at wrapping myself in a towel and peeling off wet clothes without getting nakey in front of the boys.

When I turn back, all nestled in my towel, Liam is staring. "What? Have I got mud on my face?"

"No, but I think you might have mush for brains."

"Me? Why?"

He steps closer and leans in, his scowl increasing as he counts off on his fingers. "One, that guy's a pompous dick. Two, he assaulted you. Three, he's leaving tonight, isn't he?"

I step back, gaining some distance from the testosterone poisoning smacking me in the face. "Who pissed in your whiskey?"

It's not like Liam to go off on me. In fact, I don't think he's gone off on me since we were kids and fighting over trucks in the sandbox.

I lift my fingers and count them back to him. "One, Sloan's not that bad once you get past the pompous dick part. Two, it was a test, not an assault. Truth be told, *he* got the worse end of things during that test because he wouldn't fight back. And three, yeah, he's leaving tonight after he transfers Da and the boys their powers. So, what?"

Liam makes a face, and I honestly don't get what's crawled up his ass. After a moment, he shrugs and shakes it off. "So, nothing, I guess."

I've been surrounded by men my whole life. You'd think I'd understand them better. Nope. It's a Mars versus Venus moment happening here.

He roughly exhales and when he meets my gaze, the Liam I know and love is back. "My bad. Sorry, Fi. I'm still freaked about you running off to Ireland without telling me, then the druid thing, and you disappearing for months when we didn't know…"

The pain in his eyes melts my annoyance. I realize that in the two days since my return, with Brendan's death, talking druid stuff with the boys and Sloan, and getting my bear settled, Liam and I haven't spent any downtime together.

I meet him for a hug. "I'm sorry you were scared. If there were any way to get back here sooner or let you know where I was, I would have. S'all good now, though."

He presses his cheek to the top of my head, and most of his tension dissolves. "You're forgiven. Just don't go getting yourself kidnapped by leprechauns again."

I giggle and step back. "No promises. Hey, are you here for a bit?"

"Yeah, I need to talk to you. This got delivered to my phone and I wondered if you'd seen it yet."

I read the headline of the Global News story and close my eyes. "Feckin' hell. Put on the kettle. I'll get cleaned up and be right down."

CHAPTER TWENTY

"Sloan, I need you." I straighten from calling over the railing into the basement and plunk back into my seat in the kitchen. Liam hands me a mug with tea and honey. I take a sip, staring at the screen of my laptop. "This is so bad."

As much as I want Liam to argue and tell me I'm over-reacting, he doesn't.

Sloan's long stride takes the stairs two at a time, and he joins us seconds later. He stalks right up to me, holds out his phone, and smiles. "Would ye mind sayin' that again? I want to keep it for posterity."

"What? Oh." I laugh and shove his phone away. "Not a chance. Knowing you, me needing you will be twisted into something torrid, and I'll get a reputation in Ireland as your new world chippie."

He blinks. "I don't have chippies."

"Ha! I met Ciara. She is a disgruntled chippie." Before he can get a comeback out, I point at the screen. "So, how does the Ancient Order handle it when a druid's animal companion mauls and kills three people?"

Sloan bends down to read the article. "Feckin' hell."

"Exactly what I said."

"Och, this is bad."

"Ye think?"

Sloan straightens and scrubs rough fingers through his damp hair. "This is way over my pay grade. Those weren't fae he killed. They were humans. We need to call Lugh."

"What? No. There's no way I'm telling him that less than seventy-two hours after I get back to the city, I lost control of my bear and he killed three people."

Three bad people.

I jump out of my seat and look around the kitchen. I don't see him, but he's here. "Where are you, bear? Living room, right now. I want to see your furry face while I explain a few things to you about how things are done around here."

Our house only has a few rooms big enough for a massive brown bear to materialize. The living room is the closest place we can have this discussion until I sort through some of the clutter in the rest of the house.

The first thing I did when we got home was to enlist Dillan's and Emmet's help to move my furniture and make space in my room. As I'm rounding the corner from the kitchen to the hall-way, Da and Aiden storm in the front.

"Fiona Kacee Cumhaill," Da snaps, fighting mad. "Have ye any idea what's been happening in mid-town this morning? Three Thorncliff Thugs were found ripped to ribbons—"

"Yep. Just found out. I'm on it."

My bear materializes in the living room, and he's a bloody mess. His fur is mucked up and matted, and there's a chunk of his ear missing. He had the good sense to hang his head and look abashed.

I didn't want ye to see me like this, Red. Sorry.

"Are you sorry for what you did or sorry you got caught?" I blink and look at my father. "How many times have you said those words to me?"

"Too many times to count."

"Anyway." I get back on point. "First off, are you all right? Are you hurt?"

No.

"Okay, good. Now, what the hell happened? I sent you to see if you could find the skull-trimmed lurker, not start a gang war and kill people."

I found the male—

I hold up a finger. "You better speak out loud. I don't feel like playing telephone and relaying it all back."

He growls at me but does as I ask. "I found the male who stared at us at the pub. I followed him north. He traveled up a great black river of highway. It wound its way through treed lands and under massive metal bridges spanning great wildlands."

"That's the DVP," Aiden identifies.

I nod. "So, he took the Don Valley Parkway north. What happened then?"

"He met three other males in a secluded black clearing surrounded by woods."

"Seton Park," Da says. "It's busy throughout the day, but at two in the morning, not many people use the bike paths and archery range. The parking lot would've been very secluded when he was there."

"Okay, so four men meet up. What did they say?"

"Nothing intelligible."

Da crosses his arms over his chest, and I smile. My father might be pushing fifty-three, but he is fit and stronger than most. A fact I'm reminded of often when one of my few girlfriends comes over. *Ew* but true.

"Let us decide what makes sense, bear. We have a better understanding of the vernacular."

My bear dips his chin. "The one from the pub told the other three he had information for them. He said the man they knew as

Jimmy Blue wasn't an ex-Cliffside Crip like they thought—he was a pig. They didn't seem to take that well."

"No. I suppose they wouldn't."

"Then, he said he came from an entire family of cops. He told them to tell their boss to wipe out the lot of ye and send a message that undercovers will regret messing with them. I understood enough to know he was talking about yer family and wasn't about to let that happen."

"Shit." Sloan leans against the frame of the entranceway. "He marked ye for execution?"

"But only three bodies were recovered," Da says.

"True. When I intervened, the man from the pub vanished. I searched for his scent after but found no trace of him."

"Is that where you were all night?" I imagine my bear searching the woods and the wilds of the Don Valley for a man out to destroy our family.

Bear waves a huge, clawed paw and shakes his head. "Och, no. I found a couple of black bear sows with willing natures and beautifully broad haunches. They kept me occupied until the wee hours."

Aiden chuckles. "We should call you Badass Bear."

"No, we shouldn't," I disagree. "So, while I was worried sick and imagining the worst, you were—"

"There's no such thing as a walk of shame," Aiden cuts in. "You took out the trash, then got the girls in true Cumhaill fashion. Good one, Bear."

I throw my hands up, but no one seems to notice.

Aiden shrugs. "What? The universe rewarded him for making the city a safer place."

"The Killer Clawbearer appreciates yer respect."

That does it. "Okay, no. The names you're choosing are bad enough. Now you're referring to yourself in the third person. Not happening. From now on, you're not Bruinior the Beast or

Badass Bear, or the Killer Clawbearer. Your name is Kyle Cumhaill."

"Kyle?" Sloan says. "What kind of name is that?"

"It's the perfect name. We can say it in public without drawing attention, and it doesn't inspire images of brutality and carnage."

"Kyle isn't the name of an ancient spirit totem," Sloan snaps. "It's common and passive."

"Exactly," I say, surer of my decision by the moment. "Kyle was a friend of mine at my first job. He ate vegan foods and never lost his temper. He certainly didn't go around eviscerating gangers. Everyone likes a Kyle."

"I hate it already," the bear says.

"Good. Then, it's settled. Kyle it is."

Da has a muddled expression on his face. I can't decide if he's frustrated or relieved.

"A bit of both," he says when I ask him. "While I'll not mourn the loss of any of the gang members involved in us losing Brendan, I don't like the fact that someone has their sights set on this family. I thank ye, Bear, fer stoppin' the ones ye did, but the trouble won't end there."

"Who's the guy gunning for you and why?" Liam asks.

Da scrubs a hand over his face and exhales. "That's what we need to figure out. Fi, you're the only one who saw Skull Trim. Do you think if you sat down with Kevin you can work up a sketch?"

"I think so." I look at Sloan. "Calum's partner is an artist, and he's really good."

Da points at Liam. "Text Calum and ask him to arrange that as soon as he can. Once we have an idea of who's shadowing our door, we'll have a better understanding of our next move. We need to close ranks for the next while."

"What I don't get," Aiden responds, "is how did Skull Trim connect us with Brendan being undercover? The shooter didn't kill him because he was blown. Brenny stepped into the line of fire. That shouldn't have led back to us in any way."

Da frowns. "I'll have a chat with Brendan's captain. Maybe if we put our heads together, we can figure out how the man at the wake found us."

"If it were me," I begin. "I would've started with the coroner's office. If this guy was watching Brenny or the gang, he'd know where the shooting was and where his body would end up. If he connected Brendan to the funeral home, it wouldn't take much to find his obit and trace it back to us."

"Ye make a fine detective, Fi. That's sound logic. It could be that, or maybe our stalker knew who he was all the time and stirred the pot. I'll see what I can find out. In the meantime, I want ye to keep yer trainin' up. I'll not have ye venturin' off to the grocery store on yer own and gettin' into trouble."

"Don't worry about that," Liam states. "I'll shadow her during the day while everyone's at work."

I shake my head. "I appreciate the need to circle the wagons, but I'm the one with magic and a vigilante bear inside me. I'm more worried about you guys being vulnerable out on the street, and Kinu and the kids."

Aiden grimaces at the mention of his family.

Liam rolls his eyes at me. "Of course, you are Fi. You wouldn't be you if everyone else weren't your first impulse. Remember, though. You're not indestructible. When danger rears its ugly head, normal people duck for cover. You stand up straight and walk into the line of fire."

"This." Aiden points at Liam and nods.

"Exactly like Brendan." Da heads to the bar. He pours himself a tall glass of liquid sedation and takes a few deep gulps. "Ye did us a grand favor last night, Bear. I'll ask ye to do me another. Protect wee Fiona here from herself. She's reckless and head-strong and the beating heart of this ragtag family."

"I'll protect her with my life, Da. I swear it."

Da? Seriously? Ha! Forget Killer Clawbearer. His name should be Furry Ass-kisser. I look at the sad state of my disheveled bear and sigh. "Come outside, you big furball. I'll get the hose and clean you up."

It's nearly ten that night when Emmet and Calum get off shift and walk in the door carrying three pizzas and a case of Canadian. I point at the beer, and Sloan takes the hint while I grab the boxes. "We're downstairs. Get changed and join us when you're ready."

They both unlace their boots and tear up the stairs like a couple of kids. "Don't start without us."

"How can we start without you when you're part of the transfer, dumbass?" I turn back to the stairs and Sloan is staring. "What did I do now?"

He shakes his head. "Nothing. I was thinking about going home and wondering what life will be like without you in it."

I laugh. "Boring.

"Very likely."

"And so, I want ye all to be extra cautious," Da warns after giving the boys the lowdown on what Kyle learned and did up in Seton Park. "It isn't a bad idea to stick close to home and avoid friends fer a few weeks too. If we're the targets of retaliation, that's on us. I don't want innocent citizens getting caught in the crossfire."

There's a round of bobbing heads of agreement.

"I don't want to leave Kady alone." Dillan is sitting on the three-seater with Liam and Calum. "If I'm here, there's no one there to watch out for her."

Da nods. "If she'll come, have her stay here with us for a bit.

She'll be better protected when yer on shift if she's in this house. Liam offered to make himself available to escort the girls through the day fer a few weeks. We'll be takin' him up on that with our thanks."

Liam nods. "Of course."

"Da," I protest. "I don't—"

"Humor me, Fi. I'm not askin' him to keep ye safe. I'm well aware yer capable. I simply don't want ye alone and taken or hurt without someone else bein' aware. After the past two months and losin' Brendan, I need ye to give me this one without a fight, *mo chroí.*"

The same pleading look hits me from every male in the room. There are moments when I forget that while I was playing video games and learning dance routines to Elvis Presley hits, my family suffered seven weeks of not knowing where I was or if I was alive or dead.

"Fine. I'll play the buddy system like a good girl."

"Good then," Da approves. "That settles that. If something happens or doesn't feel right, I don't want any of ye takin' chances. Call and let us know and we face it together, understood? Respect the danger this could raise."

I stiffen. "Why is everyone still looking at me?"

Da continues. "Sloan erected wards around the house this afternoon, and I've asked him to stay on a few more days. He'll be here to get ye started on yer paths and to keep workin' with Fi. If yer not on duty or sleepin', yer here trainin', understood?"

We all nod.

"I'll not lose another one of ye to the evils of this world. It's a blessed gift that we know what's comin' fer us and we'll not waste it."

Emmet rises from the club chair and holds his beer up toward my bear sitting on his haunches on the basement rug. "To Kyle. Thank you for having our backs, man. Glad you took down some of the bastards involved in Brendan's end. And congrats on the threesome, buddy. Two days in town and you score a woodland ménage. Well deserved. Glad to have you as part of Clan Cumhaill. *Slainte mhath.*"

"*Slainte mhath,*" we all echo and raise our bottles.

Kyle raises his black, leathery nose to the air and lets out a throaty growl. Then he paws the empty roasting pan beside him, and his nails click against the enamel. "Barmaid, how about ye show yer appreciation in liquid form?"

I snort and thumb the nozzle of the keg Dillan set up for him earlier. Tipping the pan to eliminate a foam head, I let the ale flow.

Sloan chuffs. "Ye can't let yer spirit totem get liquored up every time he asks. It's not good."

"Mind yer business, wayfarer," Kyle grunts.

"Learn yer place, Bear," he snaps back. "Yer bound to serve her, not the other way around. What good are ye in a battle if yer soused and can't lift yer big, fat head? This isn't how it's done."

"And exactly how many greater spirits have ye known in yer lifetime ye tight-assed dullard? None? Och, that's what I thought."

"Okay." I compromise and only give him a few inches at the bottom of the pan. "Can we get to the main event before there's a donnybrook in the basement?"

"Hells, ya," Dillan exclaims while chewing his fourth piece of Hawaiian. "Start dishing out the magical powers."

Da shoots him a disapproving look. "If yer taking on the power, yer taking on the trainin', the mindset, and all that comes with it. I'll not have ye thinkin' a fae gift is a joyride. It's a tool and a weapon, like yer gun and yer baton. Ye need to learn how to wield it and respect it."

Dillan straightens. "Geez, Da, I was kidding."

He dips his chin. "Fer the next hour, I want ye all to smarten up and take this seriously. I mean it. Fiona made her choice, largely to save yer Granda's life. There's no need to change yer lives if yer not sure."

My brothers, to their credit, don't bat an eye.

Da nods. "All right then. Sloan, have ye got the laurels? We'll start with Aiden and work our way down. Fi will keep Brendan's spark to add to her powers. I want her to have as much power as she can, and think he would've liked that."

"He would've," Aiden says.

"Yeah," Dillan, Calum, and Emmet agree.

Sloan hands me one of the two metal crowns, and I place it on my head as I had at Granda's bedside a few months ago. Da's right. I did make my decision under duress to save Granda. I don't regret it.

Being locked into a life of servitude in Ireland would have been insufferable, but here and now, with my family and my bear and being home in Toronto...I can't imagine not having this life unfurling before us.

I sit in one of the two folding chairs Da sets out. Aiden takes the one opposite me. He winks as he sets the other laurel on his head. "What do you think? I make this crown look good, right?"

"You're killing it." I lean forward and take his hands in mine. "I guess this means Jackson and Meggie are our next-gen additions to being urban druids."

Da chuffs. "Don't get ahead of yerself, Fi. We don't know the power can survive in the city. There are too many unknowns to start dreamin' up romantic notions of a new world order fer druids."

Whatevs. A girl can dream.

I squeeze Aiden's fingers and look serious. "You ready, tough guy? This is gonna hurt like hell."

Sloan arches a dark brow but doesn't give me away. "You ready, Cumhaill?"

"I was born ready."

CHAPTER TWENTY-ONE

The loss of my brothers' powers was negligible. The loss of my father's didn't happen. When Sloan finished the spark transfers for the boys and called Da to the chair, he declined. He said he wouldn't take power from me when there was danger afoot. We argued, but, as usual, Da proved himself the most stubborn Cumhaill.

The next few days are busy with training and buzzing with excitement. I hate to admit it, but Granda was right about the level of ambient power not being as readily available in the city as it was in Ireland. There, it tingled over my skin like a warm summer breeze. It filled me with a sense of potential energy waiting to be called to action.

Here, I get spits and spurts.

Sloan says that I'll recharge in time and that I shouldn't worry. It's frustrating. It's like I was ready for high school and find myself back in the third grade. I remember my spells. They simply don't amplify my intentions the way they did on the Emerald Isle.

The most worrisome part of the sudden decline in my druid-ness is my bear—or lack of. Since the night of the transfer, I haven't been able to cast him out to physical form.

I can hear him in my head. I can feel him fluttering restlessly in my chest. I can't release him.

Kyle says I'm subconsciously punishing him for staying out all night poppin' bottles and bangin' models—note to self, limit my bear's time with my brothers—but that's not it. I'm not trying to control him. I don't have the juice.

It's concerning, to say the least.

Still, grade three power levels are better than nothing, and since my brothers are in the kindergarten stage of learning, we're good to work on the basics. Emmet set out a buffet of nuts and seeds and is working on inviting the locals. Apparently, he's okay with the community squirrels organizing as long as he's their pied piper.

"Would you look at that." Kady shifts her attention from Kevin's sketch to watch Emmet commune with his fluffy-tailed minions. "He's got them eating out of his hand. Isn't he worried they'll bite? What if he gets rabies? My cousin's friend got bit by a raccoon in the forest and had to get a whack of needles."

"He'll be okay." I hope I'm right. "Cumhaills have a way with animals.

"Well, it's certainly cool."

It is. It's *really* cool.

Kady and Kevin don't know about the druid part of things— Da told us all we're not to speak of it outside of the family—but I'm so proud of how enthused my brothers are.

We've always been a tight-knit family, but sharing this secret brings us closer in a difficult time. It's not a bad thing that our training distracts everyone from the ache of missing Brendan. It's also not a bad thing that in time, if things go sideways in the streets, they might have another resource to keep them from being killed.

Sadly, we hadn't seen Brendan for months and were already

sort of accustomed to his absence. Now, it's a matter of adjusting to that absence being permanent.

Easier said than done.

I press a hand over my chest and connect with the fledgling spark inside me that never got the chance to grow. I'm honored to be the one who gets to hold Brenny's spark. I'll commit myself to be as brave and dedicated to justice as he always was.

His sacrifice will be paid forward.

"How's this, Fi?" Kevin taps his pencil on his sketch pad. Kevin is a hazel-eyed hottie with spikey blond hair, a crooked smile, and ruggedness that both women and men find irresistible. Not that it matters. He and Calum have been together for years, and we're all anticipating they'll make it permanent sometime soon.

I check out his sketch and nod. "Can you shade his eyes a little more to make them look more sunken in?"

"Sure." He puts his head down and gets back to work.

Dillan saunters over to us with a wide grin on his face and a little terracotta pot in his hand. "For you, milady." He sets the greenery in front of Kady. "Fresh cilantro, grown with you in mind."

I hold up my knuckles for a bump. "Great job, D."

"Thank you." He hands me Da's malachite casting stone.

I leave the lovebirds to chat and take the stone inside to slip it back into the velvet bag.

Sloan and Calum are sitting at the kitchen table in the final stages of magical healing 101.

"How's the hand?" I lean over my brother's shoulder to check out the damage.

Calum shows me his palm and flexes his fingers in and out. "Good as new. Thanks, Doc."

Sloan wets a cloth to clean up the herb and honey mixture off the table, but Calum claims the cleanup and takes over. "In this house, you don't do the dishes if you did the cooking. The same goes for healing magical booboos."

I slide into a chair and look at Sloan's casting stones, and his spellbook laid open on the table. "May I?"

"The book, ye may. Not the stones. Ye never touch another man's stones."

Calum and I both snort at the same time.

"Och, that's why you're wound so tight," I say with my thick accent impression of Da. "Ye've been missing out."

Calum laughs at Sloan's scowl. "Hell, Doc, you walked right into that one."

I ignore the grunt of derision from Sloan and fasten the silk tie on Da's marble bag. "Hey, you and Gran touched my stone from Patty."

"Ye hadn't started working with it yet. Ye build a relationship with yer casting stones over time the same way ye do with an animal companion and environment. My stones work as a conduit to amplify my power signature. They know and respond to me. Everyone's energy runs on a different frequency. Cross-contact muddies the magical water."

"Don't cross streams," Calum agrees. "I get that. So where do we get ours? We're all sharing Da's. That must leave our waters pretty murky."

"Fer now, ye can cleanse the stones with the vibration of a singing bowl and setting them out fer time in full sunlight. But yes, ye'll all need to get yer own at some point soon."

I pull out my phone and add that to the Urban Druid to-do list. Find casting stones goes under, find ink-magic artist, enchanted ink, more spells, sacred grove, and singing bowl. Whatever the heck that is.

"Can I make one of my cereal bowls sing with a spell?" I scan the upper cabinets.

"No, ye'll find singing bowls at reputable spiritual shops. Mine is authentic from Tibet and gives off the most remarkable harmonics."

"Do you cleanse your stones? I thought you said you want to build your energy into them."

Sloan sits heavily in his seat and scrubs his hands over his shaggy, black hair. "This is why ye should be in Ireland trainin' with Lugh. Ye have no clue how much there is to this life. Yer a wee sea turtle flappin' yer fins on the sand. Yer miles from the ocean and the gulls are descendin.'"

I blink at him. "Harsh. Well, this little sea turtle has *hutzpah*. I can flap and flop my way to the shore like nobody's business. It might take me a little longer, but I'm a survivor. I'll get there."

I can't stand the frustration and disbelief in his mint-green gaze. Dropping my focus, I glance at the healing spell he used to fix Calum's hand. It's set on a page near the front of the book under the heading—Healing. I flip forward and skim Battle Magic and Creatures, then go the other way and see Mockers, Potions, and Protection.

This tome is thick and filled with ten times the number of spells in Da's binder, which makes sense. Sloan is an obsessively driven guy and so are both of his parents.

"I don't suppose you'd lend me this, would you?"

He studies me for a long moment, then sighs. "Ye don't ask fer much, do ye?"

"Is it a big ask?"

"In our world, it is."

There's an edge to his voice like I've put him on the spot and I'm caught between feeling bad and embarrassed. "Never mind. I didn't know it's a cultural *faux pas*. Forget I asked."

After a long minute and a heavy exhale, he raps his knuckles on the table. "Ye can't have my book, but I won't leave ye empty-handed either. Get me a business directory, and I'll get ye sorted. Have ye got money to burn? We're gonna need quite a bit."

Calum pulls a card out of his wallet. "My line of credit is empty. Have at it. Fi, you know the password."

Sloan stands, tucks his spellbook under his arm, and his casting stones into his pocket.

"Road trip!" I bound to my feet.

Sloan casts a locator spell, and Calum and Emmet watch wide-eyed as the pages of our phone book flip themselves. When the thin, onion paper pages fall still, he makes a few calls, and we head out. "What the hell is that racket?" he asks when I start up my car in the back lane.

"Molly is a little under the weather at the moment, but she's a good car. Jettas have long lives and great safety ratings."

He arches a haughty brow and looks exactly like the kind of guy who was raised in a castle. "This is not the kind of rumble ye want coming from yer car, Cumhaill. Do ye have noise ordinances here?"

I check the cross-traffic and wait until there's an opening. Merging with the mid-day flow can be tricky. "It's not half as bad as before Dillan duct-taped the hole in the exhaust."

"Yer not supposed to tape it. Yer supposed to fix it."

"Oh, is that where I went wrong? Thanks so much for clearing that up."

"I'm serious. Ye need to maintain yer vehicle better."

"Are you volunteering to be my sugar daddy?"

He reaches to the controls and fiddles with the A/C. "Does this work?"

"Nope. Didn't you know retro is cool? Use the window."

"Nothing about this car is cool. It's a sweatbox."

I click my indicator and turn west onto Queen Street. "We don't all have the powers of apparition, wayfarer. Some of us need to use more modern modes of transportation."

"Let me know when we get to the modern part. This chunk of moving scrap metal need not apply."

I pat my dash, giving my old girl some love. "Weren't you the man extolling the virtues of the aged and weathered, telling me I'd do well to start appreciating the mold and decay of your castle as character? Well, Molly has character."

He chuckles. "If ye say so."

We chug along Queen at a walking pace—because of traffic, not any deficiency of my car—until he points for me to pull into one of the street parking spots after we cross Spadina.

I turn off the engine, lock up my Jetta, and push a loonie and a toonie into the slots for our meter. "Three bucks gets us an hour."

"That should be fine."

We walk to the crosswalk at the corner of Queen and Spadina and stop for the light. I thumb the pedestrian button to activate the crosswalk and loop my purse strap over my head.

While we wait for the lights to change, I glance across the street and read the sign a few units up the block. "Geologic Gallery Boutique."

Outside the storefront, I read the welcome. "Celebrate the beauty of nature and create your oasis of peace with our world-class collection of high-quality mineral specimens, fossils, and spiritual items. Adorn yourself, your home, and your sacred space with a gift from the Earth."

Sloan shrugs. "The locator spell said this is where we need to be to find quality stones."

"Okeydokey. Let's spend Calum's money."

Forty minutes later, we stash our bags in the trunk and drop onto the faux-leather seats of my car, which are now—without exaggeration—hot enough to melt the backs of my thighs off my legs.

"Jaysus fuck." I arch onto my feet and flail into the back seat for the tea towel I use on such occasions.

Sloan shakes his head, circles his finger in the air, and blows down the length of his Peter pointer. A refreshing breeze cools my seat and puts out the fire singing my legs. "How many times do I have to say it? Ye need to start—"

"I know. I know. Thinking like a druid. It's not that easy. I've been a normal girl for twenty-three years and a druid for two and a half months—seven weeks of which don't count because I was in a dragon lair fast-forward. Gimme a break."

He snorts. "I doubt ye've ever been normal."

"Point to you. That might be true." I start up the car, and we head out to the next address on the list. It's still on Queen Street West, but not close enough to walk. "Now that we have the stones, what's next on our list? Where are we headed?"

"A fae bookshop."

I laugh and peg him with a look. "Seriously? There's a fae bookshop in Downtown Toronto? What happened to Granda's big, 'ye can't do magic in the city' speech?"

"If ye recall, Lugh said there aren't druids in the city because our magic can't flourish here. There are many other members of the fae who do fine in urban settings."

Huh. Many other fae in my city.

"Are there leprechauns?"

"Maybe."

"Fairies?"

"Sure."

"Witches?"

"Many."

"Vampires?"

"Not fae but possibly. Demons, monsters, and the undead are an entirely different caste of magic. Druids and fae don't usually intersect with them if we can help it."

Hubba-wha? How am I ever going to get a handle on all this on my own? Sure, Da will know lots, but he's been outta the loop for four decades. He also isn't accessible all day and night to me like Granda and Sloan have been.

"Thanks for your help. I'm seriously impressed at how much

you know about this stuff and am thankful you helped this noob as much as you have. I won't let you record me saying it, but you're one helluva talented druid."

Sloan chuffs. "Being a druid isn't just who I am. It's the only thing I've got. Where yer family has water fights, dance lessons, and barbeques, my parents took me to pagan ritual events and meteor sites. I don't pretend to understand how yer father walked away and gave it up. I do, however, respect what he did fer his kids. Yer life is filled with joy and appreciation fer one another. I'd trade knowing the gemstone indexes fer that any day of the week."

I track the rising building numbers, studiously not looking at Sloan. That sucks ass. Who would I have been without my brothers and Da? Even having Ma love me for eleven years affected so much about who I am.

"There it is." He points to a shop as we pull up in front of it. "Myra's Mystical Emporium."

Out of the car for our second stop, I lock things up, and we set off. A stiff breeze hits my back and swings the painted shingle hanging perpendicular to the building.

Suspended over the concrete sidewalk, the sign pivots on the old-fashioned iron rod. It squeaks and creaks like something from a horror novel and my gift tingles to the fore. I ignore the prickle of hair standing up on the nape of my neck and read the lit sign in the green-tinted window.

Myra's Mystical Emporium
Augury, Alchemy, Astrology,
And all Implications of Same

The hair on the back of my neck is still standing with awareness. I use the reflection in the glass to check out my surroundings. Nothing.

Red? You okay? Yer anxiety is climbing.

It's good to hear his voice. It's the first Kyle has spoken to me since our fight about whether or not him being trapped inside me is intentional. It's *not*, but there are so many things he wants to experience that my lack of magical mojo is cramping his style.

I don't blame him for his frustration. If I'd been alone since the extinction of my species fifty years ago, I'd be raging horny and excited to dive into a new life, too.

"I'm sorry, what?" Sloan looks both baffled and amused. "Why are ye tellin' me yer ragin' horny?"

I blink and feel heat surge to my cheeks. "I didn't. I'm *not*. I was thinking about Kyle and didn't mean to talk out loud. I'm not horny and I'm not anxious. I'm fine. Both of you focus."

I push through the entrance and the brass bell over the door jingles as the door strikes it. A high-pitched cheery chime announces our arrival.

An icy chill runs the length of my spine. I don't know what's triggering my Spidey-senses, but I feel it to my depths.

Something wicked this way comes.

CHAPTER TWENTY-TWO

"Come in. Come in. I've been expecting you two. Welcome. Like it says on the sign, I'm Myra, and this is my beloved establishment." We follow the woman's voice deeper into the shop and find her standing at a long, wooden display counter near the back wall.

Myra is a spry old girl in jeggings and a smock shirt. She's beautiful, as I learned most fair folk are: tall with vertically slit eyes as electric-blue as her funky hair. The playful style is cropped on a severe angle from shaved and short on the left side of her head, to shoulder length on the right. Her skin is pale, almost silver, but when I look closer, it's cracked with darker tones beneath. The effect reminds me of the bark of a birch tree. It's odd but cool.

I have no idea what she is other than fascinatingly pretty. "Been in business in this location nearly forty-five years now, so you can put stock in my practices and discretion."

Forty-five years?

I study the interior of the space and believe her. I might even give it a cool century. As Sloan would say, the architecture and finishes have character.

Despite looking like a quaint curio shop from the road, Myra's Mystical Emporium has a cavernous interior and makes the Disney library that Beast gave Belle look rinky-dink.

The overhead lights are off, which is fine in the bright daylight of late-summer because the ceiling is entirely crafted as an artisan piece of stained glass. The colored panes cast elongated shards of green, gold, ruby, and indigo across the spines of more books than I've seen in any public library.

Bookcases line the walls on each level of three stories, from the pocked hardwood floor beneath my sneakers to the domed ceiling high above. Wrought iron railings and platform walkways allow catwalk access to the second and third levels.

"Um, wow. This is so weird."

"What's weird, duck?"

"I'm a local. I've gone up and down Queen Street a thousand times and never noticed this place. How did I miss it?"

Myra smiles. "That's not weird, that's magic. Only the people who need my wares find me. Until today, there was nothing you needed from me. Now there is. So, here you are."

It seems to be a poor business model to exclude window shoppers and only be accessible by those who specifically need something, but who am I to argue?

"Now, tell me what you need." Her smile is honey-sweet. "Is it a matter of life and death, or simply desire? My offerings vary based on the need of my patrons."

"I'd like to sire my book." Sloan holds out his leather-bound book of druid spells.

Myra takes it and brushes a hand over the tree of life emblazoned on the cover. "Oh, he's beautiful. Confident. Content. He has the utmost respect for the way you handle him. Well done, young man."

Sloan dips his chin. "Is he willin' to produce a copy?"

Myra strokes her hand over his cover again. "Yes. Come

around the counter, and the three of you can pick one of my lovely ladies in waiting."

I'm only half-following the gist of the conversation when she opens a shallow drawer, and I look at the covers of a dozen more leather and suede books. "Do any strike your interest, Fiona Cumhaill?"

I startle at the sound of my name. Sloan shakes his head almost imperceptibly, and I interpret that as a "don't ask." Fine. He doesn't seem alarmed and isn't tensing up to call on his powers, so I let it slide and direct my attention back to the books.

The moment my gaze washes over the selection, I'm drawn immediately to a midnight blue book with the triquetra symbol on the cover. "Ooo, this one is beautiful."

"She is at that."

I hesitate to pick it up, but Myra nods for me to go ahead and I do. The suede is ultra-soft, and it feels like it almost purrs under the stroke of my fingers. "How much is it?"

Myra frowns and tightens her hold on Sloan's book. It's now vibrating in her hand. "Who are we to put a price on true love, duck?"

I'm about to argue that while that's a sweet notion, my brother won't be pleased with me if I fall in love with something pretty that blows the bank.

Myra beats me to it. She takes the blue suede book—Ha! Blue suede, maybe my Elvis infusion isn't over after all—and sets it and Sloan's book in a deeper, empty drawer.

The moment his book is released, it flips my book's cover open and—"Are they..."

"Oh, yes." Myra grins. "A very good match."

Sloan meets my bafflement and frowns. "In the fae world, books aren't mere inanimate objects. They're made of all-natural materials, paper, hide, string, and glue. Like all things in nature, they have a life and magic of their own. They have awareness and desires."

I eye the happy couple and laugh. "Wow, they're really going at it. And Kyle accused me of cock-blocking him. You gotta let your boy out a bit more, surly."

"Grow up, Cumhaill."

"Come. It's best not to interrupt." Myra shuts the drawer, and we leave the books to their cavorting. "Anything else I can help you with?"

I'm still distracted by the rustle and bump going on at a steady clip in that drawer. I hold up my finger. "No seriously, how does this get me my spellbook?"

Sloan rolls his eyes. "Do ye honestly need me to spell it out fer ye?"

"Um... Yep, I think I do."

He exhales and drops his chin to his chest. "Well, when a male book and a female book take a fancy to one another—"

I chuckle, finding this entire situation hilarious. "I'm good on this first part."

"Well, when my book reaches its end, he'll spill into yer book and all his wisdom will fill her pages."

My jaw drops, and I clap my hand over my mouth to try to contain my amazement.

Sloan looks at the closed drawer and frowns. "He's a great deal lonelier than I realized. We might be here for a while."

I giggle and shake my head. "Well, your book better treat Beauty like the treasure she is. She deserves a skilled and giving lover. Is this a one-time thing or do we need to update their relationship status?"

He shakes his head. "Yer so incredibly strange."

While the bump-and-grind continues behind Myra's counter, Sloan and I gather a pretty brass singing bowl painted with blue symbols, several embroidered medicine bags, a marble mortar and pestle, and a reference text on natural herbs and remedies.

"Ye'll need a cauldron once ye start with potions."

"I have a big corn pot. Can that work?"

Sloan winces. "Druids do not make magical potions in old corn pots. Get a cauldron."

"Fine, Mr. Snooty Pants."

He carries our basket to the counter and unloads our purchases on the wide wooden surface. "Have ye any druid ink or know of a ritual artist who can ink spells?"

Myra tilts her head this way and that. "I might. I'll have to check with her and see if she's open to take on any new clients. Tell me your number, and I'll get back to you."

"Do you want me to write it down?"

"Oh, no, duck. If I teach you one thing in this life, let it be this. Never write your details and leave them behind for others to find. That's how you get yourself killed."

I scratch my head and wait to see if she's screwing with me. Nope. Okay, so don't leave my deets with people—big checkmark beside that one. Instead, I recite the digits of my cell number. "And you'll remember?"

"Haven't forgotten a number in a hundred and ninety-four years."

I wouldn't have pegged her as any older than Gran and Granda. "One-ninety-four! Wow. You're killing it, Myra."

That wins me a glowing smile for the entire time it takes her to bag everything and tally the bill. I point my key fob toward Molly, and she beeps unlocked.

Sloan takes everything out to the car while we wait for the enchanted spellbook marathon sex to come to its climactic, info-spilling end.

Geez. Between horny bears, delivering basilisk sperm, and now banging books, my life has taken on a bit of a tone.

I'll have to ask Da what that's about.

"You're a lucky girl," Myra says before Sloan comes back. "You know what they say about a book's stamina and his owner."

Oh, gawd. It continues. Okay, can't resist. "No. What?"

The bell above the door jingles and we both clam up.

The sudden silence is shocking.

I look over the counter, and all remains quiet. "Hey, they're done. Good timing."

Myra opens the drawer a little at first, then fully. "Yes, they are. Hello, you two." She lifts them out of the drawer and sets them one atop the other on the counter. "Shall I wrap them together or will they part ways now?"

"Together, please. They can ride out the afterglow on the trip home." She sets them on a large swatch of beige muslin and folds the fabric over them before tying a red silk ribbon around the center. I accept the cloth bundle and hug them to my chest. "I'm glad you two had fun, but it's time to go."

My thanks are on the tip of my tongue when I remember Gran's and Granda's lesson about that. "You've been kind and so very helpful. I look forward to coming back soon."

"You are most welcome to return. Until next we meet, Fiona, namaste."

I turn toward the door and reach into my pocket for the keys—

The hit comes from behind, a blunt strike to the back of my head and left shoulder. I stagger sideways and drop the books to bring my hands up to catch myself against the wall.

Instinct more than thought allows me to drop out of range before the next hit lands. Groping fingers brush past my face as I roll and scramble behind the next shelf of books.

"Get out of my—" Myra's silence and the heavy *thunk* on the wood floor strikes me cold.

I haven't got time to worry about her yet. I'm back beneath one of the sliding ladders and hustle to the next section. My mind is fuzzy. I think it's from the rush of adrenaline more than the hit.

Red, what's wrong?

Bad guys. Under attack.

Let me out.

I run to the end of the next aisle and duck behind a tall display case. *Please, let me be recharged enough to do this.* My heart is hammering, but I close my eyes and try to release my bear. Nothing happens. Dammit!

"Come out, come out, wherever ye are," a man with a thick Irish accent says. "Tell us how ye called the mark, little girl, and we'll let ye live."

Called the mark? He knows who I am? How?

I thought this was a magical bookstore shakedown, but it's more than that. This is about me.

The store holds more ambient magic than anywhere I've been since I came home, so I pull in some of the power. I cast my voice to protect my hiding spot.

"I didn't call the mark. How do you know it appeared?"

I rise enough to peek through the glass of a display case. A hard-bodied, curly-haired brute is edging my way. I need a weapon. Granda and Sloan have been working with me on defending myself with whatever is close at hand.

The Spanish cutlass in the display case will do in a pinch.

"I know a lot of things, Fiona. I've been watching you."

"There are laws against that." I ease the blade out of the case and make sure not to knock it into anything. "Why me? I'm not that interesting."

It's not Brute in front of me who's talking, but I don't know where Bad Guy Two is. I slink around the far side of the display cabinet and slide between the shelves of Mythical Creatures and Occult Symbology.

Now that I have a weapon, I swallow the panic choking me and text Sloan. *911.*

My sneakers make no sound on the hardwood, and I am almost back to the cash counter when I see Myra. She's bleeding from what looks like a magical wound on her shoulder and isn't moving. When I look closer, her shirt rises and falls in a shallow rhythm.

Skull Trim is standing over her.

Dammit, that makes three of them.

"Fiona, run!" Sloan portals into the middle of the store and goes straight for Skull Trim.

There's nowhere to run. Brute's in front of me, and Bad Guy Two is coming fast from behind. Before I'm trapped, I rush forward and swing between the end of two aisles.

I slice the cutlass through the air as I round the corner.

My hold on the grip is tested as I hit something solid. I don't stop to see what it is. I roll to my knees and scramble behind an antique harvest table.

The hiss of a man is a good sign, the crash of body to floor even better. I think I'm good until heavy footsteps thunder behind me. Bad Guy Two has a gun.

And it's pointed at me.

Think like a druid. I throw up my hand, expecting a basic shield to divide him from me. It doesn't come.

Dammit. I lash out with the cutlass.

A shot rings out, and the world both explodes into fast-forward at the same time everything around me seems to stop.

I fall forward with the sword in my hand, and whether it's fate or a fluke, we collide. The cutlass finds purchase, lodges in his belly, and twists out of my grip.

The world spins, and I'm on the hardwood, my legs pinned beneath his weight. Brute makes his reappearance, and I scramble against the floor with my hands.

Sloan shouts something and sweeps his hand toward me. His words are lost in the thundering rush of blood barreling through my eardrums, but suddenly Bad Guy Two's gun is in my hand.

I aim like Da taught me. Point and squeeze.

Bang. Bang.

The look of shock on the man's face is almost comical. He falls against the corner of the table, then flips backward onto the floor in a weighty crash.

I keep my aim up, waiting and listening.

"Duck? Are you alive?"

I scramble through the blood; my sneakers once again destroyed from struggling for purchase in a plasma slip and slide. Gross. The fae world has a high yuck factor.

"Myra? Are you all right?"

I collapse more than lower myself, but she's already sitting up. "I'll be fine. Your man and the third one grappled onto one another and vanished."

"Damn it." I pull myself up to stand and search the empty aisles of the store. He probably thought transporting Skull Trim away would keep me safe. Stupid man. "Sloan's a wayfarer. They could be anywhere."

"Go, duck. Get home or somewhere safe."

I look toward the two men I've either killed or almost killed and shake my head. "I can help. My father's a cop and a druid. He'll know what to do."

Myra places her hand over mine, and I'm washed with a calming rush. "I know what to do. You don't live almost two centuries and not come up against a bad one now and again. Go on now. Gather your things and get somewhere safe. If your man comes back for you, I'll send him along."

"But the bodies—"

"—are fine where they are. Finders keepers, as they say."

Finders keepers? "That might apply to dropped money or a trinket, but I don't think dead bodies are on the list." The words slip off my tongue without thought, and Myra's gaze narrows. Something slips in the veil of my perception, and I see and feel an aura of power I missed before.

Damn. I know nothing about this woman, and here I am pissing her off and defying her wishes in her store. "You're sure?"

In a blink, she appears as she had—colorful and fun. "Of course. Off you go now."

Yep. That's my cue. My bloody sneakers squeak on the floor

when I stop to pick up my book bundle from where I threw it minutes before. "It's okay, you two. We're going home now."

Fae, witches, vampires, monsters, and who knows what else. What have I gotten myself into?

And where the hell is Sloan?

"Come on, Molly." I ram my key into the ignition and bring her to life. I set the books on the seat beside me and buckle up. "Let's get out of here."

A glance in my rearview and my blind spot has me gunning it to squeeze into an opening that, in truth, isn't big enough for me to try for.

There's a squelch of brakes and a long, roar of a horn behind me. There is no neck-snapping jolt or crunch of steel-on-steel, so I unclench my girlie parts and offer what I hope is an apologetic gesture. "Sorry."

"Damn. Damn. Damn," I mutter while pulling around a taxi easing to the side so I can make the light. It flips amber as I enter the intersection and I cruise through the—

I'm still worrying about Sloan and what kind of creature Myra is when that crunch of steel-on-steel I was worried about hits out of nowhere.

The spellbooks fly off the seat, and I'm half-reaching for them when gravity shifts and it's only my seatbelt holding me to the cushion. My back flares with numbness that spreads from my Fianna mark until it swallows my entire body.

My shield.

Over and over I go until a massive bang has me rocking violently and my brains rattling. Something slams into me with bone-breaking force and a foul smell.

A sharp pain follows... Then nothing.

CHAPTER TWENTY-THREE

Red, sweet mother of mercy, wake up.

It's the panic in Kyle's voice that cuts through the darkness and brings back images of being t-boned and rolled in the intersection. That shouldn't have happened. I still had the right of way. Da's going to kill me. No. First, he'll tell me he loves me more than life—then he'll kill me.

"Are you okay? You didn't get injured in the crash, did you?"

Are ye daft? I'm a feckin' spirit bear. In this form, I'm nothin' more than air in yer lungs.

Right. "Sorry. I'm not firing on all pistons. What happened? Was anyone hurt? The other driver?"

The other driver was yer Skull Trim bastard. It wasn't an accident, Fi. He plowed into ye to stop ye from getting away. Yer not in a hospital. Yer his captive.

The horror of that reality stirs me fully awake.

I'm lying on a cot within a clear, acrylic cage.

"Sloan!" I roll off the cot, and thankfully it's low to the ground because my legs are Jell-O and don't hold my weight. I hit my knees hard on the concrete floor, but the flash of pain is a drop in the pan. I feel like I've been run over.

Oh yeah… I have.

I send up a prayer of thanks to whoever or whatever blessed me with a magical Fianna shield. I have no doubt that without it, I wouldn't be moving at all right now.

I manage to crawl to Sloan. He's slumped over and bleeding on a second cot. "Wake up, surly." I press two fingers to the side of his neck and draw a steadying breath. He's alive. "How long has he been unconscious?"

Sorry. When yer out cold, all I get is darkness.

"Okay. Then we'll figure this out together."

I sit back on my heels and take stock. The cell is a ten-foot cube with a line of two-inch air holes running along the ceiling and a steel beam barring the door on the outside.

The prison is set in the center of a much larger space, the walls of the bigger room stark white and nondescript. Everything in both the inner and outer areas is either metal or plastic or acrylic.

"Homey."

The significance of my surroundings clicks. Nothing in the space carries natural energy. It's a druid magic dead zone.

"Who are you?" I shout. "What do you want?"

Static crackles above my head and I stare at the speaker built into the thick, acrylic ceiling. The line opens, and everything goes quiet. "I'm known by many names, Fiona. And as fer what I want…well, that's quite simple actually. I want everythin' due me."

I can think of a few things he deserves, but that isn't likely what he means. "Uh-huh, and how did I get mixed up in your quest of entitlement?"

"Ye called the mark. How?"

I roll my eyes. "Seriously, you sound like a broken record. I didn't do anything. One night I'm drinking at a pub. I go out back to toss the trash, get suckered into a brawl in the back lot, and whammy, the mark came to life."

I honestly have no idea if this is one of those moments Myra mentioned about not sharing personal details if I don't want to end up dead. If so, oops.

"Quid pro quo, asswipe. What did you do to Sloan?"

"Nothing compared to what I will do if ye try anything."

I'm not sure how I'm supposed to pose a threat when I'm stuck in a sealed box.

"You sure are a pretty little thing, aren't you?"

I laugh. "Does that line work on any of the girls you stalk, run over with your car, then kidnap?"

"I left a bottle of water on the floor beside the cot. You should drink it. You're likely dehydrated after the accident."

"Hard pass." I glance at the bottle. "I was mistakenly roofied once at the bar. It's no fun. Nothing bad happened, and it was awful. I'm not about to volunteer for a second round. What did you put in it?"

"Nothing terrible. Just a wee something that makes my guests a little friendlier. We are friends, aren't we?"

"No. Friends don't roofie friends."

"Poetic. Ye should put that on a t-shirt."

I ignore the playful banter and check on Sloan. He's still out cold. With no idea why he isn't waking up, I turn him this way and that and do a quick inventory to make sure he's not bleeding or anything.

Huh. I find two small red dots on his collarbone.

Either a vampire bit him or two very talented mosquitos lined up perfectly before feeding. Man, if Sloan hadn't opened the door to that particular vault of crazy a couple of hours ago, I wouldn't have gone there.

But he did...and I do.

I stare up at the speaker cover, which now that I think of it is weird. There's no reason to talk to the speaker. After dropping my gaze, I sweep the white room around me. "If we're done with the get to know you session, I'd like to leave."

"I'm afraid that won't be possible. You see, there are a great many projects in the works right now, and the knowledge of a Cumhaill druid setting up in town is bound to chuck a wrench into the cogs."

"So, you try to solicit a gang of criminals to wipe out my family? Not cool, dude."

"Yes. You seem to have a knack for foiling my plans."

"Aw, shucks, you give me too much credit."

A phone rings on his end, and the speaker makes the same squelching sound as it shuts off. It seems rude that he can listen to my conversations and I can't listen to his.

"Mmm." Sloan stirs.

Yes. His mint-green eyes crack open, but there's no focus. His head lolls to the side like it weighs a million pounds.

"Hey, Mackenzie, it's me. You're okay." When he tries to sit up, I press a firm hand on his chest. "Give it a minute. I think you got whammied by a vampire."

"Fer fuck's sake," he mumbles, his eyes still closed. "What is it about you that draws this level of crazy?"

I don't think it's a real question, so I don't attempt to answer it.

"Where are we?"

"In Skull Trim prison."

He manages to lift his head, so I help him sit. Because he's wonky, I sit beside him to prop him up. "What happened? One minute you were tackling him and the next, you poofed him away."

"He poofed me." His voice is groggy. "Do ye honestly think I'd ever leave ye in a fight when there were more of them after ye?"

I never really thought about that. "No. You wouldn't."

"What about the other two that had ye surrounded?"

"Dead. I got one with a cutlass and shot the other with his gun."

He nods, then winces as if he regrets the motion. "I got

portaled out and was wrapped in a fight when a second man joined the fun. By his strength and the fact that he bit me and knocked me out, I'd say our Skull Trim is friends with at least one vampire."

"He knows about the mark of the Fianna, and can portal, too. Do you think he's a druid?"

He lifts one shoulder in a lackluster shrug. "Hard to say. Maybe... But he's more. His power has a foul stink to it that bodes of black magic."

I remember the stink from the car accident right before I passed out. "Yeah, like mothballs trying to mask the reek of rotten, maggot-ridden garbage."

"Otherwise known as black magic." Sloan smiles a little and turns his attention to our surroundings. "We need to get out of here."

I nod and clamp my hands around his wrist. "Okeydokey. Let's go. Beam us out, Scotty."

Except we don't go anywhere.

"Are you broken? This is not the best time to be offline."

He stabs me with a look and balls his fists. "Could ye feck off fer five seconds and give me a chance to clear my head?"

I give him some space. "Okay, dialing it down a few notches. Sorry. Maybe you haven't noticed, but when I'm nervous, I get snark-happy."

"I've noticed." Sloan stares at the airholes.

I follow his gaze and try my best to be quiet, which lasts all of five seconds. "Oh! I have an idea. Come. Sit with me."

I point to the concrete floor and strike the meditation pose, knees crossed, and shoulders loose. I shake my hands to release the tension, and he's still sitting lopsided on the cot.

"You're not joining."

No. He's frowning. "I get that we need to have cool heads, but I've recently been snacked on and drugged by vampire venom. I don't think I'm in the headspace right now for meditating."

I point to the floor again. "Humor me. I did more than play Animal Crossing and learn Elvis tribute routines from Patty. That little Man o' Green taught me a few things that might come in handy in this situation."

With a groan of submission, he slides off the cot and ass-plants in front of me. He crosses his legs and, knees to knees, I take his hands gently in my fingers and swing his arms loose. "I'm going to take you into my happy place. Then, I'll tell you my plan. Ready?"

Sloan exhales heavily. "Why must I be trapped with a pint half-full cheerleader? The Fates hate me."

"Nonsense. Breathe with me. Here we go."

When Patty first showed me how to retreat into myself, he described it as sending my consciousness into the trunk of my body. Like a tree, there is a hollow where those with magic hold and nurture it.

It doesn't matter whether it's a spark like the druids or essence or root power or whatever, fae energy must be stored and protected somewhere within.

Patty said it could be in someone's mind, their heart, their lungs...it doesn't matter. Mine is in my chest. The tricky part is taking a visitor. I'm not sure if I could do it if Sloan weren't as powerful and well-trained as he is, but that's a question for another day.

Right now, we need to get outta Dodge.

When I open my eyes, he and I sit on the dance floor in Shenanigans, still with our legs crossed, still gently holding each other's fingers.

Behind Sloan's head, Da is at the bar pulling the tap. He fills a pint glass and hands the draught across the bar to—I lean to the side to see around Sloan and suck in a breath.

Brendan.

My big brother laughs at something Da says, and the sound of his voice fills me with joy. Gone is his undercover scruff. His dark hair is cut, and he looks like he always did.

"How is he here?"

Sloan stands and grips my elbow to help me up. "Ye hold his spark inside ye as well as yer father's. I suppose they're here because their magic is here. Ye've manifested them the way ye remember them."

I squeeze Sloan's arm. "Does that mean he'll stay here? That I can see him when I need him?"

Sloan shrugs. "I can't say. This is yer trick, remember?"

Movement in one of the booths draws my attention to the wee man raising a pint to me from atop the table. I offer Patty a wave and wonder why he's here. Did I manifest him? Is he here because I carry his gift? Because he showed me how to get here and has been here with me before? Or because I inadvertently created a bond of gratitude with him by thanking him outright for my stone?

I'm mulling over all the possible reasons when Sloan taps my shoulder. "Hello? Ye said ye wanted to show me something. Is that still yer plan?"

"Right." I look around and close my eyes, willing another to join us.

"Hello, Red." Kyle lumbers close.

He bumps me with his muscled shoulder, and I bend over and hug the ruff of his neck. "Hello, Bear. How about we bust out of this prison? I think I figured out a way."

"Do tell," says Sloan.

"Kyle wisps out the airholes of our prison in his spirit bear form. We wait until someone comes into the outer room to feed us or talk in person, then he does his Killer Clawbearer shredding on them."

Sloan eyes my bear. "If it's a vampire who comes through the door, ye'll need to decapitate him, Bear. Not much else will stop a vamp."

I try not to imagine that and get back to my plan. "Once whoever comes in here is out of commission, Kyle unlatches the bar locking us in. Then it's a matter of exiting the cleanroom and you poofing us the hell home."

Sloan nods. "I give ye points for the plan. There's only one problem. Ye can't cast yer bear."

"Unless she is holding me in on purpose and she can."

I roll my eyes. "I'm not. I told you that, but I think that in here, we can merge our powers enough that maybe I'll be able to. Da? Brendan? Will you two come over here for a sec, please?"

The two of them set down their glasses and join us on the dance floor. In my head, I know this isn't really Brendan, but he's a manifestation of my memories of him. I'll take it. Before I explain what I want, I give him a big hug.

"What's this about, boo?"

I smile. Brendan always called me boo when I was little. "I love you."

"I love you too, chickypoo."

I drink in the sight of him for one more second, then pull back and explain what I need.

"...and so, I think if the four of us join hands around Kyle, we can amp my energy enough to set him free. Does that make sense?"

"I'm game." Brendan grabs my hand and reaches for Da. My father takes Brenny's hand, then takes Sloan's. Before I close the circle and take Sloan's, I reach into my pocket and take out the peridot stone that Patty gave me.

"You said it clarifies the mind and increases willpower. We can use both right about now."

Sloan closes the circle by taking my hand with my leprechaun casting stone pressed between our palms.

"Okay, give me all you got, boys. Let's set this bad boy loose.

And Bear? You don't have to kill them if whoever comes isn't lethally dangerous. If you can knock them out or maim them, that's good too. Except for the vampire... On second thought, you can kill Skull Trim too. He's too dangerous to give a second chance. Him, you should definitely eliminate if the chance presents itself."

Sloan frowns. "Yer a scary woman, ye know that?"

"Why, because I want to survive and not have a maniac targeting my entire family? If you expect me to feel bad about one less bad guy on the streets, you'll be disappointed."

I meet the gaze of the others and nod. "Okay, on one. Three. Two. One."

CHAPTER TWENTY-FOUR

"Fi, thank the stars. Where have ye been?" Da is on his feet the moment we materialize in the living room and rushes to hug me. "*Are ye all right, mo chroi?* The police tracked yer plates to us, and we saw what's left of poor, wretched Molly. How are ye?"

"Sore." I release Sloan's hand and lean heavily on Kyle. "It's been a day, I tell you."

"Sit, baby girl." Aiden escorts me to my chair. "Are you guys hungry? Can we get you anything?"

"Can I get a ginger ale? I'm nauseous from whatever spell Skull Trim hit me with."

Sloan shifts sideways and sinks into the club chair. He looks worse than I feel. Still, he got us home, so he gets bonus points for that. "I'll take one as well, thanks."

"Why do you smell like smoke?"

"We escaped by killing a vampire." I accept the can of soda Calum hands me. "Sloan wanted us to burn the body so he didn't revive or resurrect or whatever they do."

"You were taken by vampires?"

I shake my head. "No, Skull Trim. The vampire was the jailor he put in charge of watching us."

218

"Skull Trim again?" Dillan confirms. "When Da got the call about the wreck, and we learned neither of you was anywhere to be found, we canvassed the witnesses. He T-boned you in the middle of an intersection in the middle of the day, and no one remembered seeing a thing."

"We knew it had to be a magic thing," Calum adds. "Other major cities might have problems getting witnesses to speak up. That doesn't happen here. If somebody sees it, we know about it."

"Yeah, it's all a crazy blur. He whammied me with black magic, so that likely affected the witnesses too. I was so focused on getting away from the bookshop and getting home that I missed it. The truck came out of nowhere."

"Why were ye in a hurry to get away from a bookshop?" Da asks.

"I wasn't at first. I wanted to call you and wait for Sloan, but Myra said no. She wanted to keep the bodies, and I didn't want to know what she wanted to do with them—"

"Bodies?" Aiden repeats.

"What bodies, Fi?" Da's expression darkens.

"The two guys I killed."

The boys reel and I realize I'm not telling the story well. Adrenaline is pumping hard through my body, and my thoughts are barreling out like a runaway train.

Da stands before me and takes my hands. They're shaking. Is it me shaking or him? I think it's me. "Fi, what bookshop? Where were ye? Start at the beginning."

"We went to a magic bookshop where Sloan copied—oh, the *books!* Did you rescue them from the wreckage? Are the spell-books all right?"

Emmet blinks. "Are *you* all right?"

I look to see if anyone is following. Nope. "The bundle of books in the front seat. There were two spellbooks. Are they hurt?"

Da points to the front hall. "Yer car was a write-off. I had the contents collected and boxed. Fi, we were talking about ye killing two men. Can the books wait?"

I hustle into the front hall and find two boxes sitting on the shoe bench. I pull the flaps of the first open and see the purchases from the crystal shop, a blanket, an ice scraper, and my emergency kit. I leave the box with the contents of Molly's trunk and open the second box.

The muslin-wrapped bundle is there, and I lift it out and head back into the living room. After setting them on the coffee table, I untie the red silk ribbon that still holds them wrapped and pull away the fabric.

"Are you guys okay?" Yes. Maybe they have a little magic of their own because they seem undamaged. I look at Sloan to reassure him that his book seems unharmed and my stomach churns even worse. "Shit. Sloan?"

With all eyes in the room on me, no one noticed that our wayfarer guest has slumped over to one side in a sweat. I'm the first to get to him, and I lean him back to see what's happened. "Shit. He's out cold and drenched. Get him to the couch and lay him down."

"What's wrong with him?" Da asks as Aiden and Emmet move him.

"I don't know. He hasn't been a hundred percent since he woke up in our cell. I checked him over then—Ohmygawd! Is he turning into a vampire?"

"What?" Emmet grips me under my arms and pulls me back. "Okay, you seriously need to rest. First, you're worried about books, and now Sloan's turning into a vampire?"

"I'm fine." I pull free and place a hand on Sloan's forehead. "After the accident, I woke up on a cot sealed in a druid magic-free cell. Sloan took longer to wake. He said when he and Skull Trim were fighting, he got *poofed* away and sedated when a henchman snacked on him and drugged him with vampire venom."

"Vampire?" Dillan peels back with a groan. "I thought you were in shock when you said that. Seriously, Da? Do ye not think we shoulda known about this shit before now? We're out on the street every day."

I undo the top buttons of Sloan's shirt and put a little throw pillow under his head. "Focus, people. What will venom do to him?"

Da frowns. "Nothing good, I'm sure."

"You don't know?"

"Fi, I left the preternatural life when I was eighteen. Vampires, witches, zombies, and the monsters of the other magical sects never came into my training."

"Zombies?" Emmet repeats, the pitch of his voice unusually high.

I ignore my brothers. "Then we need Granda's help."

Da pulls out his phone and makes the call. He puts it on speaker and holds it toward me. A moment later, Gran picks up. "Hello, dear. It's nice—"

"Gran," I blurt while taking the phone from his hand. "Sorry, I don't mean to be rude, but I need Granda. Is he there?"

"Och, one moment, luv." She sets down whatever she was doing and shuffles through the house and out the front door. "*Lugh!* Fiona needs ye. It sounds urgent."

"Hi Gran," Emmet shouts while leaning over the coffee table. "This is Emmet."

"Hello, luv. Okay, Fi, here's yer grandfather."

"Fiona, what's the matter?"

I give Granda a crib notes version of what happened and end with Sloan being unconscious on our couch. "Is he turning into a vampire?"

"No, likely not. It would help if I could see him. Can ye call me on my new cellular and switch me to video?"

I balk at that. "Wow, you got a cell phone?"

"Sloan helped us pick it out," Gran says from the background. "We have a laptop, too."

I can't imagine but now is not the time. "Yeah, give me your number, and I'll call you right back." Emmet writes it down as he recites the digits and I do as he asks. When the call connects, I hold the phone over Sloan's face so he can see. "Press his lips up off his teeth. Let me see his gums. How do they look?"

Dillan takes the phone, so my hands are free. I push Sloan's lips up from his teeth and let Granda take a look.

"Press the gums over the roots of his incisors. Did his canines descend at all?"

"No. They seem normal."

"What about his blood? If ye cut him, does the wound swell with scarlet blood as ye'd expect?"

I look at Aiden. He always carries a pocket knife. He takes it out, sits on the coffee table to get a good angle on Sloan's arm, and draws the silver blade's tip across the tender flesh of his palm.

Staring at the line he draws, I've never wanted to see someone bleed so much. When the blood swells, I let out a heavy breath. "Okay, that's normal too. It's bleeding as it should."

"Then it's likely only poisoned him."

I frown. "Oh, is that all? Then great, why worry?"

"Watch yer tone, missy. Sloan is important to me, too. I'm tryin' to help ye."

I take a breath. "Sorry. What can we do?"

My new spellbook bangs its cover on the table and flips her pages until they fall open on the section marked Poisons. "Good thinking. Thank you, Beauty."

I look over the section she's shown me and find a sub-section marked Monster Venom. "Granda, in my spellbook, I have a potion, but I don't know what half of the ingredients are. Can you help me?"

"Read them out, luv." Gran grabs a notepad and her spellbook. "I'll look things up while yer talkin'."

I start reading the ingredients out and get about halfway down the list before Granda drops his gaze, and Gran stops writing. "What? What's the matter now?"

"Adder's fork is the tongue of a European viper, and lionfish spine is literally the separated vertebrae of a lionfish. Both will be immensely hard to locate, and even if yer proficiency with potion work wasn't nil, neither ingredient could get to you in time."

"Would Wallace have the ingredients?"

"Likely so. He has an extensive clinic and prides himself on being prepared for anything."

"Okay, then send Wallace here. He fixed you up and patched me up more than once. Surely he can gather what he needs and leave Ireland to save his son."

Gran milling her hands isn't a good sign.

"What?" I ask. "Why can't Wallace fix this?"

"There isn't time, Fi. A flight to Toronto wouldn't get him to ye—"

"Find someone to portal him. The McNiff heir from the alley fight. He's a wayfarer. Send Wallace with him."

Gran frowns, and I know the reason why that won't work before she says a thing. "Shit."

I meet the confused gazes of my brothers. "Wayfarers can only transport to somewhere they've been previously. It's a GPS thing. Their inner compass needs to sense the exact coordinates."

Calum curses. "I don't suppose the McNiff guy Fi mentioned has been to Toronto? Maybe he's a Blue Jays fan?"

Granda shakes his head. "No. The McNiffs are purists. No member of their clan has ever left the enchantment of fae grounds. They pride themselves on that fact and never let us forget it."

"Okay, so what do we do?"

Granda's pursed lips make my panic triple. "Ye make him

comfortable. If he was bitten hours ago, he'll be gone in a very few hours more. I'm sorry, *mo chroi*. Ye did yer best."

"No." My mind reels. "We can't give up and let him die."

"There's nothing to be done, Fi," Granda repeats. "If ye were here, sure, there are greater fae to bargain with, and possibly one might help for a price, but so far from home... There's nothing fer ye to do. I'm sorry."

An hour later, I'm sitting on the edge of my bed, pressing a damp cloth on Sloan's forehead. Aiden and Da took off his shirt, shoes, and socks to help cool his fever, but it's a bandage on a bullet wound situation. Kyle is curled up on my rug. He's not sleeping, but he hasn't said a word since we came upstairs to wait things out.

A knock on the door brings all four of my brothers into my room. Aiden's got Da's bag of marbles in his hands, and Calum and Dillan each carry one of the spellbooks.

Emmet shrugs. "There's a section in here about sacred death prayers. We thought maybe we could offer him safe passage. You know, to let him know we care."

I blink back the sting that brings tears to my eyes. "That's very sweet, you guys. Thank you."

"It was Da's idea," Aiden says, as my father comes into the room to join us. He's wearing a white button-down dress shirt, a leather kilt, and a jewel-hilted sword at his hip. It's the stuff he keeps stuffed at the bottom of the trunk in his closet.

Somehow, embracing his heritage seems like a bitter victory. "You look every bit as handsome as any of the druid men at the Tralee festival, Da. Thank you."

He dips his chin. "Sloan's been a good friend to this family and risked his life to keep ye safe more than once. He has our undying respect fer that."

Aiden sets Sloan's spellbook on his chest and places his hands over the top. "Peace be with you, brother."

The boys empty Da's bag, and everyone takes one of the marble casting stones and kneels beside the bed. Da stands at the footboard with Beauty in his hands and starts to read the prayer. I pull out my peridot and stare at the beautiful green gemstone.

How can this be the end of Sloan?

His warm brown skin has a gray tinge to it that makes me ill. This is my fault. If he hadn't gotten dragged into my drama... If he hadn't portaled me home... If I hadn't asked him to copy his spellbook and get me set up...

If any or all of those things hadn't happened, he'd be in Ireland, healthy and surly, and lauding himself over the peons.

I'm sorry about this.

I wish I had a bit of Sloan's magic to hold him in my happy place and visit him once in a while. I think he and Brenny would get along. Likely Patty, too.

I rub a thumb over my peridot. It's warm in my fingers, its energy bolstered since I used it to release Kyle for our escape earlier. Used to clarify the mind, and increase willpower, well-being, and vitality. I push with everything I have, wishing for Sloan's health and life. Nothing helps.

It hurts to lose him so soon after Brendan.

With my heart aching, I withdraw from my consciousness and leave my brothers and my father to say the farewells. Instead, I open my eyes and find myself in Shenanigans with Brenny and Da at the bar. Patty sits absently in the corner booth. I point at the jukebox, and *Suspicious Minds* comes on. Patty straightens and meets my gaze.

"Hey." I join him in his booth. "Sorry I didn't get to say hello earlier. I was busy escaping from imprisonment in a magic-free zone."

"Not a problem. So yer free? All is well?"

"Yes, I'm free. All is far from well. Remember when I told you about my friend Sloan?"

"The druid stickler that lives to look down on ye?"

"That's him. He got poisoned by vampire venom while saving my life. I tried to get him help, but there's nothing and no one close enough to where we are to save him."

Da brings over a couple of pints of green Guinness, and I thank him. "A tribute to yer friend. Yer always up fer a pint, aren't ye, Patty?"

"I am at that." Patty raises his glass.

It's funny. I've never had a lot of friends beyond my brothers and a few girlfriends. Now, I have Kyle, Sloan, and Patty. I look around and smile.

"A bear, a druid, and a Man o' Green walk into a bar."

Patty chuckles and uses both hands to lift his glass to his lips. "I'm sorry yer life turned on ye, Fi. Don't forget to speak the word."

I swallow a mouthful and close my eyes, tracking the descent of the icy chill down my esophagus and into my belly.

What's that? What did Patty say to me as I was released from my detainment in the dragon cave? *If yer future turns on ye, speak the word, and we'll make it right.*

"I wish you could make it right, Patty."

He sets his glass on the table, and his eyes glitter behind the rounds of his frameless spectacles. "A wish, ye say? Then let's hear it. Make it plain."

"Are you..." I know leprechauns are greater fae powers, but... "Is saving Sloan from the poisoning of vampire venom within your powers, Patty?"

"That depends."

"On what?"

"A bargain with a man of my ranking is a complicated thing, Fiona. Don't consider it without considering that. Because I like ye, I'll lay it out fer ye. Properly made, greater fae bargains hold great power, but they must be weighed and balanced. If I save yer friend, what do you offer me of equal importance? Ye see the rub? Do I want yer first-born? I don't think I do, but I could ask it. Do ye understand?"

Oh, yeah. Okay, that's a scary thought. "Is there anything you want or even think you want? Sloan hasn't long to live. If you are his last hope, we need to come to terms quickly."

He takes his hat off and sets it on the table. "As of now, yer new to all things. Yer power is fledgling. Yer knowledge is low. Yer contacts and connections uninspiring."

"As pep-talks go, this one bites."

He holds up a stubby finger, and I make the gesture of locking my lips and throwing away the key.

"Yer new to it all, but I like playin' the long game. I have faith in ye, wee girl. In six months or a year down the road, ye'll be a very different druid. That Fiona might well have somethin' I value."

"So, you want a blank-slate raincheck? That's terrifying, Patty. What if Her Slitheriness gets a hankering for Canadian? I won't give you one of my brothers to feed her."

"Now yer catchin' on. Good on ye, Fi." He arches up one of his bushy eyebrows. "No. I'll not put ye in that spot. Let's agree that what I can ask of ye must be a favor or an action. I'll not claim the life of one ye love. I promise ye that."

A favor or action. Is there anything I wouldn't do to save someone I love? "I won't forfeit the lives of family or friends, and I won't kill innocent people."

"Agreed. I'll not ask ye to."

I raise my glass and think about it some more as I down a few swallows. "Okay, you heal Sloan Mackenzie of Stormcrest Castle of the vampire venom poison taking his life. In return, I agree to fulfill a favor or action in the future as long as it doesn't cause me to lose any family or friends or kill any innocent people."

I try to get as much information in the agreement as I can.

Gran said words hold power in the fae world. I want to make sure I honor that.

"Shall we seal it with a kiss?" Patty answers.

I give him a wry glance. "Is that customary?"

"No, but I thought it was worth a shot."

I chuckle and lean over the table, propping myself up on my elbows. Before my lips meet his, I smile. "It's a deal."

My eyes open and I'm kneeling at the side of my bed. My brothers are still focused on their stones, and Da is still reading the prayer from the pages of my pretty new spellbook. I stand, and Patty's there, sitting cross-legged on the pillow beside Sloan's head.

"Is this him?"

The startled grunts and bewildered looks of my family are hilarious. I deserve another Oh Henry! bar, if only it were a prank. "Yes, this is Sloan."

"Consider our bargain sealed."

I'm about to thank him when I remember Sloan's warning about that. "Your actions in saving his life won't be forgotten, Patty. You are a great man. I count myself lucky for knowing you."

Patty smiles. "That's a girl. Now yer suckin' diesel."

And with that, Patty and Sloan vanish.

CHAPTER TWENTY-FIVE

"What did ye do, Cumhaill?" I hear the worried frustration in Sloan's voice and tuck my cell between my ear and shoulder. "A bargain with a Man o' Green? Yer nowhere near skilled enough in the nuances of fae communication to be posing a trade."

It's been a week since Patty *poofed* Sloan off my bed and back home to his father. Wallace said he arrived home cured of the poison, but there was a great deal of damage done to his system— injuries that might've killed him if Patty hadn't deposited him home.

"You're welcome," I retort, although I don't need him to thank me. I did it as much for myself as I did it for him. He had my back, and I wouldn't let him die because I was out of my depths. "How are you feeling?"

He huffs, and I picture him all stressed out and annoyed. Hilarious. "Do ye know what ye've done?"

"I do, although I'm alone in my opinion of what that is. I think it was a bargain well-made and worth what comes."

I head back into the stock room to grab the next box. Like the one in Gran's and Granda's house, there is a tree growing from the ground in the middle of the reading area off the main store. It seems like the building that houses Myra's Emporium was built around it to preserve its fate.

"You're alive. That's a solid check in my win column."

"But at what cost?"

I set the box of books on the long wooden counter and use the box-cutter to open it. "A cost I'm willing to pay at a later date. Look, you can save the lecture. I've been getting it from all sides for days. Da thinks I'm blind to danger and determined to get myself killed, and Granda thinks I'm an uneducated fool who doesn't know better, *annnnd* who's also going to get myself killed."

He chuckles. "Well, at least they agree on something."

"Go me! Bridging the gap of a forty-year estrangement."

"Speaking of strange. I heard yer bear is living large."

I unpack the box, transferring the books onto the counter for pricing. "He is. He doesn't appreciate being trapped in me while I suffer through magical brownouts. He's opted to hang around the house and go out to the forested areas of the Don at night to get his groove on."

"Ye realize yer setting a bad example fer the rest of the folks that have battle beasts, right?"

I laugh. "Live and let live. He has time to make up for, and so much he wants to learn about life in Toronto. As long as there are no news headlines the next morning, I'm certainly not going to stop him. Besides, the whole family loves him. Aiden even brought Kinu and the kids over to meet him."

"His wee ones spent time with the bear? So, none of ye have any sense, then?"

"Kyle won't hurt anyone unless they try to take a stab at us. Then, it sucks to be them because he's our secret Killer Claw-bearer weapon."

"Let's hope he remains a secret." Such a pessimist griper. "And yer recovered from the accident?"

With the contents of the box unpacked, I break it down to put in the cardboard recycling bin with the others. "Mostly. The left side of my face is a pretty gross yellow from slamming against the window during the rollover, but I'll survive."

"Ye know, they have an invention to keep that from happening. It's called an airbag. Perhaps I'll send yer Da a quick text suggestin' that yer next car be up to safety standards."

The brass bell rings over the door, and I straighten. "Okay, that's my cue. I gotta get back to work."

"It's early to be at the pub, isn't it?"

"It would be, but no. This morning, I started working part-time for Myra at the bookstore. You've told me a million times I have a lot to learn. I figure spending time here with her, surrounded by magical books, and talking to magical folks, I'll learn tons."

"And at the same time, soak in the ambient magic."

"You got it. Later, surly. I'm glad you're not dead."

Sloan laughs on the other end of the line. "Me too. Try not to get dead yerself."

"I'll try my best."

Myra sweeps in from the front of the store carrying two Tim Horton's coffees and a box of Timbits. A celebration tribute, she called it, for the beginning of my new job. "Vanilla chai latte for you and a medium double-double for me."

"Awesome. Perfect," I respond, in lieu of thanks. With no idea what Myra is and not on close enough terms to ask, I err on the side of caution to not create a bond of gratitude with another fae.

"I brought ye something else too." She clears the aisle and steps aside to reveal my father following her. "Found him outside staring at the building looking confused."

"Hi, Da. What's up?"

His scowl of worry is firmly locked in place. "My daughter left me a note that says she's starting work in a magical book-shop instead of stayin' home and out of trouble. Since this is where she was attacked last week and forced to kill two men sent to kill her, I thought I had the right to come and check things out."

I crack the plastic tab on the lid and take a sip. "I expected as much, and already told Myra what to expect and to keep an eye out for you."

"That predictable, am I?"

"That dependable." I chuckle and offer him a donut. "So, official intros. Myra, this is my father, Niall Cumhaill. Da, this is Myra."

He dips his chin. "Yer a meliae, are ye not?"

Myra smiles. "Fiona said you left the life over forty years ago. I'm surprised you picked up on that so quickly."

"My father is Lugh Cumhaill, Master Shrine-Keeper of the Ancient Druid Order. I suppose some of his meta-composition runs in my veins. I don't forget much."

"No. I don't suppose you would."

I watch the exchange, not sure what to make of it. There is tension in the air, and they're sizing one another up, but I can't tell if it's going well or not.

"What's a meliae?" I wonder aloud.

"An ash tree nymph," Da informs me.

I brighten. "So, the tree in the back?"

Myra nods. "That is my home tree, yes."

"Cool. My grandparents have a tree in their house, too."

Myra takes the lid off her coffee and pours it into a wooden mug with an intricate handle. "It's not uncommon for nature folk to include established growth in their homes. It speaks to the kind of people they are."

Da is watching Myra, and he seems to conclude that she's worthy enough to spend time with me because he relaxes and looks around. "Fi says ye've been here almost a half-century?"

"That's right. The builders were moving up this block and had designs to cut down my tree. We saw things differently. In the end, I won. I bought out this section of the block and designed a building to encompass my tree."

"Nice." I pop a chocolate glazed Timbit into my mouth. Soft and sweet, the beauty of Timbits is that the little round balls of donut perfection are the perfect size to pop in your mouth. "Way to fight the man, Myra."

Da crosses his arms over his chest, and I roll my eyes. This is his standard interrogation stance. Here it comes. "The fight that took place in here where Fiona fought for survival. Have ye any idea who the men were?"

"No. It was the first I'd seen them."

"How did they find this place, do you suppose?"

"I've been thinking about that." She blows across the surface of her coffee. "There were three of them. I only saw the two Fiona left behind. Maybe the third knew where the shop is."

"Fi says yer spell allows only those who need yer wares to find ye."

"That's right."

I swallow. "Then maybe they felt they *needed* to find me and gained access because I was here?"

I see by the look on Da's face he doesn't buy that. "I knew where ye said the shop was, but couldn't see past the fog of the spell to come inside. In fact, I was havin' a hard time fightin' the urge to move along. I think the logic of the third knowing where is sound. He likely brought the other two."

"Show her the picture of Skull Trim. Maybe she'll recognize him."

Da reaches inside the lapel of his jacket and pulls out the sketch Kevin drew up for us last week. None of us recognized him, and we haven't had any luck figuring out who he is or why he has such a hate-on for our family.

Myra holds the sketch at arm's length. It doesn't take more than a glance, and she hands it back. "Him I know. He's been here a good many times. He goes by the moniker Barghest."

I swallow my drink and grab another glazed chocolate ball of bliss. Da doesn't look happy. "What am I missing?"

"Barghest isn't a name. It's a mythical, monstrous dog that serves as an omen of death."

"There's no way that works out in our favor. So, that's why you said moniker and not name."

Myra nods. "I can't imagine anyone having that as a natural surname, no."

"Barghest," Da muses. "All right, well that gives us something more than we had. I don't suppose he's paid for any purchases with a credit card or ordered anything delivered that we might be able to trace back?"

Myra shakes her head. "No."

I recall something she mentioned. "Has he ever given you his number? You said you never forget a number."

"No."

"Do ye recall what he's purchased?" Da urges. "Maybe if we can't find where he is, we can discern what he's up to."

Myra sets her coffee down and pulls a large black ledger from under the counter. "That I can tell you. I track what brings back all of my repeat customers." She flips to the back of the book and flattens the page open. "Here you go."

Da looks over the list, his finger running down the page. "Would you mind if I take a picture of this?"

"If it helps you find the man responsible for invading my home and attacking my guests and me, you're welcome to anything you need."

Da takes the picture and checks that it's in the gallery. "Very helpful. What time are you finished, Fi? I'll have Kyle and one of yer brothers come to pick ye up."

The rest of my week is split between the bookshop and home. With Barghest, a.k.a. Skull Trim still at large, when we're not working, we stick close to home. Calum's been staying at Aiden's to help cover Kinu and the kids. Dillan's been working day shift and spending his nights at Shenanigans watching over Kady, and that leaves Emmet and I reading the spells in Beauty and trying to become proficient before we're attacked again.

"Fuck me." Emmet flops back on the grass of our backyard and stares at the gray sky. Summer is hanging on by a thread, the late October chill threatening to drain the last of our autumn warmth. "Nothing happened."

"Don't worry about it." I try not to let my disappointment show. "We still don't have enough fae energy to do three-quarters of these spells."

"We need more power!"

"I'm givin' her all she's got, Captain!" I flop on the grass beside him and stare up at the clouds. "I'm sorry it's so much less fun for you guys than it was for me in the beginning."

"It'll come, Fi. In the meantime, we can kill it at a party."

"I wish you could feel how it was at Gran's and Granda's. There, you can feel the potential energy pulsing from the ground and trees and wildlife. It's in the air and fills your lungs with this tingle. It's like living life on a whiskey buzz."

"Do you think we'll ever come close to that here?"

"I did. In true Taurus form, I thought I could bull my way through any obstacle. Now, I'm not so sure."

"Three-legged dog." Emmet points at a cloud overhead. "I miss Brenny."

I take his hand in mine and squeeze. "Me too."

The rumble of a big truck coming down the back lane has us both sitting up. When the brakes squelch right behind our house and four burly guys spill out of the cab, we both roll to our feet.

"Can I help you?" Emmet meets them before they open the gate.

The guy with an electronic pad looks down and taps his screen. "I've got a work order here for trees to be planted, a prefab gazebo to be constructed, a koi pond dug, and there's a note here to landscape the yard to the point of being lush."

Emmet and I lock gazes, and we're both bewildered.

"Who ordered it?" I ask.

"Name on the invoice is Kyle Cumhaill. Name on the credit card is listed as Calum Cumhaill, the same address. Are either here? Can I get one of them to sign off?"

Can my grizzly bear sign your work order? No.

"I'll sign for them." I take the iPad and remove the stylus. I look at the total and grimace. Damn. I'm sure Calum didn't mean for the druid thing to cost him that much.

"Do you know what you want where, or would you like Garish to help you? He's our landscape designer. With such a big job, he tends to come along to see if he can be of help."

I hand him back the signed work order. A pickup truck pulls in behind the landscape truck, and another guy with three girls in the same uniforms join the fun.

"Holy shit," Emmet says.

"True story." I nod. The one talking to us is staring. Right, he asked me a question. "Yeah, sure. By all means, let's talk to Garish."

"We needed it," Kyle growls that night. He stayed out of sight for the entire day but finally materialized for dinner. "After centuries of living in the Blessed Isle, I'm accustomed to a certain level of ambient energy. I'm not expecting things to be the same here, but if we can dial up the power a notch or two, we need to try. Ye'll never be the druid yer meant to be if ye can't put fuel into yer tank. I talked to Sloan about it, and he agreed."

"How did you talk to Sloan about it?"

My bear sways his head and crinkles his nose at me. "He called while ye showered a couple of days ago."

"And you answered my phone?"

He gives me what I assume is a feigned look of indignation. "What, I'm not allowed to check on him after he almost died? We escaped prison together. We hung out in yer happy place together. He's grown on me."

Liam stops in mid-process of stacking the dirty plates and scowls. "Wait. Go back. What does that mean, Sloan hung out in your happy place?"

Cue the arched brows around the room.

Dillan's catcall whistle cuts the tension. "Are you holding out on us, Fi? Are you and McSurly doing the dance of twenty toes?"

"Seriously? No. It's not like that with him."

They all let out scoffing laughs.

"It's *not.*"

"Does he know that?" Liam sets the plates on the counter. He turns his back on the sink, leans against the edge, and crosses his arms. "From my seat on the sidelines the week he was here, that's exactly what it looked like."

Okaaay, Liam is genuinely mad.

I want to wave away the crazy, but don't want to dismiss Liam's feelings. I haven't had any quality alone time with him since I got back. In all honesty, I've been too wrapped up in my life changes to notice what's going on with him. "Did I do something to piss you off? What am I missing?"

"Do you really want to know? Are we doing this?"

"Hey! Who wants to see the backyard?" Calum grabs his beer and stands. Emmet and Dillan jump out of their seats like their asses are on fire to follow.

"Come on, Bear." Emmet hustles him out of the room. "Let mom and dad fight in private."

I'm standing there, feeling like someone fast-forwarded

through the movie of my life, and I missed a critically important part. "Why are the rats abandoning ship? What's going on?"

Liam's body language is closed and hostile, and I don't like it. I step right up in his grill and force him to look at me. "If I did something, and there's something you need to get off your chest, spill it. I know we haven't had time—no, change that—I haven't *made* time since I got home, but—"

He moves so fast I don't register anything until—holy hell, he's kissing me.

For the briefest moment, my sense abandons me, and I enjoy it. Liam's a good kisser. His lips are soft yet firm, and the anger he feels tingles through me with heady passion.

Then my senses return.

I step back, a hand on his chest as I catch my breath.

He stares at me and doesn't seem any less annoyed. "Say something."

I swallow and try to think. "Why'd you do that?"

"Are you mad?"

"No. I uh... I just don't understand." There were times in my late teens when I wondered what it would be like with Liam. But then, the family ties overruled, and the curiosity passed. "What changed?"

There's a tentativeness in him I'm not used to. We've always been at ease with one another. "When you left without a word, I was angry and hurt. Then you went missing..."

Gawd, this again. "I'm sorry. I hate that you all suffered through that, but I didn't have a say in the matter."

"I get that, but during those weeks, it dawned on me that we're more than an extended family. You and I have always been a good team, but by the time I figured out there was more, you were gone."

"But I'm back."

"Yeah, and when you came back, I wanted to talk to you about it. Every time I came near you, he was here. You may not realize it, Fi, but you've got a crazy, chaotic draw to you. I don't blame Sloan for getting caught up in it, but I was caught in it long before him."

My mouth opens and closes a couple of times, and I feel like a goldfish.

His mouth quirks up in a crooked smile. "You can't tell me you never thought about it."

I pull a chair under my ass before my knees give and I end up on the kitchen floor. "Sure, I've thought about it."

"And?"

I run my fingers through my hair and try to draw enough oxygen into my brain to say the right thing. "I agree we're a great team and I love everything about you. I think... It's just the past couple of months have been a *lot*. With all the changes, I'm not in the headspace for dating. Not you or Sloan or anyone. I'm focused on my druid stuff. That's my passion right now."

Liam nods. "That's fair. And it's cool. Consider the door open if or when you're ready to walk through it."

"And if I want to remain besties and family?"

He shrugs. "We're a lock either way."

Liam bends and kisses my forehead. It's a chaste brush of his lips. Then he grabs his beer and heads out to join my brothers in the yard.

I take a long swig of my beer and close my eyes. "Okay, so that happened."

CHAPTER TWENTY-SIX

The next day when Da and the boys are working, Liam hangs out with Kady and me and plays the part of our chauffeur. Thankfully, it's not weird. He's the same Liam he's always been, and I'm relieved. The two of us drop Kady off at Shenanigans for the lunch shift. Then he takes me to the emporium for my mid-day start with Myra. "You can't see it, can you?"

I watch as he squints at the storefronts. His brow is pinched, and his eyes narrowed. He gets the same look on his face when one of his migraines is taking hold.

"Don't hurt yourself. I wondered."

He abandons the attempt and breaks his gaze. "No. I don't see it. I think I should be going."

"That's normal. Myra's spell has a bit of a get along now kick to it." I gather my purse and my snack bag and get out. "Thanks for the ride. You're working the bar tonight?"

"Yeah, nine until close."

"Cool. I'll see you tomorrow."

I stride toward the shop, relieved that the romance issue is over, and I can focus on being the first urban druid to figure out what it takes. One thing about Ireland is that there are ley lines that create access points and a transfer of energy.

"I need something like that in Toronto," I tell Myra twenty minutes later. "Have you ever been to Ireland? The feel of the magic is so different there."

I pull the last of a half-dozen books from the shelves—a regular customer called in the order and will be by to pick it up before three—and take them up for Myra to double-check and wrap up.

"Never been." Myra uses the pricing gun to ring in the books. "I get my strength from my home tree. As long as he thrives, I thrive."

I think about the landscaping work Kyle instigated. For all the pushback I gave him, he's not wrong. We need it.

"Hopefully, that will work for us, too. You should see my backyard. I thought Da was going to shit bricks when he came home last night. He's been good about the whole thing, though...considering."

"Considering?"

I shrug and straighten the spines of some new arrivals. "Considering I became a druid against his wishes, got my four brothers caught up in it, am taking over the backyard, have a grizzly bear living in the house, and generally smashed to bits any sense of normalcy and order he established over the past forty years."

"Is that all?" Myra chuckles as she finishes with the order and writes up the bill. Then she copies the titles into her ledger for regular customers. "Did your father find out anything more about Barghest?"

"Nothing yet that I know of. Between work, Brendan's death, and worrying about our safety, he's spread thin." I notice a few books tilted and head over to the shelf to straighten them. My promise to the boys to watch how much Da's drinking resurfaces. I need to pay better attention and pull him back from the brink a bit if it comes to that. "He's not himself."

"I know the pain of losing a son." Myra closes the ledger. "It's not something that ever truly eases. Your father may never be the same man you knew before. In my experience, the only thing that fills the gaping loss of a loved one is adding more love."

"Well, we've got lots of that."

The computer *bings* a little notification, and Myra writes down the name of the book someone ordered. "This is up on the third floor over the reading section. Will you fetch it down for me?"

I take the slip of paper and read the digits.

"While you're up there, maybe look through the books on ley lines and see if there are any you'd like to flip through. That might help with building your power source."

"Great idea." I walk through the entranceway in the sidewall and climb the black, circular metal steps that coil up to the third floor. "Do you know how ley lines form?"

"No," Myra calls back. "Good thing this is a bookstore. Maybe you can find out."

Har-har.

After fetching Myra the book she needs to fill her order, I find four books on ley lines that look interesting. I pull them and settle in on one of the leather sofas under her home tree. The whole concept of Mother Earth's chakras is fascinating. Still, I don't see them helping me here in Toronto.

"Fiona, can you come up to the cash, please? I have someone I'd like you to meet."

I stack the books and leave them there to come back to. When I get up, I place my hand on the trunk bark of Myra's home ash tree and thank him for our time together. He's old, wise, and completely devoted to Myra.

He's also worried about her.

"Coming."

Hustling through the store, I hear the deep, husky voice of a visitor and find Myra chatting with a woman in fuchsia leopard-print pants and heels. The newcomer towers over me and, compared to Aiden, who is six-foot-two and the tallest one of us, she beats him by a couple of inches of purple hair.

When she turns, I recognize her from the billboard posters outside a drag club down on Queen East. The club isn't far from where we live in Cabbagetown, and I pass by it nearly every day. "I recognize you from Queens on Queen."

"Pan Dora." She flicks a swath of violet curls behind her broad shoulder and extends a manicured hand. "Nice to meet you, baby."

"Nice to meet you, too. One of my brothers' ex-girlfriend went to your Merry Queens and Scots event last year. She said it was outrageous and so much fun."

She beams and squeezes my fingers. "Glad to hear it. We aim to please."

Myra folds her hands together and leans on the counter. "Dora agreed to discuss taking you and your brothers on as inking clients. She's the most talented artist I know and has the magical experience to imbue your spells with druid energy. The question is, what do you offer her?"

The fact that she's still holding my fingers is a little awkward, but I go with it. "I don't know. We're very new to the workings of the fae realm. Do we pay you or do you take payment in trade? If I should know this, I apologize. I'm sorta flying blind here."

"I suppose you are," Dora agrees. "I was quite surprised when Myra said we have a family of start-up druids in the city. Breaking the mold, are you?"

"Trying to." I scratch at the tingle on my forehead. "My

Granda doesn't hold out much hope for success, but I don't agree. I think the city can be as powerful as any rural Eden. I have to figure out what will work for us and tap into it."

"Bravo." Dora steps back and eyes me up and down. First, her gaze is direct as she looks at me. Then, her gaze shifts and she looks through me. When she finishes whatever she's doing, her bright, fuchsia lips part in a smile. "How good are you with a ladle?"

"Excuse me?"

"A ladle. You know, a big scoopy spoon?"

"Right. I know what a ladle is, but how good am I?"

Myra giggles. "Dora and her co-stars run a drop-in soup kitchen in the building next door to the club. I think she's wondering about you volunteering there as payment."

"Oh, sure! That's totally doable. And my brothers are strong, hard-working boys. You can put them to work, too."

Dora tilts her head, and her attention falls to my right arm. A zebra-striped fingernail drags down the sleeve of my t-shirt and stops on my upper bicep where my armband tattoo hides underneath. "May I see it, baby?"

I lift my sleeve. "How'd you know?"

Dora leans closer while eyeing the wyrm dragon encircling my arm. It glitters in the same iridescent blue of the male wyrmlets. When she touches it, I get a surge of energy tingling through my cells.

"You've been favored by a Cyteira."

"Who?"

"The Lady of Wyrms. She can be a snappy bitch at times, but she likes you. What did you do that placed you in such high esteem?"

"I helped her fertilize her eggs."

Dora's brow arches. "Wyrm dragons have hatched and thrive once more?"

"Seventeen had hatched when I left her lair. There were twenty-three eggs in total. I assume they're thriving."

Dora turns me to face Myra and presses her hand flat on my back. "And marked as well? I must admit, I'm shocked. And it's been a great many years since I've been shocked."

"Is that good?"

Dora turns me back, and after another thoughtful study of me, she nods. "Very good. I like you. I will help."

If someone told me three months ago that I'd be stoked to have my drag queen tattoo artist lined up to ink me with Celtic symbols, I would've spat milk through my nose.

Funny how life changes things.

She sensed my armband and my Fianna mark without knowing they were there. I don't know what she is or where her powers stem from, but I don't need Sloan to tell me she has power. Lots of it.

It doesn't feel like the tingle I get from other druids or my nymph boss. It feels more like the energy I sense from Kyle. Considering he's an ancient totem god, I figure Pan Dora has serious juice and likely an ancient existence.

I wait inside the door of the emporium until Calum pulls up. "See you tomorrow." I wave back at Myra.

"Have a good night."

It's after six, and my stomach growls like rolling thunder as I span the concrete between the storefront and the curb. Calum is standing with the driver's door open, leaning over the hood of the car. "You up for Chinese food?"

"I could go for that."

"Good, because you're paying. You owe me, like, twenty-seven grand."

I wince at the edge to his voice, but there's no real heat. He knows the backyard landscaping wasn't my fault, but it *is* my responsibility. "Okay, take it off my tab."

A half-hour later, with two bags of wok-fried bliss in my lap, we're back on the road and heading up Parliament toward Wellesley. Calum hits his indicator to take us home, and a patrol car with its lights on gives us a quick *bloop* of its siren.

When it pulls up beside us, Aiden waves for us to follow.

"What's going on?"

Calum gets out of the turning lane and speeds up to keep pace. "No idea. But if we're following a squad car and Aiden's on duty, I don't imagine it's anything good."

We follow Aiden past the St. James Cemetery and up to the Rosedale Ravine Lands. After a while, he pulls off the beaten path, and we end up with the backs of industrial buildings on our left and forested ravine on our right. The road, if you can call it that, is wide enough for one car easy or two if they edge off to the side to pass. Calum parks behind Aiden, who stopped behind two other cruisers.

Taking in the gathering of cops and the yellow caution tape strung across posts, I agree with Calum's assessment.

This can't be good.

Calum cuts the engine, and we meet Aiden by the hood of the squad car. He doesn't look upset, so that goes a long way in taming the nerves going squirrely in my belly about this being personal.

"Hey." Aiden lays a heavy arm over my shoulder and kisses the top of my head. "Da is calling in the Lady Cumhaill to tell him what he's not seeing. We've got two bodies in the ravine, but he says he's getting that same 'move along' vibe he got outside your bookshop the other day."

I nod to Aiden's partner Dax standing beyond the tape barrier, and we step out of the stream of traffic. "If Da had his powers, he wouldn't be running at a disadvantage."

Aiden shrugs. "Moot point, right now. You have the most

power of all of us and know more about what you're seeing. If Sloan were here, I'd have him *poof* you in to look around, but he's not."

Da crests the embankment of the ravine and joins us while rubbing dirt off the palms of his hands. "Did Aiden fill ye in?"

"Sort of. You think there's spellwork hiding something in the area and you want to know what."

"That's the gist of it." He points back the way he came. "The bodies were found by a man and his dogs, down there. I felt the push of magic over there."

He points farther down the dirt lane we drove in on. "Not in the ravine lands, but on the flat grounds that way. We're looking at a number of warehouses and a lot of private property. I can't justify trespassing that far from the crime scene without cause, and I can't exactly say my druid instincts are telling me I need to look closer."

Calum nods. "So, you want me and Fi to take an unofficial look around?"

"Just Fi. Yer a cop, Calum. Ye can't be part of the trespassin', or we won't be able to pursue it."

I lift my hand to my brow, blocking the glare of the setting sun as I stare down the lane. "But I can snoop and report what I find to the police like a dutiful citizen. Then you have the grounds to take a closer look."

Da nods. "That's what I think."

"I don't like it," Calum says. "That puts Fi in there alone. Do ye forget there are two dead bodies already?"

I'm here, Red. Emmet said ye needed me.

"Not alone," I interject. "Kyle's here." A breeze picks up and swirls around us on an otherwise still day.

"Stay close to her, Bear," Calum directs. "And I'll be close if ye need me. I'll walk as far as I can on public lands and be listening. If I hear a call for help, I'm well within my rights to assist."

"That ye are, son," Da agrees. "On yer toes, Fiona."

CHAPTER TWENTY-SEVEN

Calum walks with me along the narrow lane, and we leave the police teams to their investigations. "Da's right about the presence of magic. Do you feel that?" We're three or four hundred yards from the entry point into the ravine where the police are working, and fae power tingles over my skin.

"The sensation of bugs crawling over my skin? Yeah, I feel it. What is it?"

"It's a spell." We stop at the edge of the lane, and I study the trees. The growth is thick. I can't see more than forty feet in from where we stand. "Kyle, can you take a preliminary sweep into the trees to make sure I'm not walking into something horrible?"

Happy to.

"And buddy?"

Yes.

"No Killer Clawbearer if we can help it, yeah?"

And just like that, ye suck the fun out of our adventure.

I chuckle. "Sorry. Once we're in the trees though, you can take form and scare bad guys stupid if you want."

Calum laughs. "There's a chocolate bar in it for you if you make grown men who think themselves badasses piss their pants.

248

I always love it when perps get hauled in wearing pee pants. It sets a good tone in lockup."

Challenge accepted.

I wink at my brother and start tromping through the scrub, zeroing in on the repelling spell. Working at Myra's bookshop all week, I've stored enough power in my cells to pull off a few magic moves confidently. I call on Feline Finesse and the spell-symbol flares on my back. My steps grow quieter in the under-brush, and my senses heighten.

"This was way more fun in Ireland when I was hunting down Sloan," I say to a chipmunk bounding through the groundcover. I giggle to myself while thinking of the hedgehog quilling his ass.

I enjoy being a pain in his fine ass.

Is Liam right? Is Sloan into me? I honestly didn't see it, but the hostility has transformed into angsty banter. And when we had our water hose fight, he loosened up and laughed more freely than I've ever seen him.

He's kind of fun once you tunnel through his bullshit.

I push that thought out of my mind. What I told Liam is true. I've got a long way to go to become the druid I want to be, and to prove to Granda and the Nine Families that being an urban druid is a viable alternative.

No guys needed for that—except my brothers.

We are Clan Cumhaill, and when we lock onto something, we get 'er done.

I'm a couple of hundred feet from the road when I stop at the outer edge of the warded barrier. With a hand raised in the air in front of me, I test the spell's density. It's more of a fog than a barrier. I read about this. It's called myst.

On the other side of the myst, my beautiful bear sits on his wide, furry haunches. *All clear. I know where we're headed, and yer not going to believe it.*

"And you're not going to tell me?"

Why ruin the surprise? Come on. There's no one here.

The travel is slow since I'm lifting my feet over knee-high grasses and climbing over downed trees and uneven ground.

There's easier access off a private road to the east, and the land at the back rolls straight down to where yer da's men found the bodies.

"Do you think someone killed people up here, then rolled them down the embankment into the ravine?"

That's what I thought, but there are no tracks or blood.

"That could be a simple disguise spell."

I follow Kyle through the thick forested brush. After slogging another ten minutes, he leads me to a wall of dense growth. There's no way this is natural. It feels more like the thick hedge that grows around my grandparent's property.

I call on my connection with nature and ask the hedge to allow me entrance. The leaves and branches split, granting me passage. "Thank you." I rest a hand on the greenery as I step through.

On the other side, I take in the site and my mind fritzes. "Hubba-wha?"

Riiiight? I knew ye'd be surprised.

"Standing stones? I did not see that coming. I was expecting an abandoned shack or warehouse or something."

But that's not at all what we're looking at.

Before us, a two-hundred-foot clearing plays host to a ring of standing stones.

If I'm not mistaken, it's a perfect replica of Drombeg Circle in West Cork.

"What's it doing here?"

I haven't the foggiest.

"Do you think the dead guys were set upon while worshiping and flung down the hill?"

Kyle's massive head swings as he slogs along beside me. *Based on the blood gathered in the urn at the circle's center, I think they were offerings slaughtered on the altar.*

"Seriously?" A chill races from the back of my neck down the vertebrae of my spine. "That's very medieval."

This scene is very medieval. I lived when these rituals were performed regularly back home but haven't seen anything like this in four or five centuries.

I notice he remembers being much older than he told me he was but let that slide. Whether he's coming back into his own or trusting me more, doesn't matter. He's telling me now, and that's good enough.

It's hard to grasp.

Seventeen stones, each reaching about eight feet from the ground, encircle a stone slab with a hole in the center. Beneath the opening sits a wide-rimmed earthenware urn buried in the earth below. "That's where blood would collect from the sacrifice?"

It would.

I stroll around the rugged-cut stones. The closer I get, the more the stanky stench of black magic singes my nostrils. When I complete a full circuit, I pull out my phone to call my father.

"Fi? Are ye all right?"

"Fine. Tell me about the bodies. What are they wearing? Are they both men, women, one of each? Do they seem to be down a few pints?"

"Why do you ask?"

"Because I think I'm standing in the primary murder scene and it looks like a ritual offering of some kind. We found a stone circle a la Stonehenge, and if Kyle's right, it's a replica of Drombeg Circle in West Cork. Does that mean anything to you?"

Da curses on the other end of the line. "It does. Drombeg Circle is also known as the Druid's Altar. It's an iconic and mystically powerful site fer us. Get out of there, Fi. Whatever's going on, it's dangerous and worth killing over."

"Don't panic. I'm fine. There's no one here. I want to take

some pictures and look around a bit more. Don't worry. I'll call Calum to join me. S'all good."

"Except fer ye standin' in the center of a ritual kill site."

"Well, yeah. There's that. What about the bodies?"

"One man. One woman. Both naked and both bled out from their femoral artery."

"That's high in the leg, right? In the thigh?"

"It is."

I eye the stain on the altar slab and the position of the hole over the urn. "That fits with what I see."

"Get Calum, take yer pictures, and get out of there."

"Will do." I end the call with my dad and call Calum. "Yeah, I've got a ritual circle, and I'm pretty sure it ties back to Ireland and druid sacrifice. You're good to join."

"I'm on my way in. How far did you go?"

"In three or four minutes, you'll come to a foggy wall. It's called myst and other than giving you the heebs, it's harmless. Push through that, and I'll send Kyle back to lead you the rest of the way in."

"No. Keep the bear with you. I'll find my way."

I look back the way we came and doubt that very much. "No, you won't. I'm sending him now."

After Kyle flips into his spirit mode and wisps away, I pull my phone's camera. First, I take shots of the stone slab altar. Its surface is scored in measured rows angling toward the hole in the center. Along the outer edge, in line with the draining hole, there are two round depressions about the size of a dollar coin.

The round indents give me the impression that something is missing. Like two circular components get snapped into place for some reason. I imagine a woman's body there and figure it would be where her hands fall.

Maybe they have something to do with restraint?

It's easy to see how the blood flows to the urn instead of off the sides and into the grass. The stone table stands three feet off the ground, and I stand close and raise my phone over it to get some shots down the hole to the urn.

Next, I take shots of the seventeen stones that make up the circle—particularly the two largest stones with ancient Celtic symbols etched in the outer faces.

I select my grandfather's new cell number and Sloan's and make a What's App group. Then, I send the pictures to them for translation. *Got a ritual kill site in town, a dead, nakey couple, and a whack of stanky black magic. What do these symbols say?*

Lastly, I climb the old oak near the north entrance of the circle to take a few shots from above. If there's one thing I learned when climbing the trees in Granda's grove, it's that things look different when you change the perspective.

With Feline Finesse still buzzing in my cells, I scale the tree and step out on a wide branch like a leopard in the wild. Freaking awesome. This will never get old.

From this angle, overlooking the entire circle, and with the sun sinking toward the western horizon, the site holds mysterious magic. Even knowing two people were murdered here, it stirs a level of awe inside me.

A flash of headlights catches my attention as a car swings into the little clearing near the two etched stones. I squat on the branch and tuck myself in behind some foliage, then text Calum. *Hold your position. I've got company.*

I'm coming.

No. I'm good. Stay. Don't scare him off.

Sending Kyle.

As much as I want to be a super druid warrior ready to take on any evil that I come across, knowing that my bear is returning is a relief. Despite what Da thinks, I know I'm not indestructible. My run-in with Baba Yaga and the Queen of Wyrms taught me that.

I'm an itty-bitty minnow in an ocean of sharks.

The sun drops below the horizon and dusk continues to take hold. In another twenty minutes, it'll be dark.

I gauge my power levels and frown. My spell is draining my magical energy. If I end it and get spotted, I don't think I'll have enough juice to manage a defensive shield. If I leave it in place, I'll be out of power in less than ten minutes.

I decide to keep it running. If I get spotted and knocked out of the tree, I'll get seriously hurt. Best not to be seen. If I run out of power once I'm on the ground, I still have the fighting skills and survival instincts bred into me as the daughter of Niall Cumhaill.

I'm here, Red.

Awesome. We've got two men in the car.

Why are they sitting there?

Maybe their favorite song is on the radio. Ghost them and see what they're saying.

I'm an ancient bear spirit, not a ghost. A little respect would be nice.

My bad. Depart, my beloved totem spirit. I beseech you to assess our foes in this moment of danger and adventure.

Yer brothers are right. Yer an ass.

A smartass? Wiseass?

Pain in the ass.

Bear, go!

I'm going. I'm going.

The energy in the air dissipates with his departure, and I focus my gaze on the car. Thank you, Fae Powers, for my bear. He's awesome.

My legs ache, coiled in a crouch so long, but I don't dare move. I'm well-hidden and won't risk being seen. What's a few burning muscles next to catching magical murderers?

Shit—

The world explodes as everything happens at once.

The branch beneath my feet dips and I spin to see a man climbing out after me. A rush of wind morphs into a massive flying bear right behind me. And a dagger flies end over end at my head.

I throw myself backward, arch into the air, and spring clear of the tree. The flash of silver steel narrowly misses my throat as I plummet. I don't have enough power to cast Slow Descent, but my Feline Finesse holds out, so at least I stick the landing.

There's a roar of fury and the scream of a man.

My knee comes down hard on the ground, but I have no time to worry about the pain. I roll away from the tree and into the stone circle.

Calum breaks free from the woods as a clamor of falling bodies ends in a thud to our left. "Kyle's got that one. We're going to lose the others."

The futile *rer-rer-rer* of an engine not turning over has the two men abandoning the car and hoofing it. I smile as Calum and I close the distance. "Well done, Bear."

As we run, I feel as much as hear the thumping gallop of my bear as he catches up...*annnd* passes us. His powerful frame carries his weight, his stride building like a juggernaut on the attack. One of the guys sees him coming and freezes in place. Kyle roars, and Calum and I go after the other.

Chocolate bar for me.

I laugh as I pass. I'd piss my pants too if I were that guy.

Our guy books it down the private drive and rabbits back into civilization. It's dark now, but the streetlights are on, and the moon is bright. Calum and I beat feet like we're freaking track stars and the full-tilt feels good.

We're hot on his trail. He ducks down a side street edged with broken skids, dumpsters, and the metal back stoops of a strip plaza. The reek of black magic is strong in the air. Whether that's from the area or coming off him, I can't tell.

"He's moving too fast to be normal." Calum pulls away from me. He's gaining a few inches with each stride. Man, my brother can run.

I'm twenty or thirty feet behind and losing ground. Neither of them seems to be struggling with the uneven concrete, but I trip once and almost tumble ass over end.

I save my stride, but it costs me time and momentum.

The man drops out of sight after veering between a pair of industrial buildings that sit in full darkness. When Calum disappears around the corner, too, panic allows me to pull an extra burst of speed to try to keep up.

I access my bond with Kyle.

We need backup. We've never tested the distance of our internal communication. I don't know if he'll hear me.

I turn the corner and Calum is closing in on the guy—too quickly. Our rabbit doesn't look hurt. Is he deliberately slowing his pace? Every alarm bell I possess clamors at the same time. It's a trap.

Calum is focused on the chase—too focused.

"Calum, stop!" I can't tell if he hears me or not, but he doesn't slow. His police training has him pushing to take down the bad guy and make the collar.

Except, I'm pretty sure this bad guy is a vampire.

I reach into my pants pocket, grab my peridot, and focus every ounce of energy I have left on the concrete beneath my feet. Driving my fist into the ground, I send off a rippling pulse of earth like Gran did during the attack on the back lawn.

The asphalt tidal wave rolls toward my brother as our bad guy turns and launches. Knocked off balance as the ground beneath his feet heaves, Calum buckles out of the way before the vampire strikes.

The gust of air rushing past me sets my world right again. "Decapitate him, Killer Clawbearer."

With pleasure.

A moment later, the bad guy's head clunks to the ground.

Yay team.

CHAPTER TWENTY-EIGHT

"Da, yes. We're *fine*." I assure my father for the eighth time in the span of a three-minute phone call. "We're back at the stones now. Calum is questioning the one we have in custody and Dillan is on his way. Honestly, Kyle did the dirty work and took the vampire down faster than you could believe."

My bear raises his chin and lets out a throaty grunt before his mouth splits with a smile. *My pleasure.*

That's what scares me.

The Killer Clawbearer is pretty pleased with himself. No matter how badly I don't want to view him as a ruthless killing beast, Bear, the native spirit totem is said to stand as a strict enforcer who punishes with brutal force.

My mind burps up what he told me back in Ireland. *I accept who ye are this minute. Ye needn't put on airs and be what ye aren't.*

He accepted me for who I was, and I haven't returned the favor. If I love him—and I do—I must accept the brutal side of him and realize there are different rules in the magical realm.

Trying to sanitize him to fit my life isn't fair.

Dammit. I hate judgy people who hold their ideals over others. He deserves so much better.

I end the call and cup my hand under his broad chin. "I'm sorry, buddy. I haven't been fair to you. You earned your gritty, brutal names and I had no right to try to change them to fit the way I thought you should be. How about a compromise? Instead of trying to get out Bruinior the Beast, what about Bruin for every day? It's a bear word that is a bit more modern, and there's a hockey team named after it. I could get you a hat."

I've never had a hat.

I look at the size of his furry round head and his velvety, oval ears, and frown. "Or maybe a scarf—"

Can ye call me Killer Clawbearer when I'm allowed to shred bad guys?

"Yes."

And do ye think Bruin is a name that can blend?

"Yes."

And can yer brothers call me Badass Bear if they want to?

I chuckle and nod. "Yes."

A long, pink, ribbon of tongue comes out and swipes up my face. *Thanks, Red.*

I nod. "Sure. Thanks for the save, big guy. I'd hug you, but you're gross, and you reek of black magic."

When yer safe home, I'll go down into the Don River and wash up.

I chuckle. "Yeah, I bet it's a bath that you're interested in down in the Don."

"Hey, Fi." Calum straightens from talking to the guy trapped in one helluva mangled car. Instead of killing the man who froze in place, Bruin forced him inside the vehicle and crumpled the metal around him so he couldn't escape. "Come listen to what Mr. Pee Pants is saying."

I snort at the joy he gets from saying that and remind myself to stop at the convenience store on the way home and buy Bruin an Oh Henry! bar.

A deal is a deal.

When I get to the crushed car-ball, I bend over to see into the pocket where our captive is trapped. Aside from looking pissed and pretzeled, he seems fine. "Hello, in there."

"Tell her what you told me. What's your name?"

"I am Barghest."

I bend down again and frown. This guy has an Eastern European complexion and black hair. "If you're Barghest, who's the red-headed Irishman that I assume is the druid in your little raiding party of criminals?"

"He is Barghest."

Calum chuckles at my expression and points to the trees. "And who's the dead guy the bear mangled in the woods?"

"He was Barghest."

"You're all named Barghest?"

He nods.

"Is this like a weird George Foreman kinda thing or did your leader watch too much Walking Dead?"

"I know, right?"

"Doesn't that make it difficult when your head honcho is doling out duties? Barghest, you kidnap people to sacrifice. Barghest, you pick up the grocery order. Barghest, you recruit more Barghests. Seems confusing to me."

Calum nods. "I'm with you. Is there a number system maybe? Are you Barghest 6?"

"I am Barghest."

I rake my fingers through my hair and sigh at the pressure building behind my eye. All I wanted to do tonight was share some Chinese food with my brother and scald my skin in a hot shower.

We step away from the car and head over to the two biggest stones at the entrance to gain some privacy. "If they all go by Barghest, we've got nothing."

"Pretty much."

"Well, that sucks."

"Yep. And if you like that one, wait for it..." Calum pauses for effect. "What do we do with him? We can't haul him in. With you depleted, we won't get him out of the car without the jaws of life. And we can't let him go."

I press my fingers against my eye. "If I have an aneurysm, tell the paramedics it was pressure under my right eye that blew my brain."

"Will do. Until then, what's our plan?"

I stare off toward where I hid in the tree. "What happened here, anyway? Why'd it go to hell?"

"We tripped a ward when we crossed the myst," Bruin says. "After I disabled the workings of the car, I spirited inside. Barghest and Barghest were talking. A third man, Barghest, I assume, spoke through a villainous black spirit box. He said he'd found ye in a tree and was moving in to eliminate the threat. I didn't want ye dead, Red."

"I appreciate that. I'll try not to die."

"I'd appreciate that."

Calum chuckles. "We all would. Bear, how's your night vision? Can you see in the dark?"

"I can."

"Do you think you could find the villainous black box that the tree Barghest used to communicate with the two in the car? They come in pairs, so Fi's tree attacker had one too. If it's a two-way radio, maybe we have something after all."

"And it's safe to approach?"

"I promise." I cross my heart with my finger. "It's a device similar to our cellphones."

"Very well. I trust you."

Bruin waddles off, and I remember the guy still lying dead in the woods. "We need to find a paranormal cleaner to hire to dispose of bodies."

Calum arches a brow. "Okay, John Wick, settle yourself down. How many dead bodies are you expecting that you think we need to have a guy on speed dial?"

I shrug. "All right, what do you suggest?"

He looks around and frowns. "I say we get out of here. The head honcho will realize his men never came back from the perimeter alarm and he'll send another team. They can find the guy in the car and the mulched man in the woods. Let them deal with it."

My feet ache, and I step closer to lean against one of the etched stones. I point at the car as I take a load off. "We can't just let him—"

A jolt of power shoots up my arm like a rocket, and I'm thrown into the air. Distantly, I hear Calum hollering and wonder what's going on. I am weightless, flying backward like a bug flicked off a giant's arm.

I assplant hard in the scrub and come to a violent stop when I hit the trunk of a tree, twenty feet away. My breath exits my lungs in a rush and leaves me gasping.

I lay on my back, my throat pulling aimlessly for oxygen.

"Fi. Shit, Fi, look at me." Calum kneels over me, and I try to give him a sign that I'm only down, not out.

I have nothing.

As suddenly as the power surge hit me and knocked me on my ass, another hits and I can breathe again. I blink, but it's not Calum kneeling over me now, it's the ruddy face of a blond, weathered warrior.

The ends of his braids brush my shoulder as he bows over me and smiles. Then he clasps my wrist and pulls me to my feet with an ease that speaks of his muscled strength. "Fiona Cumhaill, blood of my blood, be not afraid."

His Irish is laden with a heavy accent, the consonants and vowels clashing together with an ancient rhythm.

Blood of my blood? I glance around, and we're standing among the same seventeen stones erected in a circle where I was a moment ago, but also not.

Instead of a forested section of the Don Valley River System, we're surrounded by the sage green and beige hills of the magic-infused Emerald Isle. I breathe deep, and the ambient energy of fae power fills my lungs and feeds my cells. It's the first real breath I've taken in weeks.

"Why am I here? Am I here or did I crack my head on the tree when I was knocked on my ass?"

"Yer here, and yer not."

"And who are you?"

He places a scarred hand against the wide leather belt around his middle and bows. His thick cloak drapes forward with the motion, and I recognize the Fianna crest on the two bronze shoulder brooches.

"I am Fionn mac Cumhaill, yer great-granda of sorts if ye trace it far enough back."

Hubba-wha? Okay, that's trippy.

"Why am I here?"

"The two of us are sharing an *airneal.*"

"No offense, but I was in the middle of a bit of a sitch. I'm sure my brother's freaking out right about now. I don't have time for an evening of storytelling by the fire."

He ignores me and gestures to the center of the standing stones. In this version, instead of a sacrificial altar in the center, there's a fire burning and building strength.

When I sit on a chopped-off wooden stump, he sits on another opposite me and stokes the coals with a stick. After he's satisfied with the flames, he slides a flat pan of fish into the fire to cook. "Time works differently in the spirit plane, Fiona. When I send ye back, it'll be the same moment that brought ye here. Fear not."

I swallow. The scent of the fish sizzling on the pan makes my mouth water. "All right, so, an *airneal.* What story do you have to tell me?"

He straightens and eyes me up. "Are ye always this anxious? In my days, people were content to sit and chat with old friends and new ones. It seems ye might learn a few things from the old ways."

My stomach lets out a tortured roar and I slap a hand against my belly. "Sorry. It's been a day." I shake out my hands and tilt my neck back and forth. The *pop-pop* of my vertebrae cracking lets off some of the tension I'm carrying.

I draw a deep breath and try to sink into the moment. I'm sitting at the fire with an ancestor from over thirteen hundred years ago. "I apologize. And to answer your question, no, I haven't always been this anxious. A lot has happened over the past three months."

He grips the pan's handle and adjusts the fish in the fire. "Yer druid blood awoke when yer mark flared."

"You know about that?"

He chuckles. "I know everything about it, my fair Fiona. That's why yer here."

I straighten as my pulse kicks into high gear. He knows everything. Oh, thank you, baby Groot. "Tell me," I demand a little more aggressively than I meant to. "Tell me everything."

"Well, the tale begins at the turn of the seventh century. My sire was Cumhaill mac Trenmhoir, of the tribe of Ui Thairsig. My mother was a beautiful maiden by the name Muirne Muinchaem. She was the granddaughter of the high king and his wife, a deity of the Tuatha De Danann."

Seriously? "We have the blood of the Tuatha De Danann running in our veins?"

"That is correct."

"What are we talking about? Greater fae? Leprechaun? Dragons?"

"Mother told me Gran was a goddess of the fair ones."

I scratch my forehead, still not a hundy percent sure I'm not lying knocked out with my brother kneeling over me.

Fionn pauses, and I get the feeling he senses my mental spin. "Mother possessed a strong will and unshakable passion. To her parents' horror, she fell in love without consent. Cumhaill asked for her hand but was devastated when denied."

"You're here, and I'm here, so I guess it worked out in the end, eh?"

"In a fashion." He pulls the pan from the fire and sets it on a rock to cool. "Deciding they were destined, he kidnapped her, and they lived happily for a short time. Until her sire petitioned the high king, had Cumhaill outlawed, then killed."

"That's terrible. I'm sorry."

Fionn bows his head. "When her sire took Mother home, he found her to be with child and ordered her burned alive."

"Oh! This guy was a piece of work."

"The high king wouldn't allow it. He said revenge was served with my father's life taken. He could not have the life of his daughter and by extension, me. Mother was placed into the custody of Cumhaill's sister, Bodhmall. My auntie was the youngest of six with five brothers before her, like you. She was a great and practiced druidess, and that is where I learned my skills."

He uses his dagger to cut the cooked fish and places half on a broad, waxy leaf, then reaches forward and passes me my share. "I lived as the bastard child of an outlaw for a great many years, but in the end, I was given a chance to prove myself. You see, there was a fire-breathing man of the Tuatha De, who wreaked destruction on the lands each year during the Samhain festival. No one wanted to face the beast, so I volunteered."

I pull at the fish on my leaf with my fingers and pop it into my mouth. It's salmon, and it's hot and oily, but also very good.

"At the time, I was a young servant of the king, and few thought I could succeed. The high king, however, wanted the destruction ended. He awarded me an enchanted spear named Birga."

"Did you win?"

He chews his fish and dips his chin. "When I defeated the fire-breathing foe, the king recognized my heritage and gave me command of the Fianna. Once I grew to be feared and respected, I returned to my maternal grandsire and demanded compensation. I was awarded the estate of Almu, the present-day Hill of Allen, in County Kildare."

"I've only been to Ireland once, so I'm afraid I don't know much of the landscape. Is Kildare near Kerry?"

"Kildare is a slogging, ten-day ride from Kerry on a good steed. I ask that ye rally yer brothers and set off to my land. The site has been raped and quarried to great depths and breadth. The destruction guts the hill but has not yet impacted the underground fortress of the Fianna. Go there, Fiona. Take yer brothers and claim yer heritage."

The mere thought of the fortress of the Fianna has images popping into my head unbidden. I picture the layout of the caves, the coordinates of the entrance, and where the weapons keep lies within.

"How is this happening?" I ask as the bombardment continues. "How do I know all these facts about your fortress?"

He smiles and holds up his last bite of salmon. Licking the oil off his fingers, he swallows it down. "If ye ever find yerself at a loss fer answers, go fishin' in the River Slate. It flows through Ballyteague and is home to a fish of knowledge that only a druid can catch. There's a secret to catchin' the Salmon of Wisdom, though, and I never whispered it to another soul. Always cast yer line from the Ballyteague side of the river. Once ye eat of its meat, the answers ye seek will come to you."

I can't believe all the information flooding into my mind. It's like I'm a living Google search of the Fianna and the life of Fionn and his descendants. "How long does it last?"

"As long as it takes to pass through yer system. Yer best to write things down that come to ye because once it's gone, ye won't remember it fer the life of tryin'."

"Thank you." I reach down to my feet and wipe my fingers on the grass. "Will I see you again?"

"If the Fae Powers smile upon us, perhaps. In the meantime, if ye save my treasures from ruin or discovery, I'll be in yer debt. They are more than our things—they are our brothers, and we owe them a debt of loyalty. Prove to me that yer every bit the woman yer auntie Bodhmall was, Fiona. Take the gifts I awoke in ye and do great things in the name of the Fianna."

"I'll try my best."

I blink, and I'm lying on my back with Calum's panicked face hovering over me and the moonlit night sky playing the backdrop of my view. "I'm okay." I grip his elbow as he pulls me up. "You'll never believe what happened."

CHAPTER TWENTY-NINE

I sit at the kitchen table, writing down as much information as I can sort through. It quickly becomes apparent that the magic fish wisdom isn't all-powerful. It doesn't tell me who is the power man behind Barghest or who the next winners of the Superbowl will be. It's specific to the topic Fionn gave me for my quest.

The Fianna fortress.

Calum and I pick up Kevin on the way home, and he helps me draw the floor plan of the underground fortress and where to find the entrance.

I write down the spells I need to trigger the hill to open and disengage the booby-traps set inside.

"Fi," Da pushes a plate of heated-up food toward me. "Take ten minutes and eat. Yer looking awfully pale. Ye can't keep pushin' yerself without refuelin' the tank."

I take a scoop of chicken fried rice and chew as I keep writing.

Emmet comes in and frowns. "You're still at it?"

Calum snaps a fortune cookie in two. "Yep. I feel like we're stuck in a scene from Rain Man."

"Three minutes to Wapner."

"Wednesday is fish sticks. Green lime Jell-O for dessert."

"Eighty-two. Eighty-two. Eighty-two."

I take another stab at my dinner and give them a middle-finger salute. "You two are hilarious."

My brothers yuck it up.

I look at the spells spilling onto the page, the list of herbs for the potions needed, and the instructions to find the hidden keep. "Okay, I might be channeling a little Rain Man."

Aiden came over after he tucked the kids in bed. He's sitting on the kitchen counter having a plate of food. "Can we rewind a bit? Could one of the Nine Families be behind the stones and the sacrifice?"

Da shrugs. "Anything is possible, but I can't imagine it."

"The Nine Families are made up of a bunch of purists. I can't see any of them venturing this far from Ireland."

"Hot off the presses." Dillan jogs down the stairs like a stampeding elephant. He brings in a stack of eight-by-ten glossies and spreads them on the other end of the table. "Take a gander at these beauties."

"What the hell?" Kevin stares at a picture of the blood-stained altar stone. "Where were you two tonight?"

We all glare at Dillan who realizes too late he's muddied the waters for Calum. "Sorry. Crime scene stuff. I'll take these in the living room."

He starts to gather them, and Calum backhands him in the arm. "He's seen them now, you dolt. You might as well leave them where they are."

"What's going on?" Kevin leans back in his chair. "Calum's been weird for weeks, Fi's on some kind of Tomb Raider high, and now you've got pictures of bloody Stonehenge and a car that looks like the Hulk crumpled it like a tinfoil ball. Will someone let me in on the secret?"

Calum flashes Da a pleading look but gets a head shake in return. "I'm sorry, son. It's police business. Yer gonna have to trust us. The less you know, the safer ye are. There's trouble brewin', and we don't want ye caught up in it, do we Calum?"

Calum stares at the pictures and bites his lip for a long while before he lifts his gaze. "No. Of course not. I shouldn't have dragged you in this far, Kev. I'm sorry."

Something heated passes between the two of them, and a moment later, Kevin rises, rips the pages we were working on out of his book, and takes his leave.

Calum curses and follows him out.

"Why can't he know, Da?" Emmet pushes. "Liam and Auntie Shannon know."

"Let's see where we are once we get a handle on the Barghest and we'll revisit. We don't know enough about any of it yet. Study these shots and see what we're missing."

I'm lying awake on my bed when I hear Calum creep upstairs shortly after two. "Hey," I call when he passes my door. "You get things sorted with Kevin?"

"He's mad. He thinks I'm lying and keeping things about my life from him."

"He's a perceptive guy."

"Yeah. Lucky me."

I roll onto my side and prop my head on my hand. "There's nothing that says you can't tell him and brave Da's annoyance. You're a grown man."

"I get that, but it's not only my story to tell. If the others want it kept quiet and aren't telling the people in their lives, why should I get to break the silence?"

I flop back down onto my pillow. "Well, if it comes down to the wire, you have my consent to tell him whatever you want."

"Thanks, Fi. Get some sleep."

"Night." I track the sound of his shuffling feet down the hall and sigh. "We need to figure this out and clean it up so we can get back to normal around here."

Bruin lets out a throaty noise, which I assume is a laugh. *And what does normal look like around here?*

"Yeah, well, there's that. Good point. Night, Bruin."

"Good night, Red."

By eleven the next morning, I've gotten everyone off to work except Emmet who's on afternoons this week. The two of us water the trees and gardens in the back, feed the koi and work on a couple of low-level spells. I read over my notes from last night's brain-dump and can't believe it all came from me.

"Fionn was right." I wipe down the kitchen table while Emmet unloads the dishwasher. "Once the salmon was digested, the power of knowledge was gone."

"The next time you're in Ireland, you'll have to plan a fishing trip. Can you freeze magic fish for when you need it?"

I snort. "No idea. He wanted us all to go. He was specific about us going to reclaim the treasures of the Fianna before they're discovered or destroyed."

"What kind of treasure do you think we're talking? Like, pot-o-gold treasure or gems or what?"

"The Fianna were warriors but also considered outlaws—the Robin Hood and Merry Men of the seventh century. I think maybe relics and ancient objects. He mentioned his enchanted spear named Birga."

Emmet closes the cupboard and frowns. "What are the odds that all five of us put in for vacation days and can go? I'm the new guy on the block. I don't get much say on my schedule yet."

I rinse the dishcloth and hang it over the dividing wall of the sink to dry. "We'll figure something out. Maybe we fly over when you're off rotation and Sloan portals you back. It would save on travel time."

"Did he or Granda respond to the photos you sent them?"

I check the time on my Fitbit. "It's four o'clock there. Let's see if we can talk to them before they sit down to dinner." I take out my phone and send a text. A moment later, I get the ping of response. "Zoom call."

Emmet snorts. "They go from a party line to a cell phone to Zoom? The grands are on fire!"

The two of us are jogging up the stairs laughing when I hear the prompt to connect. I sit down in my desk chair and join the meeting room. "Hey, Granda, good to see you."

Emmet sits on the end of my bed, and I shift so he's in the frame. "Hello, Granda. I'm Emmet."

"It's good to put a face to the name, son. Howeyah."

While the two of them have a quick chat, I search the background of his office. "Is Sloan with you?"

"He's not. Why? Do ye need him?"

"No, I just thought... You know..."

"Know what?"

"Well, you're Zooming on your laptop. I thought he might be there helping you."

"What, ye think me a Luddite? With our electricity restored and my energy stabilized, I'm as modern as the next."

I snort. "Somehow, I doubt that."

"Fiona met Fionn mac Cumhaill last night." Emmet steals my thunder. "He transported her through the Druid's Altar to have an *airneal* in ancient Ireland."

I throw him the stink eye. "Blurt much?"

He scrunches his nose in a funny face. "Sorry. I got excited. Go on. You tell him."

I fill Granda in on what happened and what Fionn told me about the mining of the estate of Almu, and how the present-day owners of the Hill of Allen are about to destroy the fortress of the Fianna.

"He needs us to reclaim the treasures."

Granda's face pinches in that scowl he makes when I've become too much for his head. "*Mo chroi*, yer the only one who could tell me such a tale and have me believe it. It's like the god of chaos himself kisses ye daily."

"Right?" Emmet agrees. "We noticed that, too. She's always been more trouble than she's worth."

I roll my eyes at both of them. "Anyway, you can expect an influx of Clan Cumhaill as soon as we can arrange it."

"Och, my heart." Gran comes into view. "Tell me yer not coddin' us. All of ye? We'll all be together?"

"That's the plan, Gran." Emmet waves. "And I, for one, am stoked. Can't wait to meet you both in person. Fi has only the nicest things to say about her time there."

Gran fills to bursting with a look of pride.

Such a charmer, my Emmet.

"I'll get to work right away figurin' where to put ye all."

"Don't panic, Gran. The boys are fine on the floor with a foam pad beneath them. Seriously, don't put yourself out."

My plea falls on deaf ears as I knew it would.

"Och, settle yerself Lara. If they don't come fer months ye'll be in quite a state by then. It'll be grand, ye'll see."

"It will," I say. "Granda, can we get back to the inscriptions? Were you and Sloan able to decipher what they say?"

"We think so. What they say versus what they mean is the worry. The wording is simple enough. The one on the left reads, 'While these stones bask in sun, trees will grow, and water will run.'"

"Oh, okay, that's not bad. And the one on the right?"

"It says, 'Marked by the past, ordained the exalter, magic released by death on the altar.'"

Emmet's smile turns to a scowl as he pulls out his phone.

"Exalter means one who is raised in rank, power, or character. Shit, Fi, I don't like the sound of that death on the altar part."

I see the worry in my grandparent's expressions and swallow the burn of bile rising in the back of my throat. Marked by the past—check. Ordained the exalter—check.

"Yeah, I'm not too keen on that part either. That sucks."

I excuse myself for a moment and splash cold water on my face. Staring at myself in the mirror, I go over the words again. Maybe there is more than one interpretation of one of the symbols. That happens, right?

In the eighth grade, I went on a school trip to the Royal Ontario Museum when they featured Egyptian tablets. I remember our guide saying that often Egyptian symbols have more than one meaning. The ankh was the symbol for life, but it also meant heaven, male and female, the morning sun and the earth.

"Maybe the same can be said for ancient druid symbols. Maybe I'm not prophesized to be gutted on the altar to be drained of my powers."

I pat my face dry and draw a steadying breath. That has to be it. Granda and Sloan goofed on the translation and missed a secondary meaning of one or more symbols. Druid magic is pure, nature power.

Blood magic is black magic. Not the same at all.

Convinced I can table the panic for the time being, I go back to ask Granda to check out other possible meanings.

Emmet is in his glory talking to Gran about coming to visit, so I leave them and go down to the kitchen to pull out the leftovers from last night's Chinese food.

"You hungry, Bear?"

"No. Could do with a drink, though. Is it dry in here? My throat is scratchy."

I laugh. "No. It's not dry in here, and I told you that we don't drink in this house until noon or after. And until Da's feeling more himself, we'll be cutting back after noon too."

I feel his power tingle over my skin and straighten. "What are you doing?"

"Nothing." His eyes are wide with innocence. "But, I think if you check the clocks, you'll see it's past noon, and I should be allowed to have some ale."

I look at the wall clock, then the timer on the stove and microwave, and my Fitbit. All of them say five minutes after twelve. "You think I'm falling for that?"

The doorbell rings and I close the fridge door and head out to the hall. "Put them back. We have a lot of schedules to keep in this house. You can't mess with the clocks to get your way."

I'm still laughing about that when I open the door to... nobody. *Huh.* Thinking we might have an Amazon delivery, I step out on the porch to see if a package has been left behind.

With my gaze down, I miss the man who portals onto the porch until he grabs me around the shoulders. "Hey! Get off me—"

My house disappears.

In the flash of a moment, I'm standing within the seventeen stones of the Druid's Altar, surrounded by men in hooded cloaks. They each stand with their arms raised to prevent my escape and an assortment of sharp and pointy weapons gripped in their fingers.

Shit. "Boys, you should've told me there's a dress code. You stay here, and I'll pop home and grab a robe. Nothing worse than being underdressed at a party, amirite?"

The man who grabbed me pulls back the hood of his cloak, and I'm staring into the eyes of my old friend, Skull Trim. "Barghest, I presume."

He lifts his palms, and I bend at my knees, readying for the attack.

CHAPTER THIRTY

"Be at ease, Fiona Cumhaill. We are honored ye chose to join us and do yer part to fulfill the prophecy of the Druid Altar. There need not be more bloodshed here than necessary."

I assess the group. There have to be almost thirty men, most of them armed, all of them dangerous. "Chose? I think you're using that word with a great deal of poetic license."

"But it *is* yer choice."

I know there's a trick to this somehow, but I play along. "*Okaaay*, then I choose to leave."

"That's yer option, of course, but I think ye should wait until I've shown ye what yer choosin' between. Gentlemen, show her what I mean."

He turns sideways and the sea of men in black cloaks parts. At the east end of the circle, four men step out from behind the stone pillars. When they step into view and emerge fully, I see that they're pulling—

"Let them go!"

Skull Trim flicks his hand and my father, Aiden, Calum, and Dillan are all forced to their knees. Da's head flops to the side as he's shoved down to kneel. The boys look drugged too, their eyes glassy and unfocused.

If it's another run of vampire sedation, I'll never be able to save them all. "What have you done to them?"

"Remember that wee something that makes my guests a little friendlier? I told you about it before."

"And I told you friends don't roofie friends."

He chuckles. "Ye proved ye have no interest in bein' my friend when ye killed my men and burned down my building."

"We set fire to your vampire's corpse. If the fire spread, that's on you for having poor safety measures in your evil lair workplace."

"How did you end them, anyway? I came back from answering to my master and couldn't believe the havoc ye wreaked. Ye cost me quite a bit of money and a fair bit of respect in the eyes of my higher-ups. Ensorcelled vampires aren't easy to come by. I had two. Now I have none."

"My da always says, 'Ye never bet what ye aren't willing to lose.'"

He frowns. "It's not only them you killed. There were two others in the bookshop and two others here."

"There's a fix for that. Stop sending men to kill me, and I'll stop ending them."

"But *how* did you end them when you don't have the power? My master and I both find that interesting."

"Maybe you and your master underestimate me. Maybe I got lucky. Or maybe there's something inside me that longs to get out and slaughter douchebags like you. Ask your master to join us, and I'll tell him. No offense, but I'd rather deal with the head honcho than his minions."

He chuckles. "I assure you I'm a very well-established minion. My master trusts my judgment."

"But, should you trust his? I mean, naming you all Barghest?

Lame. And what kinda cult is this guy running if a little girl who just became a druid is piling up a body count?"

His eyes narrow and he nods to the man holding Aiden. The blade of his dagger glints in the sunlight and buries into my brother's stomach.

Aiden doubles over and thuds to the ground.

I launch forward, caught by the bruising grip of two men. They yank me back and root me in place. "You fucking psycho! Leave them alone."

Skull Trim smiles. "I too can pile up a body count, Fiona. You need to understand who's in charge here. I watched ye long enough to know that yer family is yer weakness."

"Says the man who surrounds himself with Friar Tuck wannabes." I pull at the holds on my arms, and when Skull Trim nods, they let me go and step back.

Red, I'm here.

Hearing Bruin's voice in my head sparks hope that maybe not all is lost. *Stay hidden. We can't get through all of them in time to save everyone. We have to play it out.*

Fingers snap in front of my face, and Skull Trim eyes me more closely. "Where did you go?"

I smile and feign more confidence than I possess. "Remember when I mentioned that beast inside me that longs to get out and slaughter you all? Well, he's anxious to get the bloodshed started. I told him to hold on and maybe not everyone here has to die."

The pinched brows and skirting gazes among the minions is exactly the response I'm hoping for. Some of these men don't want to die for the cause. That works in my favor.

"You're lying."

I shrug. "Like you said. How does a little thing like me kill not one but two of your vampire servants?"

His jaw flexes as he glances at the four men holding my family hostage. "If anything happens, kill them."

I was ready for the threat, but even so, it hits me like a physical kick to my insides. "What exactly are we doing here? What does your boss want?"

"Nothing he hasn't earned. Being a druid in his domain was a mistake on your part. You people have Ireland. You overstepped when you thought you could start up here."

Rustling in the old oak has me reaching out with my senses. A red-tailed hawk senses our connection and is curious about what's going on.

I send him reassurances and try to explain. Thanks to my fireside chat with Fionn last night, my druid stores are replenished, and I'm not nearly as helpless as they think I am.

I'm worried about Aiden. He hasn't moved since he collapsed to the ground. I need to speed this dog-and-pony show up. I point at my father and three brothers propped on their knees with daggers poised to strike. "I assume that if I let you kill me on the altar, you agree to let my family go. Then you plan to stab me and bleed me out for the prophesized 'release of power.' Have I got the gist?"

"You have."

"And when I'm dead, you kill my family anyway so no druids can rise in Toronto. Am I close?"

He frowns at me.

"You didn't think I'd figure that out? Have you ever watched TV? That's the climactic scene of every action movie or show evah. Your originality underwhelms me."

"You need to stop talking."

"You're not the first person to tell me that. Honestly, I doubt you'll be the last." I glance over at the blood-stained stone altar and amend that. "Or maybe you will."

Skull Trim growls and points to the altar. "Strip her and put her in place."

They start to grab my clothes, and I pull back. "Nowhere in the prophecy does it say I'm naked. If you want my cooperation, my clothes stay on. If you want to be mulched by my beloved Killer, keep it up."

Skull Trim rubs a rough hand over his face and throws up his hands. "I don't care what the fuck you do. Just get her up on that slab so I can end this."

I take a certain level of pride in the fact that my tormentor isn't enjoying his moment of torment.

Serves the bastard right.

Rough hands grope my hips and brush my boobs as they hoist me onto the slab. The stone is cool and coarse where it touches exposed skin. I was hanging at home in shorts and a tank, so there's plenty of that.

Skull Trim grabs something from the ground behind the slab and rises at my feet holding an ancient spear. It sings to me somehow, and I stare at the pointed tip.

The high king, however, wanted the destruction ended. He awarded me an enchanted spear named Birga.

Fionn's words sing in my head, and I wonder if he's here somehow, giving me a sign. Then, I hear Sloan's voice from Myra's shop when we copied his spellbook.

"Like all things in nature, they have a life and magic of their own. They have awareness and desires."

"Hello, Birga." I focus on the spear. "I am Fiona Cumhaill of the Clan Cumhaill. How did you end up so far from home?"

The men look at me like I've grown another head.

"What? Talking to an incredible weapon isn't crazy. An ancestor of mine said recently, 'They are more than our things—they are our brothers, and we owe them a debt of loyalty.'"

I wonder if that debt goes both ways.

Before I can figure that out, the men holding me press my hands to the slab at my sides. I pull back with a hiss.

There are now metal plates with brass spikes along the outer edge, where I noticed those two round depressions.

"Nail her down," Skull Trim orders.

"Gross. How many hands have you impaled on these?"

"They are cleaned between each sacrifice to ensure there is no energy transfer between conduits."

Conduits? He talks about the people found at the bottom of the hill like they weren't people, like they were merely a means to an end in his hunt for more power.

His guys fight with my wrists and try to pry open my fingers. "Screw you," I growl while fighting back as hard.

"It's in your best interest that they're there, Fiona. The potion they're soaked in will sedate you for the bloodletting."

Awesomesauce. "What exactly do you get out of killing me? What does 'magic released' mean? And if it's released, what makes you think it'll be of any benefit to you?"

"Not me," he disagrees. "Barghest acts for the benefit of all magicals within the city."

I stare down the side of my body and take another look at those spikes. They are longer and sharper than I first thought. Well, at least they seem to be now that we're talking about spearing my palms on them.

"What if I promise not to move?"

He raises his hand and two more cloaked men on each side of me grab my fists to force my fingers open.

Now? Your heart rate is higher than I've ever felt it.

No. Not yet.

In another two minutes, it might be too late.

I think I have a plan. Don't do anything until I say so.

I cry out in rage as my palms thrust down over the points of the spikes. Wait. It doesn't hurt. I'm not sure if my brain fritzed out or my pain receptors are on the blink but giant brass tacks stabbing me isn't anything I can't handle.

At first.

After a moment, everything changes.

Hot tendrils of magic worm their way into the open flesh of

my hands and my bloodstream. They wriggle up my arms and fill my veins with a fiery burn.

It's the sedative potion.

I close my eyes and find myself drifty. It's an otherworldly sensation, and I get sucked into a swirly fog. After all the tension and drama, it's a relief not to feel the angst and worry that's driven me for months.

My eyes roll back into my head, and I let out a heavy sigh. "Now we're talking."

"Give it a minute to take her over," he directs.

Take me over? Somewhere in the back of my mind, I know I should care more about what's happening to me—but for the life of me, I can't remember why.

Red, ye gotta fight the effects of the sedation. They're plannin' to gut ye.

Right, that's it. They're going to sacrifice me.

Hells no. Shaking my brain loose from the fog, I try to move. My head weighs a million pounds, and I can't lift my limbs. Ow... my tattoo is on fire. Does that mean my shield is burning away the sedation? Man, I wish I knew more about my life.

With nothing to do about my body, I focus on what Sloan taught me about Astral Projecting. It's one of the two disciplines I came up short on during the junior trials, but with the floaty fog in full effect, I'm sure I can get the hang of it.

Skull Trim's voice gives me a focal point, and I send my spirit self beyond the confines of my body.

I'm not sure how it works, but it does.

He's holding out a parchment and reading off his spell for the ritual. It's not a long scroll, so I have to think fast. Rising from the altar, I go straight to Aiden at the furthest stone.

He's curled up in the grass with his fingers clutched against his side. Thankfully, it's not his belly.

Movement outside the ring of stones catches my eye.

Emmet's here with Sloan and Liam. Yesss!

Bruin. Quietly. While everyone's watching the ritual, help the rescue team get Da and the boys to safety.

I get nothing back.

Do I have to be in my body to talk to my bear? Assuming that's the issue, I hightail it back and repeat my instructions.

What about you?

When I know they're safe, I'm free to fight, and you've got carte blanche, Killer Clawbearer.

You say the sweetest things.

Before I open my eyes, I activate Feline Finesse and call on the red-tail hawk. *On my mark, buddy.*

The drum of magic pulsing in my body steps up its tempo. My shield is doing its thing, and I feel like I'm going to puke. At least I recognize this feeling. I open my eyes and listen as Skull Trim finishes his oration.

He hands the scroll to someone, shifts to stand next to me, and grips Birga mid-staff. With her point poised over my middle, he looks into my eyes and thrusts.

CHAPTER THIRTY-ONE

My palms scream as I rip them off the brass spikes and grip Birga with slick hands. Surprise is my biggest advantage, and I utilize it. Me moving catches Skull Trim off guard. The hawk diving straight at his face, talons bared compounds the effect. It's enough of a distraction to swing my legs and kick him in the gut.

He buckles at the waist, and I take full possession of the spear. The moment I grip her properly, I feel the connection.

Hells yeah, she recognizes me.

And through our connection, I feel exactly how excited she is to be in the hands of family once more.

My opposition to lethal force is gone. I understand now that things are different in the fae world. Druids are the police enforcing laws to keep everyone safe from evil madmen hellbent on supreme power. I'm a druid. It's my job.

Nope. Granda would say—it's my duty.

Skull Trim rallies on the ground below me and tangles my feet. I stumble as he rises to his knees. Rolling to brace for impact, I tilt Birga's spearhead into the air between us.

The shock on his face as he launches forward and impales

himself speaks to my point earlier. "You underestimated me, asshole. If you make it a kill or be killed sitch, I'll choose kill. Every. Damn. Time."

The circle explodes into a ring of shouts, the clang of weapons, and bolts of magic shooting through the air like colorful lightning. I watch as Bruin rears up on his hind legs and plows through the Barghest Merry Men.

My distraction costs me. Skull Trim grips the spear's staff with both hands and rocks backward, pulling me off balance. I stumble forward, and he lands a solid kick to my stomach. The power of his attack throws me back against the stone slab of the altar.

The sudden collision of my back against stone forces the air from my lungs in a gust. I gasp and drop to my knees. Heaving for breath, I try to draw oxygen into lead lungs. I cough as pain and panic uncoil.

Movement in my periphery has me diving to the side and log-rolling to avoid being impaled. Birga spears the ground inches behind me once…twice…on Skull Trim's third stabby lunge, he falters, grabs the hole in his belly, and drops.

I roll onto my feet and throw dirt in his face.

Sandstorm.

My spell blinds him long enough for me to stagger to the side and catch my breath. Doubled over with my hands on my knees, I haul in some air.

A hit comes hard and fast from the side, and I go down again. My shoulder protests the slam into the ground, and I grunt as the side of my face scrapes the grass. My vision fritzes in and out, but I don't have time to think about it.

I flip to my back and meet his assault.

It's instinct more than intellect that has me grappling with the cloaked goon's wrists. We're rolling and fighting, and I'm focused on securing my blood-slick hold.

The blade of his dagger glints in the midday sun and I curse.

He's super committed to sticking it into me, and my arms are burning with fatigue.

Gawd, I wish I could time out and wipe my hands.

My fingers are so wet I can't get a grip. I lose my hold entirely and turn my head as the dagger arcs down at me. It catches the meat of my shoulder, and I screech.

My temper flares and I lunge, teeth bared.

No, this isn't a vampire fight, but the blood-sucker routing backs my goon off quick. He recoils and clasps his hands over his bleeding neck. "You should really get that looked at."

I grip the dagger sticking out of my shoulder and yank. Nothing. Fine. Stay there.

A solid grab and twist to his crotch give me enough distance to roll to my feet and find Birga in Skull Trim's limp grasp. I check his eyes before I get too close, and they're vacant and dim.

I can't say I feel bad about that.

Maybe the others will see their fearless leader dead in the grass and bug out. That's probably wishful thinking.

Before the next goon comes at me, I grab the spear and ready myself. My left arm is sloppy, but other than that and my hands being punctured and bleeding, and my muscles quivering like I'm about to collapse, I'm in top form.

I duck a fireball and startle when someone bumps my back. It's Sloan, and he's taking on three.

When I turn to block a parry, he gives me a critical once-over. "Ye look like *shite*, Cumhaill. Can't leave ye alone fer a second. Lugh said ye needed savin' again."

I snort while struggling to work Birga in my injured hands to learn her balance changes. She's a magnificent weapon, and I see why Fionn loved her.

"Me?" I strike away the guard of an attacker and wince as my arm lights up. I stagger to the side and stab forward, burying the spear tip into his thigh. "The last time I saw you, I was the one who did the saving."

"One time." He thrusts a palm out and knocks another man flying. "Should we start keeping track?"

"Hells yeah."

"Speakin' of keepin' things. Are ye keepin' that pig poker in yer arm as a souvenir?"

I glance at the hilt sticking out of my shoulder. "It's an unconventional accessory choice, but I think I pull it off."

Sloan rolls his eyes.

I sense the moment his magic tingles over my skin and try again to pull the dagger out. This time, it slides out like a hot knife through butter.

"Better?"

I throw the blade at the next opponent and bury it in his thigh. I was aiming for his chest, but I'm quickly running out of steam. "I had it under control."

"Of course, ye did."

"Come on, Birga. Let's shed some blood." Her energy surges beneath my tingling palms and I smile as her magic takes hold. The wounds on my hands close, my shoulder stops burning, and my muscles feel like they've been given a high-octane refuel for a second wind. "Um, wow. Fionn said you were a special girl. Thanks."

Bruin rears up on his back feet and lets out a thunderous roar. He shows his massive fangs, his maw dripping with blood. "Okay, I may have peed my pants a little."

Sloan laughs. "I won't hold it against ye. Yer wee man there is wicked fierce."

The Killer Clawbearer show sends the last of the Barghest men scrambling and hobbling away. When the rings are clear of opponents, we take a moment to catch our breath. Da always said fights end quickly. Thank goodness for that. I need to get in shape.

The moment everything quiets down, I pull my phone out of the pocket and call up our family What's App group.

All is well here. How are Aiden and the others?

Emmet responds. *Recovering. Nothing major hit. Meet you at home once they're done bandaging him up.*

Liam responds. *Are you sure you're okay? I wanted to stay, but Sloan said I'd be more useful helping Emmet.*

We're fine. Thank you for taking care of them.

That taken care of, I draw a deep breath and look back at the carnage. "I get that this place is spelled so that only preternaturals can find it, but we can't leave things like this. It'll stink. I told Calum we need a cleaner to remove bodies."

Sloan's head tilts, and he looks up at me through hooded eyes. "Cumhaill, will ye ever start thinkin' like a druid? It's as simple as a summoning spell."

There have to be almost twenty dead guys. "What are we supposed to summon to eat all these bodies? We don't have many lions roaming wild in the Don Valley."

Sloan shakes his head and raises his hands.

"Springtails, earthworms, snails, and slugs,
Millipedes, mites, beetles, and bugs,
Decomposers feast and flourish,
Soil and bodies fully nourish,
Rise from the ground in heaving swarm,
Consume the fallen, life reform."

What starts as a low rumble in the distance soon becomes a thundering racket. Bruin and I watch from behind Sloan as his massive army of creepy crawling creatures come to consume the dead. The ground heaves and rolls with a sea of squirming bodies.

"That's disgusting."

He rolls his eyes at me. "Yer a druid. Ye can't only make friends with the cute and fuzzy animals of the world. Every creature has its place and its purpose."

In five minutes, the job is done, and the horde recedes. Gone are the last vestiges of men and clothing. Left are the polished bones and abandoned weapons.

Sloan raises his hands once again.

"Bearded vultures, tortoise, deer,
Wolverine, and grizzly bear,
Feast upon the bones of men,
Restore the circle once again."

The creatures of the wild heed his call and fill the inner circle of the standing stones. When Sloan looks at me expectantly, I give in. "Okay, that was pretty spectacular."

His grin makes him ridiculously good looking. It's a good thing he doesn't smile much, or I might rethink my 'no men until I've got my druid-self sorted' decree.

Hey Red, can I join the fun?

I grimace as I look at the animals gathering to consume the bones of those men. The first few crunches make me wince. "Sure, buddy. Have at it. I'm going to head out and check on Aiden and the others. Meet us at home later, eh?"

Will do. Although, that brown bear looks like she might need an escort back to her den. Don't wait up.

As he lumbers into the ring of the stones, I turn toward the six cars in the parking lot. "Oh, crap. What do we do about those?"

Sloan shrugs. "Well, the Barghest owes you a car, since they killed yer death trap. I say pick one fer yerself, and yer brothers can figure out the others."

"Don't speak ill of the dead. Molly wasn't a death trap." Still, I study the selection, liking the idea. If Fionn was known as the Robin Hood of his time, I won't feel guilty about reaping the bad guy spoils.

My attention zeros in on a steel gray SUV with two charcoal racing stripes that go up the hood and over the roof, all the way to the back. "That one is super sexy."

I move closer, cupping my hand against the window to look inside. "Leather interior...ooh, it's niiiice. And it looks brand new." I spread my arms and hug the car. "Pikachu, I choose you."

It's not locked. Then again, why lock a car when it's in a parking lot protected by magic, and you're here with all your demented assassin buddies?

"Yep, this will do nicely." I slide into the driver's seat and breathe in the new car smell. I reach over and pop open the glovebox to grab the manual. Reading the front cover gives me a wicked case of the giggles.

"What is it? What's so funny?"

I hold up the booklet so he can read the make and model of the car. "It's a Durango Hellcat. I love it."

He snorts and arches a brow. "A fitting match, then. Now all ye need are yer keys." Sloan laughs and turns back to the bone-crunching feeding ground. "Shall we?"

"Gross. You had to ruin it."

It's nearly six that evening by the time Emmet and Liam drop Aiden at home and drive everyone else back to the house. Sloan and I have been back long enough to clean up, throw together a potato casserole, switch plates on my Hellcat, and finish the spellwork to change the ownership into my name.

Yeah, baby.

"Seriously?" Dillan and Calum say at the same time. "What? You get first dibs because you're a girl?"

I prop my hands on my hips. "No. I get first dibs because Molly got mangled and I was still standing at the end of the battle. You can take these and sort out what you want or don't want. Sloan will help you spell the paperwork."

Da shakes his head. "What happened to us being law-abiding citizens the rest of the community look up to?"

The boys look down at the keys and groan.

"Da? Can't we at least check them out?" Emmet asks. "Calum and I have been sharing for two years."

"If we can't each have one, maybe an upgrade," Calum pleads. "C'mon, Da. Let us at least look at what's there."

My father gives them one of his looks and sighs. "Fine. Yer free to look. Send me the license and registration for all of them. I'll run the plates and see if there's a Mrs. Barghest anywhere who will miss her car. Otherwise, I'll consider an upgrade."

"Yesss!" Their palms meet over their heads in a high-five. "Sloan. Do you think you can *poof* us over there?"

"What about dinner?" I demand.

"We'll be back in fifteen," Dillan responds. "Twenty, tops."

"You're going too, D? You have a new truck."

"I'm not interested in getting one, but I still want to check it out. I am a guy."

I look at Sloan, expecting him to protest, but by the look on his face, he's as eager as the rest of them. "What? I'm a guy too, ye know."

"Can we take Birga?" Emmet eyes Fionn's enchanted spear in the corner.

"Not on your life." I stare at their expectant faces and wave them off. "Go on. Safe home. Stay outta trouble."

"Yes, Mam." My brothers grab hold of Sloan's arms to hitch a ride.

When those three are gone, the house is always markedly quieter. I flop into my seat at the table next to Liam and Da. "Another exciting day in the Cumhaill household. Did you tell Granda all is well?"

Da nods. "He and Mam were horrified when Emmet heard ye scream and get taken. They sent Sloan in the blink and thank the Fates they did. He's a powerful young man."

I nod but have no interest in talking up Sloan in front of Liam. Instead, I squeeze Liam's wrist. "Thanks for helping to evacuate everyone. The worst part of the whole thing for me was having Da and the boys there and unable to defend themselves. I couldn't have done what I did if it weren't for you and Emmet getting them to safety."

Liam takes a swig of his beer. "We would have been there sooner, but Sloan said we had to drive. If he's this all-powerful transporter, he should've *poofed* us straight there."

"He can only teleport to locations he's already been. It's a GPS thing. I'm glad Emmet knew where the stones were. Only Calum, Bruin, and I had been there."

Da nods. "It was a team effort all around."

The timer goes off on the casserole, and I turn the oven off but leave the food inside. Grabbing the water jug, I open the lid and run the water cold before sliding it under the faucet. "Da? You know how you said my biggest fault is thinking I'm indestructible and refusing to ask for help?"

He grunts and offers me a wry smile. "I recall sayin' somethin' to that effect a time or two."

"Well, this is me asking for your help now." I return to the table and sit. Taking his hand, I meet him in the eyes. "I need you to take your powers back so you can help us grow stronger. I'm not good enough to lead the boys, and if they're not good enough, they're going to get killed."

"Sloan can—"

"Sloan's great," I interrupt. "I value everything he offers and is willing to teach us, but you're our da. You know us better than anyone—our strengths and our weaknesses. I need you to help me make this druid thing work."

Da pegs me with a tired gaze. "Why is this so important to ye, Fi? Ye were never interested in such things before."

"I never knew such things existed. Think about it. Someone from the fae realm is in our city amassing an army of minions for something. I don't know what the Barghest is all about yet, but Skull Trim said his master had big plans. If he attempts to take advantage in the city, I intend to stop it."

Da stares at me for a long time, his expression hard.

"Come with us to Ireland. Help us find the Fianna fortress and recover the treasures Fionn wants us to have. Please, Da, help me—help us."

He sighs, and his stern expression softens to a sad smile. "Ye remind me more of yer mam every day, *mo chroi.* She never did back down from a fight. She'd be proud of the woman ye've become."

I lay my hand on his and squeeze. "Help me. Clan Cumhaill can be the first of the Nine Families to expand out of the homeland and remain a druid force to be reckoned with. I know it. I feel it in my everything."

"All right, Fiona. If it's the only way to keep up with the chaos that is sure to ensue in our lives, I'll take back my heritage powers and help ye become an urban druid." Da purses his lips and takes another deep swallow of Guinness and raises his glass. "To the purity of our hearts, the strength of our limbs, and may our actions always match our speech."

I squeal and kiss his cheek. "*Slainte mhath!*"

Thanks for reading – *A Gilded Cage.*

While the story is fresh in your mind, click **HERE** and tell us what you thought.

A star rating and/or even one sentence can mean so much to readers deciding whether or not to try out a book. And if you loved it, continue the Chronicles of an Urban Druid with book two - *A Sacred Grove.*

IRISH TRANSLATIONS

Arragh – a guttural sound for when something bad happened
Banjaxed – broken, ruined, completely obliterated
Bogger – those who live in the boggy countryside
Bollocks – a man's testicles
Bollix – thrown into disorder, bungled, messed up
Boyo – boy, lad
Cock-crow – close enough that you can hear a cock crow
Craic – gossip, fun, entertainment
Culchie – those who live in the agricultural countryside
Donkey's years – a long time
Dosser – a layabout, lazy person
Eejit – slightly less severe than idiot
Fair whack away – far away
Feck – an exclamation less severe than fuck
Flute – a man's penis
Gammie – injured, not working properly
Hape – a heap
Howeyah/Howaya/Howya – a greeting not necessarily requiring an answer.

Irish – traditional Irish language (Commonly referred to as Irish Gaelic unless you're Irish.)

Knackers – a man's testicles

Mo chroi – my heart (pronounced muh chree)

Mocker – a hex

Och – used to express agreement or disagreement to something said

Shite – less offensive than shit

Slan! – health be with you (pronounced slawn)

Gobshite – fool, acting in unwanted behavior

Slainte mhath – cheers, good health (pronounced slawn cha va)

Wee – small

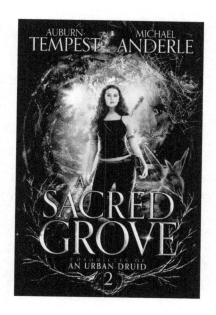

The story continues with A Sacred Grove, available now at Amazon and Kindle Unlimited.

AUTHOR NOTES - AUBURN TEMPEST

09/22/20

Thank you so much for reading *A Gilded Cage*—I hope you loved it.

In these crazy times of stress and everything in the world around us demanding our attention, I appreciate the time you took to escape for a while with Fiona and her family as she learns about her destiny as an urban druid.

What a year this has been. In October 2019, Auburn Tempest launched into the Urban Fantasy arena as my second pen name. After writing 20+ sexy/steamy romances under the pen name, JL Madore, I decided to try something different. My mom is a prolific action/crime author and we decided to co-author a witch/psychic series and mash-up our styles. I had never done a procedural book and she had never done anything fantasy. It was fun. While all my stories fall into the Fantasy/Urban Fantasy/Paranormal/Sci-fi genres, it was the first time I wrote a straight action/adventure plotline without all the pounding hearts and stirring passions. I enjoyed it.

And while I love the series with my mom, I wasn't writing them and wanted to take the driver's seat.

I approached Michael Anderle early in 2020 about putting together a collaborative series. I recognized that he and I have many the same writing goals and personality quirks and thought we'd mesh well. We both want our readers to have a fun, rollicking ride, with minimal angst, lots of laughs, and to finish a book with a swell in their hearts and a smile on their faces.

I hope that came through to you.

Now, a year later, I'm writing the 18th book under the Auburn Tempest name. It's been a whirlwind.

Having two pen names is the best of both worlds for me. It means I have two creative outlets for storytelling. For many of you, this book might be the first time you've read one of my stories. I hope you're a fan and you'll join Michael and me for the next installment of Fiona's adventure.

A Sacred Grove.

Wishing you all lives filled with laughter and love.

Hugs to all,

Auburn Tempest

First, thank you for not only reading this story but also these *Author Notes* in the back!

This series is one of my favorite fun series. It hits so many aspects that I personally look for to read on the weekend.

So when Auburn said, "We both want our readers to have a fun, rollicking ride, with minimal angst, lots of laughs, and to finish a book with a swell in their hearts and a smile on their faces, " she nailed it.

Well, at least for me.

When collaborating, I talk a lot to try and pull out of their life what appeals to me as a reader, and Auburn has had an amazing and varied life. I don't want to share too much, but I would encourage you (especially if you write a review, do it there) to ask her where she has lived and what she has done in her life.

I find I care about Fiona, and I am conflicted about her romance issues. That is a problem I'm not terribly fond of having.

Normally, I am a "one girl, one romance" type of story person.

I'm not AT ALL fond of romance triangles or any other situations when it comes to romance. I have found in this series that

Auburn has a way of not causing me nearly the amount of angst I associate when a guy tries to get the girl.

I could be because Fiona doesn't want a guy, period. She isn't leading anyone on, and she isn't waxing philosophically about this guy or that.

So, the guys all know that they are on even footing. They can wait for their shot eventually or bow out.

That's fair, right?

Well, it works for me, so kudos to Auburn for dealing with my triangle-romance anxiety issues.

So, I've read the first 40,000 words of book three. Hold on to your...uh...hats? Sure, let's go with hats because the ride is fantastic all the way through!

Let's get on with book 02. Preorder now, and you will have it waiting on your Kindle super-fast upon release! Or set an alarm / put it on a calendar to be reminded.

Trust me, it's worth it.

Ad Aeternitatem,

Michael Anderle

ABOUT AUBURN TEMPEST

Auburn Tempest is a multi-genre novelist giving life to Urban Fantasy, Paranormal, and Sci-Fi adventures. Under the pen name, JL Madore, she writes in the same genres but in full romance, sexy-steamy novels. Whether Romance or not, she loves to twist Alpha heroes and kick-ass heroines into chaotic, hilarious, fast-paced, magical situations and make them really work for their happy endings.

Auburn Tempest lives in the Greater Toronto Area, Canada with her dear, wonderful hubby of 30 years and a menagerie of family, friends, and animals.

BOOKS BY AUBURN TEMPEST

Auburn Tempest - Urban Fantasy Action/Adventure

Chronicles of an Urban Druid

Book 1 – A Gilded Cage

Book 2 – A Sacred Grove

Book 3 – A Family Oath

Misty's Magick and Mayhem Series – Written by Carolina Mac/Contributed to by Auburn Tempest

Book 1 – School for Reluctant Witches

Book 2 – School for Saucy Sorceresses

Book 3 – School for Unwitting Wiccans

Book 4 – Nine St. Gillian Street

Book 5 – The Ghost of Pirate's Alley

Book 6 – Jinxing Jackson Square

Book 7 – Flame

Book 8 – Frost

Book 9 – Nocturne

Book 10 – Luna

Book 11 – Swamp Magic

Exemplar Hall – Co-written with Ruby Night

Prequel – Death of a Magi Knight

Book 1 – Drafted by the Magi

Book 2 – Jesse and the Magi Vault

Book 3 – The Makings of a Magi

CONNECT WITH THE AUTHORS

Connect with Auburn

Amazon, Facebook, Newsletter

Web page – www.jlmadore.com

Email – AuburnTempestWrites@gmail.com

Connect with Michael Anderle and sign up for his email list here:

Website: http://lmbpn.com

Email List: http://lmbpn.com/email/

Social Media:

https://www.facebook.com/LMBPNPublishing

https://twitter.com/lmbpn

https://www.instagram.com/lmbpn_publishing/

https://www.bookbub.com/authors/michael-anderle

OTHER LMBPN PUBLISHING BOOKS

For a complete list of books published by LMBPN please visit the following page:

https://lmbpn.com/books-by-lmbpn-publishing/

Made in the USA
Monee, IL
15 June 2021

71412472R00174